Full of Trouble

STORMY FANNING

abbott press®

A DIVISION OF WRITER'S DIGEST

Abbott Press books may be ordered through booksellers or by contacting:

Abbott Press
1663 Liberty Drive
Bloomington, IN 47403
www.abbottpress.com
Phone: 1-866-697-5310

ISBN: 978-1-4582-1598-7 (sc)
ISBN: 978-1-4582-1599-4 (e)

Library of Congress Control Number: 2014908462

Printed in the United States of America.

Abbott Press rev. date: 05/15/2014

Chapter 1

A Bloody Mess

As a kid, my mother was very kind and nurturing for the most part, but she passed out at the sight of blood. As an accident-prone child, this left me to tend to my own injuries on a regular basis. Maybe that's why I ended up going in to nursing. I had experience in treating injuries and I wasn't squeamish about blood and body parts.

It was a good thing I wasn't squeamish about blood, because right now I was trying to wrestle down a 3-yr-old with a huge gash on his head, and there was blood everywhere. His mom had carried him in to the ER a few minutes earlier, saying he had fallen off the porch and hit his head on the corner of a concrete planter. I'm sure his head hurt, but I think he was mostly just mad at being held down. We were trying to wash out the wound before the doctor sutured it up.

"Ow!" he screamed and kicked out randomly, barely missing the doctor's leg. He was squirming and twisting his head side to side, making the task quite difficult.

"Logan, we need to cooperate with the nurse," his mother stated in a calm, meditative voice from her chair in the corner. "They are trying to help you and you should appreciate that." Logan was having none of it. He let out another howl and swung at my arm. I managed to avoid the hit without losing my grip on the kid. We had him on the counter with his head over the sink. His thrashing around was spraying blood, soap and water all over the counter, the floor and me.

"Logan, let's think of a happy place and go there in our mind," his mother said. At least, I think that's what she said. It was tough to hear anything over the yelling. I thought that a stern "Hold still!" would have been more effective on a 3-yr-old, but I knew better than to say that. Besides, most kids in that condition aren't listening to anything we're saying. It doesn't matter if it's soothing or commanding.

Lacey came in the room with the supplies for suturing and saw that Dr. Robbins and I were losing our battle with Logan. She slid in beside me and got a good grip on either side of his head, so he stopped twisting it around. I got his arms down by his side and used part of my body weight to hold him in place on the counter so the doc could wash out the wound. Logan was not happy about being pinned down and let out a howl. Ok, pinning down little kids isn't the funnest part of the job. I reminded myself that it was necessary and for his good. The angry, hurt glare he was giving me told me that he didn't agree.

Dr Robbins finally managed to get the wound clean and determined that it was good to suture. This was going to be even trickier than the washing was. We wrapped Logan in a blanket and carried him over to the gurney, laying him down under the bright overhead lights. I glanced over my shoulder at his mom and asked, "Do you want to come over here and try to keep him calm for this?"

"Oh no!" she cried. "I can't see that stuff! I hate the sight of blood." That brings back memories. I guess I'll have to be comforting to Logan as I'm pinning him down. I don't think I'll be very successful. I burrito-wrapped him in a blanket while Dr. Robbins set up his supplies. He looked up at me to see if I was ready and I gave him a nod.

"Ok, Logan, we're going to put some numbing medicine on here," the doc explained to the boy. He was still crying half-heartedly and his eyes were wide with fear. This is where it gets tricky. The doctor injects lidocaine into the area to numb it, and I have to make sure the kid doesn't move his head at all while the doctor has a needle in his scalp. I smiled down at him reassuringly.

"Logan, we're gonna hold really, really still for just a minute," I said. "I'm going to help you and you help me, ok?" Logan didn't reply. I hadn't won him over yet. I usually didn't win them over until I gave them the popsicle after it was all done. I gently placed my hands on either side of his head to hold it in place. "Should we sing a song?"

He didn't say yes, but he didn't say no, and I knew we needed a distraction. I started with the first song I could think of, 'Itsy Bitsy Spider'. Dr. Robbins was smiling amusedly at me over the top of Logan's head. The song is more fun if you can do the hand motions, but my hands were busy. Logan had stopped crying and was just staring at me. Then Dr Robbins picked up the syringe and I tightened my grip on Logan's head. He started injecting the numbing medication, which, ironically, burns when you put it in. Logan screamed and tried to squirm but I had him well-secured. The doc finished up the numbing quickly and without incident. I relaxed my grip on Logan's head, since we had to wait a few minutes for it to work. After this part, the kid doesn't feel the stitching, but they are usually scared enough that they cry and squirm anyway.

The spider had completed his journey up the water spout, so I moved on to 'I'm a Little Teapot.' For some reason, I could only think of songs that involved gestures. Since I couldn't let my hands free to make a handle and spout, I just hammed up the melody to entertain the kid. Luckily, the door to the room was closed to muffle the sound of a screaming child, so no one in the hall could hear me. I hoped.

Dr. Robbins started suturing in his usual calm, relaxed manner. He was talking to the mom, telling her that the edges of the laceration were very even and there would be a scar but his hair would cover it. She didn't respond and I glanced over my shoulder at her. She was sitting cross-legged on the chair with her hands folded in her lap, her eyes closed and her head bowed. She was humming softly and swaying slightly. This was somewhat unusual for a mother with a child in the ER. They are usually more anxious than the kid is. I looked back at Dr. Robbins who stared at her, dumbstruck, for a moment, then shrugged and went back to suturing. We would give her printed instructions when she left, so she would get the information she needed.

Dr. Robbins finished suturing and attempted to wipe up some of the blood on Logan's face and head. Then he decided that was a futile task. It would work best to let his mom get him home, out of his drenched clothes and into a bath.

"We're all finished here," he said, and mom popped her head up to look over at us. She jumped up and ran over to the gurney and swooped Logan up in her arms.

"Oh, you were such a good, brave boy!" she congratulated him. He was pretty good, all things considered.

"Logan, are you ready for your popsicle?" I asked. He nodded enthusiastically. "Do you want red, orange, or purple?"

"Red!" he yelled out. A fitting color for his appearance right now. Maybe people would think he was covered in red popsicle instead of blood. I headed to the fridge and returned with the hard-won prize. Logan tore into it.

"Logan, what do you say?" his mom prompted and he mumbled something that was probably 'thank you' around his mouth full of popsicle.

I smiled at him and said "You're welcome." They always decide they like me right before they leave.

I went through the instructions with his mom on how to take care of the cut and when to come back to get the stitches taken out. They walked out the door and I turned around to look at the room I needed to clean. It looked like we had butchered something in there. The easiest way to clean it would be to get a hose and spray the whole place down. Alas, there was no hose and no floor drain, so that wasn't an option. I sighed and grabbed the disinfectant wipes.

Lacey came in to help me with my task. Lacey was a certified nursing assistant, or CNA, and she was currently enrolled as a nursing student at the local college. She was 22 years old, incredibly sweet and smart, and she was going to be a fantastic nurse. I loved working with her because she was a good worker and always wanted to get right in the thick of things and help out.

"How's school going?" I asked as we were cleaning.

"Hard," she replied. "I'm in pharmacology and it's kicking my butt. There is so much you have to know!" She wasn't kidding either. There is an insane amount of information you're expected to learn in nursing school. It can be very overwhelming.

"Which section are you on?" I asked.

"Cardiac drugs," she replied.

"Well, those are the ones I know the best," I said. "I'll help you study once we get caught up here."

"Cool, Allie. That would be awesome!" she sounded relieved. I had done well in nursing school, although it didn't feel like it at the time. I struggled with the volume of homework and clinicals were a nightmare for me. The advantage I had now was 8 years of nursing experience and using the drugs in a practical application. It made a lot more sense once you used it with patients. When it was just an incredibly thick textbook filled with pages of really long words, it all started to run into a blur.

We finally returned the suturing room to its previous condition and I headed to the locker room for a change of clothes. I always came in my own scrubs, but frequently had to change in to hospital issue scrubs part way through the shift. The hospital laundry wasn't allowed to use fabric softener because it could cause allergic skin reactions, so their scrubs were really scratchy. They were also unisex, 'one-size-fits-nobody' in design. But they were not covered in blood, which was one up on my personal scrubs at that moment.

The shift ended without any further excitement, except a long discussion on the difference between beta- and alpha-blockers. I really loved being a smart chick. When I could pass some knowledge on to someone else, it just made my whole day.

I got home from work, tossed my scrubs in the washing machine and jumped in the shower. Once I was sufficiently scrubbed clean, I threw on shorts and a t-shirt. I didn't usually do too much after a 12-hour shift and I would be headed to bed in a few hours. I combed through my shoulder length hair and considered doing something cute with it, like sleeping with braids in it so it would be wavy tomorrow. Then I changed my mind and went in search of something for supper.

My phone chirped with a text message from my sister. Shelby is 4 years younger than me but we are about a decade apart in maturity. She is petite and very cute, with curly blonde hair and big blue eyes. She always has guys hanging all over her, but she manages to pick the losers out of the crowd and date them. She is currently enrolled in massage therapy school. She has previously been enrolled in dental hygiene, cosmetology, teaching, Spanish interpreter and environmental biology. She has enough college credits to make at least 2 degrees, but not enough of them are in the same subject. She keeps changing her mind about what she wants to be when she grows up. Since she doesn't seem to be growing up very fast, I guess there's no pressure. In order to pay her bills, she waits tables at a bar and grill in town called Joe's.

"Call me when you get off work" was the message and I hesitated briefly. Sometimes Shelby really needed to talk to me about her latest loser boyfriend and I had a hard time biting my tongue. Sometimes she needed someone to dog-sit her incredibly spoiled pug, Snickers. I always got guiltied into doing it, but I hated that dog. After every time, I swore I would never watch her again. Yet Shelby always convinced me that Snickers would behave the next time. I guess Shelby isn't the only slow learner in the family.

I picked up the phone and hit Shelby's number. Might as well get this over with. While the phone rang, I rummaged through the fridge. I really needed to hit the grocery store. I dug out some leftover chicken rice soup, a tomato and an avocado. That was practically a balanced meal. Meat, vegetable, starch. When you only have one person, sometimes cooking is more trouble than it's worth.

"Hi, Lis," Shelby answered cheerfully. My given name is Allison Eloise, and when I was younger, my mother insisted I be called by my full name 'Allison'. Except Shelby couldn't say 'Allison' so she called me 'Lis'. Then all my friends started calling me 'Allie' which my mother really hated. I didn't really care either way, but the only person that ever uses my full name any more is my mom.

"Hey, baby sister, what's up?" Her cheerful voice meant it wasn't boyfriend trouble, at least.

"What are you doing this Friday?" she asked. We aren't much for small talk in my family.

"Well, I don't work. I guess I don't have plans yet." Right after the words left my mouth, I cringed. *'Ask WHY, always ask why'* my inner voice reminded me. Too late. If she wanted me to dog sit, I had talked myself right out of an easy excuse.

"Tony and his roommates are having a barbeque and they want me to invite you," she said, with a smile in her voice. Tony was a prep cook at Joe's, where Shelby worked. He was tall and lanky and had a killer smile. I'm pretty sure he had a crush on me, which wasn't completely unflattering. Of course, Tony had my cell number, so sending the message through Shelby could mean that it was just a casual invitation. Either way, a barbeque sounded like a great way to spend a Friday evening.

"Sure, I'd love to," I replied. "Should I bring anything?" Tony cooked better than I did, but I could make a mean batch of no-bake cookies that always seemed to be devoured within minutes at any gathering.

"I'll ask him tomorrow," she said. "It's Jared's birthday that day, so we're celebrating." Jared was one of the roommates, if I recalled correctly. Tony and three other guys all shared a big house down by the park. It was a great location for a barbeque- great big back yard, trees, creek running by. The only scary part was when you had to go inside the house to use the bathroom. Which was about the only time I went in the house. It was very much a bachelor pad, with laundry scattered on the floor, miscellaneous auto parts on the table, empty cans stacked on the counter and dishes piled in the sink. Their fridge, however, was in better shape than mine. There was always lots of hand-cut meats, fresh herbs, gourmet cheeses and vegetables I had no idea how to prepare, like jicama. Their barbeque wouldn't be hamburgers and hot dogs, that was for sure. I was happy to enjoy their culinary skills and I was willing to risk the bathroom to do it.

"Cool," I replied. "How's school going?" I always tried to ask her how school was going. Partly to be supportive of her attempts to get an education. And partly to remind her that she was still in school. I think sometimes she forgot and just skipped classes for a week at a time.

"I'm starting clinicals next week so I need people to do massages on. Then you have to review me." The way she said 'you' indicated she expected me to be one of her practice clients. I hoped she was good at it, because I would have a hard time lying on her review form.

"Ok, let me know when." I finished up the phone call as my soup finished reheating. I sat at the table and leafed through a fitness magazine while I ate my supper. There was an article titled "Break the Sugar Habit!" and it had a picture of a donut with sprinkles, a bowl of ice cream with chocolate poured over the top and a cupcake with frosting piled on top of it. Ironic. Now I wanted ice cream. I don't think the article was very effective. I closed the magazine and finished my avocado. I didn't have any ice cream in my freezer, so I guess I'll just ignore that craving and hope it will go away. Maybe I should look at pictures of broccoli.

Or, since I'm completely wiped out anyway, I could just go to bed.

Chapter 2

Scrubs or pajamas

One of the great things about nursing is that we get to wear pajamas to work. Ok, not exactly pajamas, but close. Soft, baggy drawstring pants are just one step above pajama pants, and that's mostly because they aren't flannel. Pair them with a baggy, shapeless shirt with lots of storage space, and you have a super comfy, super practical outfit. There are no zippers or buttons or form fitting anything. The pockets on the shirt hold a ton of stuff. Right now, mine have two pens, a chapstick, some alcohol pads, a pack of gum, three quarters and a ponytail holder.

However, they are not very attractive. They pretty much obscure the feminine figure. If you're having a bad enough fat day, people might mistake you for being pregnant. Comfortable, practical, unattractive. There's the summary description of my work outfit.

At least we get to pick colors and patterns. I was required to wear the white uniform in nursing school and it was impossible to keep clean. Of course, that might have more to do with me, and my affinity for making a mess, than the clothes themselves. Either way, I have bad memories of the experience.

Today's selection is lavender with purple trim. Working ER is always a surprise as to what the day will bring, but I felt confident that today would be under control. After my last few shifts, I was due for a calm, boring day. I figured I could take the chance that I wouldn't end up with any body fluids on me, so a light color was safe. Most of my scrubs are black or navy, since it hides blood better. But I felt like dressing like a girl for a change.

I headed out the door to my car. Mr. Munson, the gentleman who lived at the end of the block, was out on his morning walk. He strode briskly down the sidewalk, arms pumping, in his navy tracksuit with reflective stripe. Mr. Munson was very concerned about staying healthy and he took this three mile jaunt almost every morning, periodically checking his heart rate to make sure he stayed in the target range. He also played tennis at the Y three days a week and swam laps two days a week. He always told me "I thank God for what you do, but I pray I'll never need you." And he looked great for 78 years old. If more people were like him, hospitals would be a lot emptier. Although there are always people getting hurt, no matter how healthy they are.

I waved at Mr. Munson and got in my car to drive to work. Mandisa was singing about it being a good morning on my radio and I had to agree with her. I was feeling pretty chipper this morning. Possibly because I get to work with my favorite crew today. And possibly because after this shift, I have four days off. Either way, it's always great to start the day in a good mood.

I walked in to work, stashed my bag in my locker and grabbed a cup of coffee. I liked to sleep as late as possible in the morning, so there wasn't time to make coffee at home. It didn't matter, there was always a hot, fresh pot in the break room. I walked up to the desk to find out how the night had gone.

"Hey, Allie, we found you a husband last night," Kara said with a grin. I looked around at the smirking faces and was afraid to ask.

"Oh yeah? Did you get me a phone number?" I joked back. "Who is the mystery suitor?"

"Remember Arnold Jones?" she asked. "He came in a couple weeks ago and you were his nurse, I guess. He was asking where you were."

I remembered Arnold Jones. Arnie was in his 40's, unemployed and lived in a local 'no-tell motel'. He spent his days drinking and smoking pot. At least those were the only recreational activities he would own up to. He had some mystery burns on his arms, so it's possible that there was some harder stuff too. His long, stringy hair was turning gray, he didn't ever smell too great and he only had about half of his teeth.

He had been in the ER a couple weeks ago because he passed out for 20 hours straight and his friends were worried he might be dead. They called 911 from a pay phone and then scattered like roaches because they knew the cops would show up as well as the ambulance. They must have cleaned out the room because the officers didn't find any alcohol, drugs or paraphernalia at the scene. Or any cash, or food, or clothes. I don't know if his friends were protecting his belongings from the cops or just took advantage of the opportunity to get some free stuff.

Arnie was conscious by the time the medics got him to the ER, but he was still drunk as a skunk. His blood alcohol was three times the legal limit and he hadn't had a drink in almost a day. It was a shame he couldn't apply that dedication to a productive activity. It takes some practice and persistence to be able to drink that much and still be alive.

Arnie had tried to put the moves on me that afternoon, but I was able to resist his charm. I couldn't breathe through my nose if I got within 10 feet of him. He could barely string together a sentence but he kept telling me I was "jus' bootiful."

After the doctor decided we should keep Arnie in the hospital a few days, we got the fun task of removing his clothes. I think they had been on him for about a week. We had to peel off his socks and I was worried his skin was going to come off with them.

Since we had to change his clothes anyway, I figured it was a good time to give him a scrubbing. So Arnie got a bed bath, which was probably his first bath in a couple months. The medics said the shower stall in his motel room was stacked full of trash. We used a full bottle of soap, four bath buckets of hot water and then a full bottle of lotion. He looked and smelled better and I hoped he felt better too.

But if Arnie was enamored with me before the ER spa treatment, he was downright infatuated after. He kept asking me to marry him and badgering my co-workers to give him my phone number and address. Jesse gave him the number of the local Catholic church as a joke. I really hoped he didn't call it.

"So what brought Arnie to the ER last night?" I asked. I was pretty sure it involved alcohol.

"He was drunk and standing in the parking lot of the motel, buck naked, yelling at something," Kara replied. "No one could figure out what he was yelling at, but when the police showed up he tried to take off running and ran smack into a parked car. He managed to gash his knee up and had to come in for stitches."

I just shook my head. There was a time when that story would have shocked me, but not anymore. This stuff happened all the time. It was funny and sad at the same time. We usually laughed about it because we didn't know what else to do.

"So did you tell Arnie that I had gotten married? Joined a convent? Ran off with the circus?" I asked.

"We didn't have to," Kara replied. "Jake was on the rig that brought him in and he told him to back off of his girl. Arnie shut right up after that." She smiled at me slyly. "I didn't know you were Jake's girl."

Jake is a paramedic with the local fire department. He likes to work out and he has the physique to show for it. He also has incredible blue eyes and dimples a mile deep. There isn't a woman in the county who doesn't swoon a little when he walks in. However, Jake is well aware of his attributes and he likes to play them up. He does flirt with me when he comes in the ER, but I don't take it too seriously. He flirts with all the women, even the little old ladies he brings in on the ambulance. Sometimes I don't even think they're sick, I think they just call 911 to get some attention from Jake.

But, at heart, Jake is a really good guy, and I could see him defending me from the advances of a drunk guy. While his intentions were good, now I had a juicy rumor running around the ER about me and Jake. Well, there was nothing to do but ignore it and hope it died down on its own. Insisting that nothing was going on was just going to fan the flames.

"How was the rest of the night?" I changed the subject.

"Busy. Nothing too major but it looks like a stomach bug is going around. Nausea and vomiting was the theme for the night." Kara added, "And the ambulance is out right now on a guy who fell and hit his head."

The EMS radio crackled to life with a male voice telling dispatch that they were on their way to the hospital with a male patient. I recognized the voice as Kent, and I knew Kent and Jake were partners on the ambulance. That meant Jake was coming to the hospital right now. My heart fluttered, even though I willed it not to, and a flush spread across my cheeks. Everyone was staring at me, which was only making it worse.

"Well, there you go, Allie. You get to see your boyfriend this morning," Kara winked at me as she grabbed her stuff to head to the locker room. "I won't stay around and ruin the mood."

The fire department worked 24-hour shifts and they changed shift a half hour after we did. That meant Jake was just finishing 24 hours of work and had been up most of the night. But he would still look incredible. Boys have it so easy like that. I would look like the bride of Frankenstein after that shift. I reminded myself that it didn't matter what Jake looked like, or what I looked like. We were all just here to do our jobs.

I walked over to the EMS radio to get report while Lacey opened up the trauma room. I identified myself as ER and said "Go ahead" in the calmest voice I could manage.

"Well, good morning, Miss Allie," a deep voice drawled. "I was hoping you would be working today." Jake wouldn't care about being professional or squelching rumors. In fact, if he knew they were teasing me about him, he would probably be flattered. I certainly hoped he never found out.

"Good morning to you, too, Jake," I replied cheerfully. Jake was a great guy and I didn't need to give him the ice queen treatment just because my co-workers were gossipy. "What have you got for me?"

"We are coming in with a 36-yr-old male who was out for a run just before sunrise. A dog barked and startled him and he missed the curb. He fell and struck his head and may have lost consciousness for a few moments. He doesn't really remember but he does have an impressive gash on his forehead. Someone driving by saw him go down and called 911." He finished up with report, telling me the vital signs and assessment and that they would be here in three minutes.

I walked in the trauma room with Lacey and put on a pair of gloves. It sounded like I would need them.

"Well, at least he won't be drunk," Lacey said with a smile. She had overheard the tale of Arnie, and she had seen her fair share of drunks in the ER. Those experiences made for good stories after the fact, but they weren't much fun at the time.

The ambulance crew came through the door with a tall, athletic man on the gurney. He had a neck immobilizer on and he was strapped to a rigid backboard, which was usual for this type of injury. He was holding a towel to his forehead that had a fair amount of blood on it.

"Please, I'm just fine," he pleaded. "This is so embarrassing. I'm fine. Really." He seemed pleasant enough, just insistent he didn't need all this attention.

"You probably are fine, but we like to make sure," Kent reassured him. "And you need stitches on your head, for sure."

The man moved the towel and tried to look over at Lacey and me. He grimaced as the cervical collar reminded him he wasn't supposed to move his neck.

"Hi, I'm Allie," I introduced myself. "I'm the nurse." All four of us took our positions around the backboard and gurney.

"On three," Kent said and we smoothly transferred the patient on to our hospital gurney, still on the backboard.

"I'm Chris," the man offered. "And I'm fine, really."

I smiled down at him. "And you thought running was good for your health," I joked, trying to put him at ease.

He smiled at that. I lifted the towel away and saw the laceration right at his hairline. It was about 4 inches long and shaped like a smiley face. He had apparently fallen straight forward and caught his forehead on the edge of the curb. I reached up carefully and lifted up on the flap of skin to see underneath. He flinched with that but I needed to see how clean it was. I didn't see any obvious dirt. We would still wash it thoroughly. The proper term for that type of laceration is an 'avulsion'. The slang term is a 'scalping', which was a pretty accurate description of what had happened. We didn't like to use that term in front of patients, though. It was a bit graphic.

The other, less obvious, injuries to consider is that he may have done damage to his neck or spine with the trauma of the fall. He could also have bruising or bleeding inside his skull from the blow. Those were actually the more serious concerns. For now, we put some gauze pads with disinfectant on them over the gash. We would worry about suturing it after we had checked out his spine and head.

Dr. Robbins walked in as I was giving Chris the usual neurological tests, questioning him about the date, where we were and who was president. I continued checking his arms and legs for movement and sensation as Dr. Robbins began looking at his pupils and in his ears and nose for bleeding. Chris was checking out okay so far.

We gathered all four of us again to hold Chris still while the doctor removed the immobilizing equipment to check his neck and spine for abnormalities and pain. The goal was to keep his spine in perfectly straight alignment until we determined that there was no damage to the bones of his spine. He currently had normal movement and sensation, so his spinal cord was intact. If he had a fracture to any of his vertebrae, however, movement of the broken bone could damage the spinal cord. This would have devastating consequences, usually paralysis.

When I first started in ER, I thought all of this was a bit excessive. It seemed like such a minor injury and we made such a big deal about the backboard and cervical collar and complete spine immobilization.

Then, one night, we had a young man come in who had wrecked his dirt bike. He 'felt fine' and was up and walking around when the ambulance showed up. He told them he didn't need the backboard or C-collar. The nature of his accident made the medics wary, though, and they persuaded him to let them put it on. When he arrived in the ER, he had some pain to his neck, so they took an x-ray. At that point, it still all seemed like just a precaution.

But the x-ray showed a complete fracture of the top vertebrae on his spine. It was nothing but the grace of God that kept that 20-yr-old from being a quadriplegic for the rest of his life. After that, I took spinal precautions a little more seriously.

Chris didn't have any abnormalities or pain to his neck or back, so we removed the backboard and C-collar. He looked a little more comfortable after that. We still needed to make sure he didn't have a head injury. This required a CT scan, which would take a few minutes.

"Chris, do you have a family member or someone I should call?" I asked.

"You better call my wife, Jill," he said. "This is about the time I should be getting home." He gave me the number and I went out to the desk to call. This was never a fun call to make. At least I had mostly good news. Well, except for the news that her husband was in the ER. With caller ID, most people knew who was calling before they answered, and they immediately imagined the worse.

"Hello," a sleepy voice answered. I guess Jill wasn't quite the early bird that her husband was.

"Is this Jill?" I asked. It was always a good idea to make sure you had the right person before you delivered the news.

"Yes, it is," she replied. She sounded more awake now.

"This is Allie from the ER. Your husband is okay," I hurried to assure her. "He tripped and fell this morning and he got a cut on his head. He had to come in to the ER to get some stitches." I left out a few details, like the ambulance ride in and the possible head injury we hadn't eliminated yet. Family members tend to get anxious enough, and over the phone it was tough to be supportive or reassuring. I preferred to wait until they were here to fill in the details. That way I could catch them if they collapsed. Which has happened a time or two.

"Oh my," she said. "He's ok, though?" She sounded a little shaky but fairly calm, considering.

"We're still checking him out, but he's awake and talking to us," I told her. Now that she wasn't hysterical, I didn't want to make false promises. I just told her the facts that I had. "Mostly, he keeps insisting that he's ok and doesn't need all of this."

She laughed. "That sounds like him. He really hates hospitals." I hear that a lot. No one seems to like hospitals. I don't take it personally.

"Are you able to come down here?" I asked. Chris didn't seem like he needed emotional support, but he needed a ride home.

"Yeah, I'll get dressed and be there in about 15 minutes," she replied. She disconnected the call and I walked back in the room to tell Chris that she was on her way.

"Oh, she doesn't need to come down here," he protested. "I'm fine, really."

"Well, you don't have a way to get home," I reminded him. I ask family members to come in anyway, because I think people in the ER shouldn't be alone. But I would downplay that for him, since he was already embarrassed at all the attention.

"Oh. That's right," he said. Little things can slip your mind when you've just bounced your head off the sidewalk. The CT tech walked in just then to transport Chris down the hall for a CT scan of his head. He explained that the test took only a few minutes and he wouldn't feel anything, then wheeled the gurney out of the room.

I went to the desk to chart everything that had happened. I was a bit of an adrenaline junkie and I loved it when a busy patient came in. However, I dreaded the pile of paperwork I had to fill out after it was over. I had learned to keep up the charting as I went. Otherwise, I was sitting down after 2 hours of activity, trying to remember what had happened when.

Kent and Jake had finally finished their paperwork and gotten all the blood cleaned off their equipment and out of the back of the rig. They stopped by the desk to say good-bye, both looking pretty wiped out. Their shift had officially been over for 20 minutes now. Twenty minutes isn't a long time, normally, but twenty minutes past the end of a long, busy shift is an eternity.

"Enjoy your day off," I said. I was pretty sure their day off was going to start with a nap.

"Well, you enjoy your day at work," Jake smiled at me. "Sorry we can't hang around to play." He flashed those killer dimples and then they were out the door.

The CT tech brought Chris back to his room, which signaled the doc that the scan was complete. He pulled up the image on the computer and didn't see any cause for concern. Now we could move on to the repair of his forehead. Lacey gathered up the supplies and went in to assist Dr. Robbins.

I still needed to complete a health history on the patient. It seemed a little silly to me to go in after all of that and start asking him if he had any health problems. But it was required and I got in trouble if I didn't do it. It would be a good distraction for the patient while he was getting sutured.

I let the clerk up front know where I would be if his wife arrived and went in the room with the patient. We went through all the systems pretty quickly, since Chris was a healthy guy.

I always felt a little awkward asking a guy my age about problems with his bowel or bladder. It didn't seem weird to ask a 70-yr-old, for some reason. I felt awkward asking any of them about sexual dysfunction, regardless of age. I understood it was an important indicator of possible blood vessel disease. It was just uncomfortable to ask. I sort of wondered if any of them would be honest with me if they did. I also worried that some of them might go in to detail.

Dr. Robbins had almost finished suturing when the clerk let me know that his wife was here. I walked out front to talk to her while he finished.

"Hi there, I'm Allie," I introduced myself. She had her hair scooped up in a ponytail, no makeup and sweats thrown on.

"Hi, I'm Jill. How's he doing?" she asked.

"He's doing fine. The doctor is finishing right now. He had to get some stitches to his forehead. He doesn't have any other injuries, though," I told her. Now that we had the 'all clear' on his head CT, I could tell her that with confidence.

She looked relieved. A trip to the ER is a nerve-wracking way to start the day. At least it was early and there was no one else in there. If you want to get through quickly, early morning is the best time to hit the ER. Of course, not many people get to plan their trip to the ER.

Dr. Robbins walked out of the room so I took Jill in to see her husband. She looked at him and smiled, shaking her head.

"You are such a klutz," she teased him. She walked over to look at his freshly sutured forehead and gave him a kiss. "What am I going to do with you?"

He smiled sheepishly. They looked at each other tenderly and I suddenly felt very much like an intruder. I told them to let me know if they needed anything and went back to the desk to work on the charting.

A guy sitting in an ER room with sutures on his forehead while his wife stands beside him in sweatpants running her hand through the dried blood crusted in his hair. That is a romantic scene right there. Or at least it was to me. I don't want to find a guy who will sit in a movie with me. I want a guy who would sit in the ER with me.

Chapter 3

The Cowboy Way

T racy, the clerk up front, called out "We need a nurse, we have a guy who is short of breath."

Now, 'shortness of breath' is a cause for alarm. If you call 911 and say you have shortness of breath, the ambulance comes screaming with full lights and sirens. Not being able to breathe has the possibility of ending up in a pine box, and death isn't usually the goal in this field.

However, 'shortness of breath' can also be very subjective. You'll have those people whose only physical activity is walking from the couch to the fridge who suddenly decide to climb up Hobson's Canyon to see the spring daisies and they get 'shortness of breath'. Shocking, I know.

Then you'll have those people who are hacking and coughing and gasping that they are short of breath, when their clothes reek of smoke and the pack of Marlboros is right there in their front pocket. It's a pretty easy conclusion as to what is causing their 'shortness of breath'.

But then you have guys like Mr. Jergins.

I walked up to the desk, to see a tall, lanky gentleman in Wranglers, boots, Western style snap front shirt and

Stetson hat, leaning against the wall about halfway across the waiting room. His shoulders heaved and his neck muscles bulged with every breath he was gasping for, which was about once every 3 seconds.

I rushed over to his side, asking him what was wrong, as if I didn't know already. He gasped "I. just...can't.... catch....a....breath" with about 2 gasps in between each word. His lips were a dusky blue-purple color. I yelled for Tracy to get a wheelchair and an oxygen tank. Then I realized he didn't have anyone with him.

"How did you get here?" I asked, afraid of the answer.

"Drove," he gasped.

I looked out at the parking lot to where a dusty work pickup was parked at least 50 yards from the door. He had driven to town and walked himself in from the parking lot, the whole time barely able to breathe.

"Didn't you have someone that could bring you?" I asked. Sort of pointless to ask that now, but I couldn't help myself.

"Didn't... want...to.....bother...." He trailed off in exhaustion. Gotta love cowboys. They sure aren't whiners.

We wheeled Mr. Jergins in to Room 3 and got busy putting him on the monitor and getting some oxygen tubing on him. His heart rate was 135 and his oxygen saturation was 65%. That would explain the blue color on his lips. He was in serious distress and we needed to find out what was causing it quick. Unfortunately, the usual method of asking the patient questions wasn't working so well, since he couldn't really talk.

Dr. Robbins came in the room behind me and began assessing the patient. Dr. Robbins was pretty laid back and after 30 years working in the ER, he didn't get too excited about much. But as he moved his stethoscope over Mr.

Jergins chest and back, his brow furrowed. He looked up at me and said "We need a chest x-ray. Stat!"

Now, 'stat' is another term that can be subjective. Technically, every test we do in the ER is 'Stat' because, presumably, it is a medical emergency. However, we take care of a lot of medical issues that are not emergent or life-threatening. So the 'Stat' term gets a little slack. But this 'Stat' was an honest-to-goodness, 'life may be in jeopardy' STAT.

I called over my shoulder to Tracy to call radiology right away. I heard her on the phone with them, telling them the doctor wanted the test done immediately. I overheard the words "he's kinda blue." That would get them over here quick. Blue is not a color we like in the medical field. At least not on our patients.

Just then, the cell phone in Mr. Jergins shirt pocket rang. Well, actually, played a few bars of "Amarillo by Morning", which is possibly the greatest George Strait song ever. He pulled it out, looked at the caller ID and grimaced, then handed it to me. It was flashing "Katy" and he gestured that I should answer it. I flipped it open and gingerly answered "Mr. Jergins phone, can I help you?"

"What?! Who are you? Where is my dad? Is something wrong? Why isn't he answering his phone? I want to know what's going on here!" Her voice got louder and shriller with each phrase.

I finally managed to break in "Ma'am, your dad is in the emergency room and I'm his nurse. He's having some trouble breathing."

"What? Why? Why would he have trouble breathing? He's in great shape! He's never smoked. That doesn't make any sense!" Her sharp sentences came rapid fire, without a chance to for me to reply. "In fact, he was just out working on a new horse this morning. He was fine then. Except he left the dang fool horse running around in the corral, dragging a lead rope around behind him. Why did he do that? Ask him what he was thinking?! And why are 3 rails on the corral all busted up? I want some answers here!"

And then I realized that Mr. Jergins crisp Western shirt and Wranglers with the creases ironed in were covered down one side and the back with dirt and hay. There was also some other brown stuff that wasn't exactly dirt.

I reached over and unfastened the shirt quick. I began tugging up the t-shirt underneath and he flinched. I grabbed a pair of trauma shears and cut the t-shirt away to see a large, purple bruise starting across the right side of his chest. I looked under the back of the shirt and saw 2 horizontal red marks across his back. About the size of a rail on a horse corral.

"Did you have a little trouble with a horse this morning?' I asked him. He attempted to shrug nonchalantly but ended up grimacing in pain. "And did the horse ram you backward into the rails on the corral?"

He nodded. I grabbed my stethoscope to affirm what Dr. Robbins had already heard- there was no air moving through Mr. Jergins' right lung.

Right then, the radiology technologist arrived to take an x-ray which would confirm the diagnosis. I went back to Katy on the phone, who was still ranting away. I'm not sure she realized I had set the phone down for 3 whole minutes. Just as well.

"Ma'am?" I managed to interject, "would you be able to come down to the hospital right away? It looks like your dad is seriously injured."

That finally shut her up. She took a deep, shuddering breath and asked, "Is he going to.... be okay?" Her voice trembled with that last word.

"Yes, we're doing everything we can and this is a treatable condition," I assured her. "But he can't really talk and we need someone for information. And I think he would like to have someone here with him."

He made a funny face when I said that, so perhaps he would have preferred to go it alone. But family, even annoying family, is a good thing to have around in a medical emergency.

"I'll be right there. It's about a 20 minute drive from the ranch." And she disconnected. Twenty minutes. Mr. Jergins drove 20 minutes with only one lung working. Thank God he didn't pass out and take out a school bus of children.

The rad tech had finished his x-ray and headed back to the department to process the film for the doctor. In this wonderful digital age, it takes about 2 minutes and the doctor has the image up on his computer screen. Very convenient.

Mr. Jergins was looking a little less blue now that we had some oxygen on him, and his vital signs were a little better, but he still heaved with his entire torso every time he took a breath. Now that his shirt was cut off, I could see the spaces between his ribs sucking in with each breath.

"Intercostal retractions" is what those were called. One of the big words we learned in nursing school, so we could sound super smart. I know a lot of really big words, and I also know the everyday words that mean about the same thing and fit into a conversation better.

"Tension pneumothorax" was another one of those big words and it means that part or all of Mr. Jergins lung had collapsed from the trauma of getting slammed into a rail fence by a rowdy horse.

Scott, the ER tech, had put in an IV and drawn blood. Scott had been a paramedic on the ambulance for 20 years and he had seen a lot. Age and a bad shoulder ran him out of that job and in to the more sedentary, controlled environment of the ER. But he always got a gleam in his eye when any kind of a trauma patient came in. He still loved it, even though he rarely got to do it.

I liked Scott, and I really liked having him at work when trauma cases came in. He knew what to do and did it well. He had a general calming presence in the middle of turmoil. He was also good to have around on slow shifts, because he could entertain us with stories from his days on the rig.

Dr. Robbins had the x-ray image up, and even my untrained eye could see that there wasn't anything showing up on that side. His right lung was completely collapsed. He also had 3 broken ribs, which were probably responsible for collapsing the lung. Dr Robbins walked in to the room to explain the situation to the patient. We needed to re-expand his lung, which required cutting a slit between his ribs and putting in a tube that would create suction to pull the lung back open.

Mr. Jergins didn't look thrilled, but at that point, I think he would have agreed to almost anything if it would help his breathing. I assured him that we would put him to sleep for the procedure and give him pain medicine as well, and he looked more relieved.

Scott started assembling supplies and equipment while I drew up the syringes of medication for the procedure.

"Ok, Mr Jergins, I'm going to give this first medication, called fentanyl. You may feel a little woozy or a bit of a buzz." I said as I injected the first dose. "The second medication is called Versed and it will probably just make you sleepy."

He was still wide awake and watching me nervously. I injected the second medication. "Do you feel anything yet?" I asked. He shook his head. I watched him for about sixty seconds and his eyelids began to droop. Another sixty seconds and his eyes were completely closed. "Mr. Jergins?" I touched his hand. His eyebrow arched slightly, but his eyes stayed closed. Versed is wonderful in times like this.

Dr. Robbins had prepped the area and numbed it with lidocaine. He made the incision with the scalpel and air whooshed out of the opening. He wrestled the chest tube in through the opening, which is a bit of a feat.

My job is to make sure the patient stays asleep and doesn't start yelling and moving around while the doctor has a finger stuck in between his ribs. I'm pretty good at it too. A couple of the doctors here have been known to ask for me by name when they need a nurse for a procedure. Even when it's my day off.

The tube was placed and connected to the suction container. Dr. Robbins sutured the tube in place and put a dressing around the site. A small amount of pink fluid came out in the tube, but most of what was in there needing to be sucked out was just air. Air that was in the wrong spot. Dr Robbins listened to the patient's chest and nodded his head. There was now air movement heard on the right side. We just had to leave that tube in for a few days while the lung healed and sealed itself back to the ribcage.

"Allie, his daughter is here," Tracy said. "Can she come in?"

The room was still a disaster, scattered with debris from all the medical supplies we had opened. When I was a young, fresh-faced nurse, I always thought I should make the families wait while I cleaned up all the mess and tidied the room. It didn't take long to learn that families don't like to wait, wondering what is going on and imagining the worst. And they don't care what the floor or room looks like. So I told Tracy to let her in.

A tall, slender lady with strawberry blond hair and blue eyes walked in. I didn't need to ask for ID, she was obviously his daughter. She looked at him nervously and glanced at me.

"Hi, I'm Allie," I introduced myself. "I'm the nurse, we spoke on the phone."

She smiled faintly "Nice to meet you." She looked back at him with her brow furrowed. "Is he..."

"He's fine," I assured her. "He's just sleeping right now. We had to give him some sedation." Dr. Robbins walked in the room to explain everything to her. She listened quietly, nodding as he talked. She seemed an entirely different person than the lady I had talked to on the phone.

Mr. Jergins began stirring about a little. I touched his hand and said his name and his eyes fluttered open briefly. "Your daughter is here," I told him and gestured for her to come up to the bed and talk to him. She gingerly approached and touched his hand.

"Dad?" she whispered. He looked at her and then around the room. He seemed to be confused as to where he was. He looked back at her frightened face.

"Katy?" he slurred. "Is that you, Katydid?" She looked relieved to hear him speak.

"He'll be a little groggy for a while" I told her. "The meds will wear off within the hour."

"He, uh, gets a little.... Um.... goofy, sometimes," she hedged. "I mean, when they give him drugs" she hastened to explain. "After his knee surgery, he was, well-"

"All my exes live in Texas!" Mr Jergins broke out in a loud, off-key chorus, then started to giggle. He stopped abruptly when the laughing motion pulled on his chest tube. "Ow! What the Sam Hill is this thing stuck in my side?" He looked down at the tubing. "Is that thing draining in or out?"

I started to explain that this was the tube we had placed to re-expand his lung, but he cut me off. "You're cute, but you're too young for me. But I like your friend over there in the corner," he slurred. I looked over my shoulder and the only thing I saw was an IV pole. He waggled his eyebrows at it. "Tell her to come sit on my lap!"

Katy looked completely embarrassed. "Uh, this is what I meant," she said. "He's a really nice guy, but something about pain meds turns him into, well, this."

Mr. Jergins had his eyes closed and was swaying his head back and forth to a song no one else could hear. I was pretty sure he would be sharing it with us shortly, since he was working his lips around, trying to get them to form words.

"Does he get combative?" I asked. Always nice to know ahead of time if your patient might start swinging.

"Oh no!" she cried. "He's never hurt anyone!"

"Well, then I think we can tolerate a drunken cowboy for a few hours," I assured her. "We'll keep him here in the ER for a couple hours to monitor him and then he'll be admitted to the medical floor for a few days."

Mr Jergins finally got enough words of his song out for us to know he was on "Four Rounds with Jose Cuervo", which was probably about how he felt right now. But at least he wasn't in pain.

I was excusing myself to go start my charting, when he suddenly jerked his head up and looked at me. "You'd get more slots filled on your dance card if you wore something a little prettier," he slurred. "Those things look like jail garb." And then he went back to humming about Jose.

The sad thing is that I've seen some of the county jail residents come in for treatment, and their jail issued garb does look pretty much like scrubs. I get to pick my color and pattern, and I'm allowed to have pockets. That's about the only difference.

Ok, so I didn't go into nursing for the wardrobe. And I'm not trying to 'fill my dance card' when I'm at work. I didn't know if Mr Jergins would appreciate my scrubs/pajamas comparison, but given his current state of mind, I thought it best to steer clear of conversations about pajamas.

I swung through the break room to get a cup of coffee on my way to the desk. I had a lot of stuff to chart, with only a few things scribbled on a paper towel as a reference. I was going to need a caffeine boost to help me get through all of it.

Scott was in there, eating his lunch. He grinned at me around his sandwich. I guess he had overheard my patient serenading me in the trauma room. At least we could laugh about it. There were some things in this job that were just downright amusing.

I settled in at the desk, armed with coffee, and began the charting. There were a few things about this job I didn't care for too much. There were a lot of things about this job that I loved. But I hated charting with a passion, and I didn't think I was ever going to change my mind on that. Unfortunately, it was a necessary evil.

I was sitting at a spot at the desk where I could see directly in to Mr. Jergins' room. I needed to keep a close eye on him while he slept off the rest of the meds. He had laid his head back and had his eyes closed. Katy was sitting beside the gurney, holding his hand. She was talking on the phone to someone and rattling away a mile a minute.

I guess she had gotten over her shock and was back to her usual self.

"Can I get a triage, please?" Tracy said from the desk. I figured Katy would holler if they needed me, so I walked up to the front.

There was a frazzled looking woman in her thirties with four boys. The oldest looked about ten years old, and the youngest looked about four. One of the middle ones was standing next to her, holding one arm against his stomach with the other hand and trying not to cry. The youngest was sitting on her foot with his arms and legs wrapped around her leg, and the other two were having a punching contest on each other behind her.

"Hi, can we help you?" I asked the mother.

"Yes," she sighed. "David fell off the jungle gym and hurt his arm." She gestured to the boy next to her. I imagined this was a familiar scenario for her.

"Ok," I replied. "David, do you want to come in to the room with me while mom gives some information to the clerk?"

He looked at me nervously. He was about eight years old, and torn between trying to be a man and wanting his mommy. The injury wasn't life-threatening, so it wouldn't hurt anything if he stayed with her for a few minutes. I gave him the easy out.

"It's okay, you can sit up here with her," I told him. "It will only take a few minutes and then we can all go back to the room together." He nodded, looking relieved. I have a soft spot for kids. Anything I can do to make this ER visit less scary or painful, I'm more than willing to do.

Tracy started asking the mom for his name, date of birth, etc. She was stopped short when the two boys in the back tackled each other and tumbled to the floor in a flurry of yelling and swinging fists. The mother just stared at them for a moment. I think she wished she was somewhere far away. Somewhere quiet and peaceful. Then she sighed and reached down to grab each of them by their shirt. She hauled them to their feet in one smooth motion, which was impressive.

"Stop it! Now!" She commanded them. They both looked at her for a moment. They must have seen something in her face, because they didn't talk back.

"Yes ma'am. Sorry," they both mumbled in unison. She turned back to Tracy to finish giving the information. Her expression was completely calm, as if nothing out of the ordinary had happened.

Tracy gaped at her in awe. Tracy had a four- and two-year-old who were terrors. I could tell she wanted to ask the lady for her secret. She had tried everything short of electro-shock therapy to get her kids to behave. So far, nothing had been successful. I was pretty sure one day I would find her buying those shock collars you put on your dog. And she was allergic to dogs.

Tracy remembered what she was supposed to be doing and went back to collecting information. As soon as she was done, I let the whole troupe come back through the door. We stopped by the scale to get his weight.

"I need to see how big you are," I told him.

"Okay," he said, and stepped up on the scale. Kids are the only patients I have that are happy to get weighed. I wrote down his weight and gestured down the hall toward the 'bones and bruises' room.

"Is he fat?" his younger brother piped up.

"No, he is just the right size," I assured him. We weigh the kids in case we need to give a dose of medication, since pediatric doses are based on their weight.

"Will you see if I'm fat?" the brother asked.

"Sure," I said. "Hop up here." He stepped on to the scale and I looked at the readout. His weight was perfectly normal. I wasn't sure where he had gotten the concern with being fat.

"Nope, you're not fat," I told him. He hopped back off the scale.

"My teacher always says that if I keep eating so much food, I'm going to get fat," he explained. With his activity level, I was pretty sure he wasn't going to have a problem with that.

"Well, I think you'll be okay," I assured him. He nodded seriously and followed us down the hall. Kids are kind of fun to watch in the ER. If they aren't terrified of the place, that is. Since he knew nothing was happening to him, he was looking around at all the sights.

I got David on the gurney and elevated the hurt arm on a pillow with an ice pack on it. It was pretty swollen, so we would get an x-ray of it. I asked his mom all the usual questions about allergies and immunizations while we waited for the x-ray tech to come get David. He had a pretty uneventful health history. I asked about previous injuries and that list was a little longer. His mom kept getting mixed up on which kid had the broken ankle or dislocated shoulder or concussion. I imagine with those four, she had a constant stream of injuries.

The x-ray tech arrived to take David to the x-ray room. On critical patients, we can take a picture with a portable machine, but the quality is better if we take them to the main machine. He looked frightened at being taken away from his mom. This was a dilemma, because she couldn't go with him and leave the other three here.

"David, if you can be brave and go get a picture of your arm, I'll give you a popsicle when you get back," I bargained with him. That caused an eruption of shouting from the other three that they wanted a popsicle too.

"I only give popsicles to brave patients and brothers who sit still and be quiet," I told them. The mom looked relieved that I could bribe them to behave while they were here. I knew they would be all sugared up when they got home, but maybe they could run laps around the block to burn off the energy.

David agreed that he could be brave, and the x-ray tech wheeled the gurney out of the room. They all seemed impressed with the bed that had wheels on it. They were sitting on the floor against the wall next to their mom and making a display of being very quiet. That worked for me.

I went back to check on Mr. Jergins and he was a little more alert. He was arguing with Katy that he was fine and they should just go home. She was trying to explain that he couldn't leave but he wasn't having it.

I walked in the room to help her out. "Mr. Jergins, you can't leave right now," I told him. I lifted up the side of his gown and showed him the drainage tube with blood in it and all the tape covering his ribs. "You still have this drainage tube in."

"Well, then take it out," he said, reaching to yank on the tube.

"No!" I cried out as I grabbed his hand just in time. I should have seen that coming. Ranchers are hardy and practical. Got a tube stuck between your ribs? Just yank it out. Makes sense, right?

I went through the explanation again about how the tube was re-expanding his lung and we needed to leave it in for a few days or he wouldn't be able to breathe again. He stared at me with his brow furrowed, like he didn't quite comprehend what I was saying.

Katy assured me that once the drugs wore off, he would be more cooperative. Sometimes, when patients keep trying to pull things out, we have to restrain their hands to protect them from themselves. I really don't like to do that if I don't have to, though. We would just give Mr. Jergins a little more time to clear his foggy brain. Katy said she would watch him to make sure he didn't go after the tube again.

David had returned from his ride to x-ray. I told him I just had to wait until the doctor saw the picture before it was okay to give him his popsicle. If the break was bad enough, he might need surgery, and his stomach needed to be empty for that. I left that part of the explanation out for now, though.

"When do we get our popsicles?" one of the other boys asked.

"After you've been good for the whole time," I replied. I knew better than to give the reward early. Then I would have no leverage and three boys jacked up on sugar in the ER. Their mom smiled at me. She knew that trick too, I'm sure.

Dr. Robbins came in after a few minutes with the good news that it was a simple break and would just need a splint for now. The arm was too swollen to put a cast on, so we use a temporary type of splint to start with. He told the mom that he would need to go see the orthopedic doctor in a week, after the swelling had gone down.

David didn't cry while we put the splint on. He grimaced when I had to tighten it in place, but he was determined to be brave. I gave his mom some printed out instructions on how to take care of the arm.

"Okay, guys, we're ready to go," I told the crew. "Let's go get our popsicles."

They jumped to their feet excitedly. I helped David get off the gurney and we headed down the hall toward the door. We stopped at the refrigerator and I opened the freezer door to show them the flavor options.

They each picked out the one they wanted and eagerly tore open the wrappers to start enjoying their treat. I figured it was better to devour them here than when they got in the car. My linoleum floor was easier to clean than the seats in the car.

As I held open the exit door for them to walk out, David stopped and looked up at me. "Thank you for being a nice nurse," he said earnestly, and my heart melted.

"You're welcome," I said, as I ruffled his hair. "Thank you for being such a brave patient." He smiled at me and walked out the door.

And that would be one of the parts of the job that I love.

Chapter 4

Lunch at Joe's

I woke up that morning with a craving for buffalo wings. Greasy, juicy, burn-your-lips hot wings, dripping with bleu cheese dressing. I laced up my sneaks and pounded out a 3-mile run, trying to outrun the craving. No luck. I took a hot shower, started a pot of coffee and toasted a piece of healthy, nutritious multigrain bread. Toast and coffee did nothing to curb the craving.

I threw myself in to the tasks for the day- laundry, paying bills, cleaning out the fridge. The whole time, I kept dreaming of wings. I finally caved. Self-control is not my strong suit.

It was Tuesday, which meant my little sister, Shelby, was working the lunch shift over at Joe's Bar and Grill. Joe's just happened to have the best wings in the state, so I could feed my craving and count it as family time.

Joe's was built in the 1960s and was called Smokin' Joes for 30 years. Posters of Joe Camel covered the walls and the sign outside even featured a huge painting of a cigarette. At night, a neon orange light glowed at the end of it.

But, as smoking fell out of vogue, and more diseases were linked to smoking, things changed. Joe and Patty, the owners, fell under attack from several groups who protested the blatant promotion of such an unhealthy habit. Then old Joe himself had a heart attack. Not a little one either. His heart actually stopped for a few minutes until the EMTs got it going again. The cardiologist told Joe that he had to get away from cigarette smoke entirely, or he would be pushing up daisies before his 70th birthday. This included the perpetual cloud of second hand smoke that hung over the dining room of Joe's.

So the cigarette sign came down and so did all the posters, and Smokin' Joes became just "Joe's". It also became the first non-smoking bar and grill in town. Surprisingly, business didn't slow a bit. Their food was amazing, and it turned out a lot of non-smokers were thrilled to enjoy a meal without the smoke cloud. It was especially popular for business folks at lunchtime.

Shelby liked working the lunch shift because it was busy and she made great tips. Plus, the businessmen were on a schedule. They ate, paid and went on their way. The evening crowd liked to linger, and the solo men liked to hit on her. She had little choice but to smile and tolerate it, as her tips and her job depended on happy customers. She was used to being hit on, but she preferred to be able to tell the sleaze balls exactly what she thought. Unfortunately, if she was at work, she was a captive victim. So she kept to the lunch shift most days, and tried to work weekdays.

Joe's was only 2 miles away, so I hopped on my bike and pedaled over there. I rationalized that this somehow offset the calories I was about to consume. I stashed my bike by the back door, hung my helmet on the handle bars and shook out my hair. Safety is important, but it doesn't always accommodate fashion.

I stepped in the back door and paused for a moment to inhale and savor the delicious smells coming from the kitchen. My stomach growled and I headed to the front part of the restaurant. I usually sat at the bar to eat, when I was dining solo. It seemed less lonely than sitting at a table for two by myself. I vaguely recall some classic country song about that. You know it makes for a sad situation if someone wrote a country song about it.

Shelby waved from behind the bar where she was filling glasses with iced tea. I hopped on a stool near the end and she slid one glass down the bar to me. If I tried a trick like that, the glass would probably end up shattered on the floor with ice and drink everywhere. When she did it, the glass slid as smooth as silk down the bar and came to a stop right in front of me. She's good.

"Hey, Lis, how's tricks?" she asked.

"Same as always," I replied. "Just thought I should come visit my darling baby sister."

She grinned. "Yeah, right! Wings, then? Inferno style with extra celery?" I nodded. Most people think I order the extra celery because I like to eat so healthy. Actually, I need the extra cooling for my scorched mouth and lips. Because I like my hot wings really, really hot.

Tony, the prep cook, came out from the kitchen to fill his soda glass. He saw me and smiled his slow, lopsided grin, showing off his beautiful white teeth.

"Allie, Allie, Allie" He sauntered down the length of the bar and stood across from me. "You're looking lovely today. Haven't seen you in here in a while."

I wasn't about to tell Tony that I had been avoiding the place so I could still fit in my jeans. Tony was tall and lanky and never had to worry about what he ate. A while back, I had been eating at Joe's about twice a week. Unfortunately, there wasn't much on the menu that was "low calorie". The celery with the buffalo wings was about all you got for vegetables, unless you count the tomato on the cheeseburger. But all their food was so delicious, you forgot things like nutritional value and self-control. You ate the whole cheeseburger, with bacon, and the French fries and loved every bite of it. I just couldn't do that too often or it caught up to me.

He leaned back against the counter and asked "Save any lives this week?"

"Oh sure," I replied. "A couple dozen or so." Tony liked to believe that my job as an ER nurse involved nonstop life and death emergencies. I'm pretty sure he didn't want to hear the actual details of my shift yesterday. A stomach flu with projectile vomiting, an abdominal pain that turned out to be constipation, a histrionic teenage girl with a sprained ankle and a gentleman of questionable hygiene with a nasty rash in his nether regions. And those were the interesting patients. Not exactly the stuff you find in Hollywood scripts of medical shows.

"Good, good," he nodded sincerely. I'm never totally sure if he's being serious or not.

"So, me and some buddies are headed up the canyon this weekend to shred some wicked trails. Wanna go?" he asked.

Tony and I both enjoyed mountain biking, but in different forms. I liked things like actual trails, safety equipment and the ability to see where I was going. Tony was a little more hard core than me. I went with him and his buddies once and it was not a fun experience. I alternated between worrying that I would break a limb and worrying that I would have to use my field training to patch up one of them. I didn't want to put my guardian angel through that again.

Luckily, I had a valid excuse.

"I have to work." I tried to look disappointed. "Sorry. Maybe next time," I lied through my teeth.

"That's ok. When I come in to the ER all busted up, you can take care of me." He winked at me and grinned.

"Deal," I replied. Taking care of trauma patients in the ER is easy. It's being out on the side of the mountain with nothing a first aid kit that gets me nervous. I'm out of my comfort zone.

"Here ya go, Lis." Shelby set a steaming basket of wings in front of me. They looked absolutely mouth-watering and I was done making small talk. Tony saw that gleam in my eye and knew the conversation was over. He pushed himself off the counter to wander back to the kitchen.

"Later, Allie. See you this weekend," he grinned over his shoulder.

I mumbled something in response, but I was already tearing into my order of grease and hot sauce. And it was absolutely delicious. I had to stop and cool my mouth off with some ice tea or celery every so often. I didn't bother with trying to clean the hot sauce off my fingers. That was a pointless task.

I finished the last wing and started licking the extra sauce and bleu cheese dressing off my fingers. Shelby wandered back over. She knew better than to interrupt me while I was eating wings. Plus, it was pretty messy to watch.

"So, what else are you up to today?" she asked, as she cleared away the plate stacked with bones.

"House stuff," I said, making a face. I really didn't like being a grownup some days. "I have to get some groceries and finish my laundry."

"Sounds like a good time," she said. I'm pretty sure she was joking. And possibly making fun of me. That was how we showed affection in my family.

"Yeah, I'm a party girl," I sighed. Some days, my life sounded a little boring. I reminded myself that if I finished my 'to do' list today, then I had all of tomorrow to go play. A huge bonus of working 12-hour shifts is that I get 4 days off a week. I could sacrifice one day off to act like an adult.

We made small talk for a few minutes. She reminded me that I need to schedule a massage with her for her clinicals and we picked a day that we both had off work to meet up.

She wanted to do it at her apartment, which is small and crammed full of stuff. Oh, and has Snickers running around, licking things. Mostly me. I preferred to have her bring the table to my house, which was bigger and cleaner and dog hair free. She argued that the table was really heavy and awkward to move. Since I had never moved a massage table, I didn't know how heavy they were, so the argument died quickly. I would wait until closer to the day to bring it up again. No point in fighting about it now.

A large group of people walked in and Shelby had to get back to work. I waved to Tony as I walked out the back. I fastened on my bike helmet and took off pedaling. I took the scenic route home, while I waited for the wings to settle a little. It was a beautiful day anyway, perfect for being outside.

I rode down by the creek and watched the ducks floating in the water. I pedaled casually through the park and past the school. Riding on a bike path is a lot easier than pedaling up a rocky mountain trail. I finally headed home, planning on finishing the house work I had left.

I parked the bike on the back porch and walked inside. The afternoon sun was streaming in through the living room window and spilling over the couch. I laid down on the couch and felt the warmth pouring over me. I decided I should lay there for a few minutes and enjoy it. Or at least, I think that's what I decided.

I woke up an hour later and the sun had moved on. The couch was now in the shade and I was cold and a little groggy. I hadn't really planned on taking a nap, but it's always good to catch up on a little sleep. I stretched and stood up to walk into the laundry room.

My pet fish, Oscar, started swimming around excitedly when he saw me moving. I guess he was ready to be fed. Oscar is a betta, which they say is the hardest pet fish to kill. He seemed to be quite hardy, considering how many times I forgot to feed him, or clean his tank, or turn on the heater when it was cold.

He had been part of a school project for one of my co-workers' kid and after the project was over, she was going to flush him down the toilet. I didn't want the little guy to meet his untimely demise in the city sewer, so I took him. Other people rescue dogs and cats and horses. I rescued a fish.

He was pretty low maintenance and he didn't shed everywhere, so it was a good choice for me. I dropped a pinch of fish flakes into his tank and he went crazy, chasing around and eating them. Wow, he was really hungry. I looked close to see if he looked underfed. I wouldn't want to starve my poor rescue fish. His shiny red body looked the same as it always did, so I figured he was okay.

I threw the washed laundry into the dryer and then poked around the fridge to see what I needed for groceries.

It was really bare, even for me. I had been working the last few days and I didn't do much besides work and sleep when I was on shift. That was why I had so much housework to catch up on my first day off. I made a mental list of what I had, which didn't take long. I needed to hit the store before supper time, or I was going to have to eat string cheese, pickles and Italian dressing for supper. That was about all I had in there.

I hopped in the car and headed to the store. I always started in the produce section, where I loaded up on fruits and veggies. I had seen my share of illness, and I knew the importance of a healthy, balanced diet. I had my occasional splurges, like the buffalo wings at lunch. But the majority of my diet was nutritious. Some things are going to happen no matter how healthy you live. But there were still quite a few health problems that could be prevented.

The thing that scared me more than dying young was living to a ripe old age, but having my body give out on me. It broke my heart to see people come in who lived in a wheelchair or bed, needing complete care for everything. I kept seeing the same ones over and over, and I realized these people were living for years in this state. Most of them didn't seem too happy with the situation, and I don't blame them. "Living" was a loose interpretation of the word.

I knew this could happen to someone no matter how healthy they tried to live. But I also knew that a healthy diet and exercise could at least help, if not prevent, a lot of diseases, like heart disease, high blood pressure, high cholesterol, cancer and diabetes. So I was going to put up the best fight I could.

I really liked fruits and veggies, so it was pretty easy for me to eat healthy. Unfortunately, I also really liked my sweets. And I didn't have much self-control around a plate of cookies. Or a pan of brownies. Or a box of candy. It wouldn't be too difficult for me to be very overweight, if I didn't keep active and avoid temptation as much as I could.

But in my job, I had also seen the progression of how life could go downhill when someone was extremely overweight. Not being able to walk up stairs led to not being able to walk down the hall which led to not being able to reach over to tie your shoes. And now we were back to being stuck in a wheelchair and needing help for everything.

So I guess one of the health benefits at my job is that I got constant reminders how important it was to be healthy. Which wasn't a bad thing.

I cruised through the store, loading up the cart with all the essentials. Being out of everything meant it was a pretty spendy grocery run. I stopped in the cereal aisle, perusing the options. I fondly recalled the days when I could eat Frosted Flakes every morning for breakfast. Then I picked out a high-fiber, adult cereal and tossed it in the cart. Tony the Tiger would have to peddle his wares to someone else.

I went through the checkout and loaded my bags of groceries in the car. The trunk was almost full, which was not common for me. But now my fridge would be stocked.

I got home and was starting to haul the bags in to my house. I heard voices from my neighbor's yard that were getting steadily louder. My next door neighbors were a nice couple in their fifties. Their children had all left home, so they had plenty of time to spend together. I'm not sure that was a good thing, because they had some pretty colorful arguments.

It appeared they were trying to hang a hammock between two trees in their backyard. Jim was on a stepladder trying to fasten one side of the rope, and Cathy was offering advice from the ground.

"You can't put it there, that's too low," she told him sharply. "You have to go up higher by that branch."

"It's just fine here," he snapped back. "You're gonna need a ladder to get in it if I put it that high."

"The instruction book says to hang it six feet up the tree," Cathy pointed out, holding up the paper as if he could read it from up there.

"That thing was probably written in Chinese and they don't know nothing," he snarled. "Those things are never right. They're just a waste of paper."

"Or maybe they're important because they can tell you how to do it right!" Her voice was getting louder.

"I know how to do it right and I don't need you or any paper telling me how!" His volume escalated to match hers. He was turned halfway around on the ladder and gesturing wildly. I was a little nervous he was going to fall off.

Cathy must have been thinking the same thing, because she yelled "You are gonna fall and break your neck, and then Allie will have to come patch you up!" She swung her arm in the direction of my house and then turned toward where she was pointing.

"Oh, hi Allie," she said cheerily when she saw me. They seemed to save their anger for each other, because they were really nice to everyone else. "How are you?" she asked.

"I'm good," I replied nonchalantly, trying to pretend I hadn't overheard their fight. I didn't want to get dragged into it. "Just getting some groceries." I held up the bags I was carrying as an explanation for why I needed to keep walking.

She nodded and I continued on into the house. I set the bags down on the kitchen floor and started unloading them and putting the food away. I finished unpacking that load of bags, but now I had a dilemma. There were still more bags in the car, but I didn't want to wander back outside while they were out there fighting. Unfortunately, there was frozen food out there, thawing quickly. I sighed and headed back out. Maybe they were done.

Jim had both ends of the hammock attached to a tree. Cathy was still insisting he didn't hang them high enough. To make her point, she got in the hammock. It sagged so much that her butt was touching the ground.

"See?" she snapped. "It's too low!"

"Maybe you're over the weight limit," Jim replied sarcastically. Cathy had a half-full can of soda in her hand and she chucked it at his head. Ok, he deserved that. Luckily, it missed him, so I didn't have to go patch him up. I just headed for the car and quickly gathered the rest of my bags.

I managed to get back into the house without them noticing me. I put away the rest of the groceries and then surveyed my freshly stocked fridge for something to cook for supper. I decided a salad was a good choice, to offset my lunch. Plus, it wouldn't require any actual cooking.

I ate my salad while I scrolled through e-mails. I was always hearing from diet and nutrition experts that you shouldn't do anything while you are eating. They say that watching TV or reading distracts you and you don't realize how much you are eating. But it's pretty boring to stare into silent space while you eat. And I can't really overeat, because once I finish what's on my plate, I'm done eating. So I looked at funny jokes and stupid videos on my laptop. It was good mindless entertainment.

I decided mindless entertainment would be the theme for the night. I had borrowed a movie from a friend that

I had been wanting to see. It was of those 'so stupid it's funny' flicks that didn't really have much for a plot line. Sometimes you just needed to laugh and not think much.

I changed into sweat pants and a baggy t-shirt. I made a bag of low-fat microwave popcorn and poured a glass of lemonade. I settled into my comfy, worn out couch and clicked 'Play.'

Who says I don't know how to have a good time?

Chapter 5

From a Clear Blue Sky

The morning started out so normal it was boring. I made a pot of coffee and scrambled some eggs. I ate breakfast and sat at the table, sipping coffee and scrolling through e-mails, trying to decide if I should catch up on laundry or load up the bike and head up the mountain. It was cloudy but still warm, which can be some great biking weather. Of course, that can also turn into a sudden downpour, which isn't so great for biking.

My phone ringing startled me. I am definitely a member of the texting generation and my phone almost never rings. The screen showed "Mom" and a tiny flutter of concern went through my gut. This was an odd time of day for her to be calling me.

"Hi, mom" I answered.

"Allison-" she started and then took a shuddering breath. She sounded like she was trying not to cry. "Allison, your father is in the hospital." Then she paused, while a thousand questions ran through my head all at one time.

"Is he ok?" I asked, even as my brain said 'that's a dumb question, if he was ok, he wouldn't be in the hospital'. "What happened?"

"He was feeling bad yesterday, so he came in early and laid on the couch. I thought he just needed a good meal, so I made some strip steaks and potatoes for him. But he said he had indigestion and couldn't eat. So I put everything up in the fridge, but those strip steaks never reheat well, they just get tough and-"

"Mom!" I cried out. "Why is he in the hospital?!"

"Oh. Well, he went to bed early but kept feeling worse," she continued. "About 5 o'clock this morning, he said he felt like an elephant was sitting on his chest. He didn't want to wait until the clinic opened, so we drove in to the ER."

I didn't dare ask who drove. I was pretty sure that my stubborn, chauvinistic father had insisted on driving. Even though he was probably having a heart attack. My family makes some of the worst health decisions. There was no point in a lecture right now, it was over and done with. However, we would definitely discuss this in the near future.

"So, what did the ER doc find?" I asked. I was already grabbing a bag and shoving clothes into it. The statement 'I feel like an elephant is sitting on my chest' almost always meant a heart attack, and I was going to get there as quick as I could.

My parents lived in a small town about 45 miles away. Of course, their rural hospital wouldn't keep him there, he would be transferred to a larger hospital. No matter where I was headed, I was going to be ready in 10 minutes flat.

"Well, they did a test with a bunch of wires and they drew some blood. He's feeling better now, they gave him some pills." She paused and then said, "But they think he should go to Springfield to see the cardiologist." Springfield was a city 100 miles down the highway from me. In the opposite direction from my parents.

"How long until he leaves?" I asked. My ER nurse mode was on, all business, getting the necessary info.

"The helicopter is on its way," mom replied. She seemed a little dazed by all of this. Now I really had a dilemma.

"Are you going to be able to ride in the helicopter with him?" I asked. Most rigs have space to take one family member, but it's not always a guarantee. If they could get mom to Springfield, I could worry about getting her home later.

"Um, I don't think so," she hedged. Ok, mom isn't the type that would like riding in a helicopter. In fact, mom would hate riding in a helicopter. Even one of the big, stable tourist choppers that show you cool stuff. Crammed in a tiny chopper with a flight crew and my dad all wired up for cardiac monitoring was definitely not her cup of tea. I was pretty sure she hadn't asked to ride along.

"Mom, it would really help dad to have someone stay with him the whole time." I played the guilt card. Maybe her love and concern for my dad would override her fear of the helicopter. At least I hoped it would. "They usually let one family member ride along. Can you ask them?"

She was silent for a very long moment. I could almost hear her internal struggle, deciding what to do. Thankfully, the guilt card worked.

"I'll go ask," she said reluctantly at last. I heard the phone clunk as she set it on the table, followed by a stretch of random room noise. I would have preferred to talk to my dad while she was doing that, but that hadn't seemed to occur to her. I could hear the steady beeping on the cardiac monitor of my father's heart rate.

I reached for my coffee cup and was surprised to find my hand was shaking. This particular situation was one that I saw at least a couple times a week. Except I was usually the person drawing blood and doing the ECG. And the guy in the bed was some random stranger that I didn't have any attachment to. Being on the other side of that bed was pretty terrifying. I had a sudden rush of empathy for all the family members I had seen standing in the corner of an ER room, eyes wide with fear.

I knew my dad was alive. But I didn't know anything else, I was having trouble finding anything out, and I was completely helpless to make him better. This had to be about the worst feeling in the world.

I heard a clattering as mom picked the phone back up and then she took a deep breath and sighed, "I can go." She sounded less than thrilled but I was grateful she was going with him. It would be an hour or more after he got to the hospital in Springfield before I got there, and even longer before mom could get there in a car. It just didn't seem right for dad to be alone right now. I couldn't really explain why I felt that way. He certainly wasn't about to die. I saw people survive heart attacks all the time.

At least that is what I kept reminding myself, over and over. "He's going to be ok." I'm not sure if I was chanting it inside my head or out loud. I also wasn't sure if I was convincing myself, but I tried to focus on the task at hand. I had 2 days worth of clothes, toothbrush, deodorant, cell phone and purse. I was as ready as I could get.

"Mom, I'm getting in the car and heading to Springfield," I said. "I'll see you when I get there, ok? Call me with any new information." I was pretty sure they would have dad diagnosed and whisked off to the cardiac catheterization lab before I could get there. Which would leave my anxious, frightened mother all alone in a waiting room for an hour. Knowing that killed me, but there was nothing else I could do. I could only drive so fast, and besides, me dying in a fiery car crash wasn't going to make this situation better.

"Ok. Drive safe," she reminded me, ever the mom and caretaker. "I hear the helicopter now." I glanced at my watch. 8:15. I would get to the hospital by 10:00. Dad would get there by 8:45. I grabbed my car keys and bolted out the door.

Only after I got in the car and on the highway did it occur to me that mom didn't mention calling my siblings. If I had to guess, I would say she only called me. And now she was on a helicopter and couldn't use her phone. I guess I should let them know what is going on. Even though I didn't know that much myself.

I pulled out my phone and hit the button for Shelby. She didn't usually get up much before her lunch shift started at work, but she was pretty attached to her phone. I was hoping she had the ringer on, just in case. Sure enough, after 4 rings, I got a groggy "What?"

"Dad had a heart attack. He's being flighted to Springfield. Mom is going with him." I rattled everything off fast, forgetting all my professional training about gently breaking bad news. There was such a long silence, I thought maybe the call had dropped.

"Are you for real?" her voice was sharp with concern. I knew she would take this hard. She was Daddy's little girl and she thought he was Superman.

"Yeah, mom called me a little bit ago," I said, a little slower and calmer. "He's in the ER in Madison, but the chopper was landing to take him to Springfield. He is going to the cardiologist there." I felt reassured that dad would be in the hands of experts, but I realized that to Shelby, transferring to a bigger hospital meant things were worse, not better. "He's doing ok," I hurried to reassure her. "They gave him some meds and mom said he was feeling better. He just might need to have something done."

"Like what?" she asked. And I didn't have an answer for her, so I had to come up with one of the bland, catch-all explanations we gave to families when we don't know for sure what is going on.

"If he has a blockage in an artery on his heart, they can go in with a wire and open it back up," I explained. "It's called a cardiac cath. It's really quick and he only has to stay in the hospital a couple of days."

It was an oversimplified explanation of the procedure, but I didn't have the time or energy to explain every detail of all the possible procedures he might need. "Once I get there, I'll find out for sure what's going to happen and then call you back," I told her.

"Have you called Andrew yet?" she asked.

"No, I'm calling him next," I replied. Our brother was pretty calm, so I knew he wouldn't be too upset at being called second. Shelby never would have forgiven me if I hadn't called her first. Although she didn't seem to notice that mom hadn't called her at all. Families are a funny dynamic. We hung up after a quick, but fervent "Love you" and I dialed Andrew.

"Well, hello there, Allison Eloise," a feminine voice with a fake Southern accent drawled. It was my sister-in-law, Nicole. She was an absolute sweetheart and we got along great, so she frequently answered Andrew's phone when she saw it was me calling. Sometimes we got so caught up chatting that I would hang up and then realize I never actually talked to Andrew. Today, unfortunately,

I didn't have time to joke around. My mood wasn't much for joking anyway.

"Hey Nicole. Is Andrew around?" I asked bluntly. "We have a little family emergency." Somehow, I felt I was supposed to tell Andrew first, not Nicole. Once again, I have no idea why I felt that way. Dad loved Nicole and she was definitely part of the family. She seemed to pick up on it, though, and didn't ask anything. Another reason I just loved having her in my family. She called to Andrew and told him to hurry.

"Hey, sis. What's up?" he asked. We were pretty direct and to the point in our family.

"Dad went to the ER this morning. It looks like he had a heart attack. They are flying him to Springfield right now." I still felt numb when I said the words. They didn't feel real yet. "Mom is flying with him and I'm driving there right now."

"What's going to happen when he gets there?" he asked. Everyone had questions, including me. I didn't have much for answers. I couldn't believe how helpless I felt. I couldn't help my dad, I couldn't be there for my mom and I couldn't answer anyone's questions about my dad. My frustration was building and my poor brother was about to get the blowout. I took a deep breath, and then another.

"He's going to see the cardiologist," I said. "That's all we know for now. I'll know more once I get there and I can call you back." I tried to keep calm.

"What makes them think it's a heart attack? What are they going to do? Is he going to need surgery?" Andrew rattled off questions. He's an engineer and he likes lots of details and information. I knew he was just trying to cope with the news and this was how he handled problems. But I was barely holding it together and getting grilled for answers I didn't have wasn't helping.

"I don't know!" I yelled. "I don't know yet!"

There was a long pause. "I'm sorry, Andrew. I just don't know anything. And I'm a little stressed," I offered up as an excuse. Andrew and I fought enough that yelling was nothing new between us. But I didn't want to fight right now. I wanted my whole family banded together to help dad.

"It's ok, I understand," he said. "I'm glad you're there to help with everything." I wondered how he felt right then, being so far away. Sometimes I envied him, living blissfully away from all the family drama. But right now, I was glad I lived close by. I would've had a breakdown trying to handle this from three states away.

"I'll call you as soon as I have any more info, ok?" I assured him. "Hug Nicole and the twins for me. Love you."

He promised he would pass my affections along to his family. I don't think he ever needed an excuse to hug his wife or daughters. He was the most devoted, loving husband and father. I really did admire him. Not that I would confess that to him. I usually just told him his shirt was ugly or he was getting fat. Like any bratty little sister would do.

I spent the next 20 miles of highway talking to God. Now I was the one with all the questions, and, once again, there were no clear answers. I know there is a purpose in everything that happens, but right then, it was tough to see what it could be. "Patience" is the lesson I fail the most often. No matter how many times I get the test, I still never quite learn the material. I turned up the radio for a distraction before I drove myself crazy.

What if this wasn't just a test to teach me patience?

I pulled off the highway and headed downtown to the hospital. I wasn't sure where my dad was at in there, so I went to the ER. I walked into the waiting room that was filled with a variety of people.

I wondered what it was like to work here, with a nonstop stream of patients. Some of them looked like they were in pretty rough shape. One girl was hunched over a waste basket in the corner, dry heaving. A frazzled looking mom was holding a crying, squirming toddler. A guy in his 30's was holding his arm on an ice pack. Nothing life-threatening here, but they all needed to be seen and the mountain of paperwork had to be completed on each of them. I wondered how long they had been waiting. We were very proud of our short wait times at my hospital. But we didn't see this volume of patients.

I walked up to the desk. The clerk was on the phone and I waited as patiently as I could. Curiosity and human nature got the best of me and I started eavesdropping. She was arguing with someone about when the kids needed to be picked up from school and who was going to take someone to soccer practice.

I tapped on the glass that mostly separated her from me. She glanced up at me and said, "One moment please," and went back to her conversation. I was getting frustrated. I know that our personal lives can creep over onto our work lives- it's happened to me before. But my dad was somewhere in this hospital, possibly with a heart attack, and my mom was sitting somewhere all alone. I tapped on the glass again.

She glanced up at me and then sighed into the phone, "I have to go. I'll call you later." She hung up the phone and looked at me with irritation. "Can I help you?"

"I'm looking for my dad, Robert Sanford," I said, as calmly as possible. She stared at me blankly. "He came in on the helicopter a little while ago."

"Um..." she looked around, puzzled. I was pretty sure that only one helicopter had come in this morning. "I don't know..." her voice trailed off. I couldn't tell if she actually knew nothing about the patient or if she was just torturing me. Just then, a charge nurse walked by behind the desk.

"Excuse me," I called out. "I'm looking for my dad, he came in on the helicopter." I hated to be rude but I needed to find my dad.

She looked at me and seemed to sense my frustration. "Sure. What is the patient name?" By law, she's required to ask me for the information, to make sure she doesn't share private information with the wrong person.

"Robert Sanford. He had chest pain and he came from Madison." I rattled off any information I thought would identify him.

"Oh, yeah. Um..." she hesitated, which made my heart skip a beat. We never pause before good news. "What is the last update you got?"

"I talked to my mom right before they left Madison," I managed to say. The room was starting to sway in my peripheral vision. "They thought it was a heart attack."

She seemed relieved that I knew that part. "Ok, he did have an MI and they took him to cath lab. I think he's still in there and then he'll go to ICU."

"Do you know where my mom is?" I asked. Those areas usually had their own waiting room, separate from the ER waiting room. Which is nice for the people waiting, but nerve-wracking for the people trying to find them. I had tried to call my mom from the highway, but her cell phone went straight to voice mail.

"She's in the ICU waiting room, I believe." She glanced down at the clerk, who seemed annoyed that we were having this conversation at her desk and was picking at her fingernail polish.

"I'll be right back," she told her, and walked around to the door that led out to the waiting room. "I can walk you down there," she said, and gestured down the hall to the right.

"Thank you," I said, as relief washed over me. Finally, I was about to find my mom. This whole thing still seemed a little surreal but it was getting more real with each step.

"Do you live in Madison, too?" the nice nurse asked as we walked down the hall. I appreciated the small talk for distraction.

"No, I live in Brighton. I actually work in the ER there," I replied. "Is this a busy day for you, or is this normal?" I was curious, since we sometimes transferred patients to their ER.

"No, this is about normal," she replied. "So, are you a nurse?"

"Yes," I replied.

"Oh." She smiled wryly. "So our clerk didn't impress you."

"Well, I know they're busy…" I hedged. I didn't want to start off on the wrong foot here.

"Don't worry," she laughed. "We all know she's terrible. I promise, the rest of the staff is much better. Your dad did have a STEMI and he went to cath lab about 9:20. He should be out shortly." We arrived at a door labeled 'ICU Waiting Room'. She poked her head in and then said, "Looks like she's waiting for you."

I stepped through the door and saw my mom sitting on the couch, purse on her lap, staring blankly at the TV without seeing what was on it.

"Thank you," I said earnestly to the nurse who had walked me down. So far, she was my favorite staff person in this hospital. Not that the bar was that high. I had met two people and one of them was horrible.

"You're welcome," she smiled back. "I hope everything comes out okay with your dad."

She walked back down the hall and I went over to my mom, who looked up at me, looking a little dumbstruck. She stood up to give me a hug and then she started to look a little like herself again.

"Are you doing okay, mom?" I asked. Once again, stupid question. Her husband just had a heart attack. Of course she isn't okay. But I didn't know what else to say.

"Yes," she replied. "I'm glad you're here."

"What did the doctor say?" I jumped right in to the important questions. Not that we make much small talk in my family anyway.

"I haven't seen him since they left the ER," she said. "They said something about a stem and they took him in a pretty big hurry. In fact, some of them were waiting in the room when we got here. They already knew all about him." She seemed a little awed at that.

"Well, with digital images, the doctor here could see his ECG from Madison right away." I began the explanation of things that I knew so far. "The word they used was STEMI, and it's an acronym. It means the type of heart attack that he had. They took him so fast because the sooner they can open the blockage, the better he'll do." I didn't get too in depth with anything. Mom tended to glaze over when I talked about medical stuff. She looked shell-shocked enough already.

"How was the helicopter ride?" I asked. I wasn't sure if I should bring it up or not, but I was curious what she thought.

"Not bad. Quick," she replied. "They sure are busy in there. They didn't stop the whole time we were flying. And they were really nice to me."

That made me feel better. I think most flight crews know how to handle distraught families pretty well. After all, that's almost all they deal with. When your loved one is sick enough to get a Life Flight, your stress level is pretty high. This was my first experience with a loved one on Life Flight and I didn't care to repeat the experience. No matter how nice and competent the crew was.

A tall man in OR scrubs and a head cover walked in. He looked around the room and lighted on my mom. "Mrs. Sanford," he said as he walked toward her.

"Hello, doctor," she said. "I'm sorry I forgot your name." She must have met him in the ER.

He smiled. "That's quite all right. It's Sampson. Mike Sampson." He took her hand to shake it but continued to hold it as he sat next to her. He looked over at me. "And this is?"

"Oh, this is our daughter Allison. She's a nurse," mom smiled proudly at me.

He reached over to shake my hand. "Mike Sampson. Nice to meet you." He reached back and picked up my mother's hand. I appreciated his use of touch to show compassion. I wasn't sure how my somewhat Puritanical mother felt about having a handsome stranger hold her hand. And I was getting nervous about what he was going to say that required him to comfort my mother.

"Mrs. Sanford, we found a blockage on the LAD, which is the main artery to the heart. We were able to open it up so he is getting blood flow through there now." He paused. My mother looked relieved but my sixth sense told me there was more. "But he does have triple vessel disease." He looked over at me, waiting to see if I grasped the significance of this.

Part of my brain grasped what he was saying in a calm, rational manner. The other part of my brain had clanging bells and flashing lights and I felt like I might pass out. Or cry. Or throw up. He saw the color drain from my face and that confirmed that I knew what it meant.

"Mrs. Sanford, your husband is going to need open heart surgery," he said gently. She just stared at him. I had no idea what was going through her head. "And he needs to have it as soon as possible."

"Like, now?" I managed to croak out. This was a lot to process.

"We would like to take him this afternoon," he replied. "There's a case in the OR right now, but we could go by about 1 o'clock."

Okay, deep breaths. Passing out in the waiting room isn't going to help. Mom needs me to be strong for her. Especially since she was still frozen in place. "Mom?" I asked, reaching for her other hand. "Did you catch all of that?" I wasn't about to ask her if she was okay.

She turned slowly to look at me. "Do you think it's a good idea?" she asked. I almost laughed out loud. The cardiologist said he needed open heart surgery, but she wanted me to weigh in. Surgeons might have a reputation for pushing a surgery on everyone. But cardiovascular surgeons didn't push open heart surgery on anyone who didn't need it. There were too many other, less invasive, lower risk ways to treat heart disease. If they could get by with one of those, they would.

"Mom, he needs to have this. He's not getting enough blood to his heart. He needs this to save his life." I didn't want to be too melodramatic, but I needed her to understand that this was not really optional.

"Okay, honey," she said calmly. "If you think so." I was glad she trusted my judgment. Now we had my dad to deal with.

"Have you told my dad yet?" I asked Dr. Sampson.

"No," he replied. "We don't like to spring that news on them until they have their family with them. Plus, he's still under the sedative they used for the cardiac cath. They are taking him to the ICU now. We can all go in there and talk to him."

I stood up and helped my mom gather her things. She had brought a book that looked completely untouched and her water bottle, which she carried with her everywhere. She was always worried about getting enough water.

Dr. Sampson led us down the hall to a large, secured door. There was a phone outside the door and he picked it up. It automatically dialed the nurses' desk and when someone answered, he said "This is Dr. Sampson with the Sanford family." The door buzzed and then swung open. He led us into the ICU.

I had spent enough time helping out in the ICU at Brighton County to know about most of the equipment. Every room had a cardiac monitor that the patient was wired to. It tracked heart rate, blood pressure and oxygen level. Every patient had a couple IV pumps hooked up to them. Some of the patients were on ventilators, which were helping them breath through a tube in their throat. Almost everything in there made some kind of noise at any time. Each room opened directly into a bustling nurses' station in the center of the unit. I suddenly saw this controlled chaos through the eyes of a 'civilian' as I watched my mother's face. Maybe I should have warned her.

The clerk saw us and said "He's over here in Room 6, Dr. Sampson."

We walked around the desk and in to dad's room. He was sound asleep in the bed. His cardiac monitor showed a normal heart rate and blood pressure. For a moment, the whole thing seemed like a bad joke. Here was my dad and he looked just fine.

"Mr. Sanford?" Dr. Sampson touched his hand to wake him up. Dad picked his head up, gazed blearily at the doctor and then flopped his head back on to the pillow. "He's still pretty sleepy," the doctor said to us. "I need to go check on another patient. I'll be back in about 20 minutes. Maybe he'll be a little more awake and we can talk then."

Mom stood in the doorway, looking frightened. "Mom, it's okay," I said. "Come in here and hold his hand." I moved the chair up next to the bed.

Mom remained frozen in the doorway. I have to admit, this setting is intimidating even if you don't love the person laying in the bed. I walked over and took her arm. "It's okay," I repeated as I nudged her toward the bed.

She sat in the chair, and gingerly reached for dad's hand. Once she felt his warm, rough, workworn hand, she visibly relaxed. Even though his eyes were still closed, I saw his hand squeeze hers.

I sat in the other chair off to the side. Nothing to do now but wait for dad to wake up. I needed to call Shelby and Andrew, but there was a large sign warning about cell phone use in the ICU, and I didn't want to leave mom alone yet.

Dad's monitor started chirping. It looked like a wire had just come loose, but the thing was clanging away like he was in cardiac arrest. Mom jumped about a foot in the air. "What's wrong?" she cried.

Since my dad was still pink and breathing, I was pretty sure it was a false alarm, and I reassured her of this.

A tall, thin lady in scrubs walked in the room. She didn't make eye contact with any of us, just walked over to the monitor and pushed some buttons. Then she checked the wires attached to my dad's chest and adjusted the oxygen monitor on his finger. And then she walked out of the room, never once speaking to or even acknowledging us.

Ok, I've never been an ICU nurse and I'm sure it's stressful. Considering the amount of clanging from the monitors around the unit, I'm sure they spent a great deal of time dealing with false alarms. I'm sure she was smart and qualified and an excellent nurse. I kept telling myself that some nurses just don't have much personality. But I still had an uneasy feeling.

Another lady walked in, short and rounded, with auburn curly hair. She looked at mom and smiled.

"Hi! I'm Marcia and I'm the nurse," she introduced herself. It was amazing how much that small gesture made me feel better. I made a mental note to smile at my patients more. I had never realized the effect it could have. She walked over to my mom and rested her hand on mom's shoulder. "Can I get you anything, dear?" she asked. Mom shook her head. She looked over at me, and asked, "How about you, dear?" In nursing school, they taught us to never use terms like 'honey' or 'dear'. Yet is sounded perfectly natural and nurturing from this lady. I shook my head as well.

"I think we're just waiting for the doctor to come back and dad to wake up," I told her. "Then maybe we'll go get some lunch." Eating was the farthest thing from my mind, but I had given the lecture about taking care of yourself about a hundred times. So I would try to get something down, and make sure mom did too.

"Ok, sweetie," she smiled warmly at us both. "Let me know if you need anything." She checked a couple things on dad and then left the room.

Mom seemed much better now that she was sitting beside dad. I knew we had a little while before he wore off the drugs. Dad was a complete lightweight when it came to meds. He got drowsy if he took a couple ibuprofen. I figured now was a good time to call Shelby. She would probably want to pack a bag and drive to Springfield right away.

I went to stand up and my legs barely held me. Finally seeing my mom and dad had released all the tension I was carrying in my body and now I was emotionally drained. I told mom I was going out to the waiting room to make a phone call. She nodded, never taking her eyes off my dad.

I walked out of the ICU into the empty hallway. I couldn't remember which way we came from. Walking into the ICU had been a blur. I started down the hall, but it didn't look right. I couldn't see a sign, even though I thought I remembered a sign on the waiting room. Why did hospital hallways have to look so confusing?

All the events of the day caught up to me at once. I couldn't help my dad, I couldn't answer anyone's questions and now I couldn't even find the stupid waiting room. I gave up, slumped against the wall and slid to the ground. I hung my head to my knees and let the tears fall.

Chapter 6

Who Likes Cabbage Anyway?

I was still sitting on the floor in the hallway, tears running down my face, when I felt a warm hand on my shoulder. I looked up into the kind face of a middle-aged man in a housekeeping uniform.

"Can I help you?" he asked earnestly. I was completely embarrassed to be sitting on the floor, crying like a little girl. But he just seemed genuinely concerned about me.

"I couldn't find the ICU waiting room," I sniffled, as I scrambled to my feet. It seemed like such a minor thing, but at that point, it had been the last straw.

"Oh, I can help you with that," he said, smiling. "It does get kind of confusing in this hall. The waiting room is actually down a little ways, past this other hallway."

Ok, I felt a little better knowing it wasn't right there under my nose and I couldn't find it. As he walked me down to the doorway, I saw the "Waiting Room" sign I remembered from before. Farther down this hall was the ER, where I had come in. A good thing to remember, because that was where my car was parked.

"Here you go," he gestured at the door. "Does that help?"

"Yes," I said, gratefully. "Thank you so much." He just smiled at me kindly again, and then went on his way. I was starting to take notice of these little things that made me feel better. The waiting room with a huge flat screen TV, leather recliners, and gourmet coffee bar- none of that made me feel better. But the kindness of people had a huge effect on me. This was an eye-opening experience for me.

I wiped my nose and took out my cell phone. Five missed calls, all from Shelby. I dialed her number and listened to the phone ring.

"What's going on?!" she cried, as a greeting. I guess I don't get 'hello.'

"I'm sorry, I can't have my cell phone on in the ICU," I said, still sniffling. Unfortunately, the sound of me crying and the words "ICU" sent Shelby into a tizzy.

"What's going on? Is he okay? Please tell me he's okay!" she pleaded, sounding frantic.

"Shelby! He's okay." I said that out of habit. 'Okay' in this case meant alive and able to have his heart problem fixed. It sort of skipped over the serious heart problem and the major surgery he needed.

"Well, then why is he in ICU?" she asked. I took a deep breath and tried to think of the easiest way to explain this.

"They did the cardiac cath thing I told you about. But he has disease on all of his blood vessels on his heart, and he needs to have open heart surgery to fix that. He's in ICU right now, sleeping off the meds they gave him for the cardiac cath," I said in a calm and even tone. My nurse mode was starting to kick back in. "Mom is in there with him right now, but you can't use cell phones in there, so I had to come out to the waiting room to call you."

There was a long pause while she processed all this. "And you're sure he's okay?" she finally asked.

"Yes, he's just sleeping right now or you could talk to him," I reassured her.

"Then why are you crying?" she asked bluntly.

Shelby knew I wasn't much for waterworks. I didn't cry at sappy movies or heartwarming stories or bad hair days. I was pretty calm and even-keeled. I couldn't tell her I was crying because I couldn't find the waiting room. She would think I had cracked.

"It just got a little overwhelming when I got here," I explained. "A lot has happened today."

"Yeah." She pondered that for a long moment. "Now you know how much it sucks for people in your hospital," she offered cheerily.

Well, that was true. I had a whole new perspective on the hospital experience now. Shelby made plans to drive to Springfield as soon as she could dump her dog, Snickers, off on someone. I told her I would check my phone for texts and call her if anything new came up.

It had been about 20 minutes and I thought dad might be waking up so I wanted to get back in to his room. I walked out in the hallway and had a moment of panic. Everything looked the same in both directions and I couldn't remember which way I came in. Then I remembered the nice man walking away past that purple flower painting, which meant I came from the other direction. I turned the other way and walked back to the ICU door.

Really, who designs hospitals anyway? Why can't they be easier to navigate?

I walked back in to the room and dad was awake, with the head of his bed slightly raised. Mom was still holding his hand and he still looked a little looped. He smiled at me as I walked in.

"Hiya, kiddo," he said. "How ya doing?"

It's such a funny question, when you think about it. We ask it all the time. It's a polite conversation filler. No one expects an honest answer, obviously. Because, right now, I was not doing so well. However, dad was doing worse, so I didn't think I had the right to complain.

"Good, dad," I replied. "How about you?"

He shrugged his shoulders. I remembered that the doctor hadn't talked to him yet and he had no idea what was about to happen. It felt dishonest not to tell him right away, but the doctor had answers that I didn't. We needed to wait until Dr. Sampson got back to start the conversation.

"How about you mom?" I asked. "Do you need a bathroom break or anything?" I had already figured out that my mom was not going to leave my dad's side unless we pried her away. I guess it would be my job to make sure she ate and slept and took potty breaks. Kind of like having a toddler.

"No, I'm good right now," she said. "Is the doctor coming back?" I could see the concern in her eyes. She was worried, too, that dad was awake and was going to start asking questions.

"He said he'd be back after he saw a patient," I reminded her. He had also said he would be back in twenty minutes, but sometimes the medical field doesn't like to follow a timeline. A quick check-in on a patient can result in an hour long crisis situation.

We sat around awkwardly, not really wanting to make small talk, and not able to talk about the elephant in the room. Luckily, dad was still groggy enough he didn't seem to realize that we weren't saying anything about his medical condition. That, or he knew something was up and didn't want to know.

After another twenty minutes, I was about ready to jump out of my skin. Nurses and other staff were hustling in and out of the nurses' station and other patient rooms and I was keeping an eye out for Marcia. I could at least ask her if she knew when Dr. Sampson was coming back.

However, it appeared that Marcia's other patient wasn't doing too well. The couple times I did see her come out of the room, it was to rush over and grab supplies or medications, then right back in the room. I also saw a doctor and a couple of medical residents in there with her. I was curious as to what they were doing in there and caught myself trying to look into the room.

"Allison, stop that!" my mother reproached me sharply. "How would you feel if you were laying in that bed, sick as a dog, and a total stranger was trying to spy on you?!"

Well, she had a point there. That person had a right to privacy, just like everyone else. It was a little embarrassing that my mother had to call me on it. I was supposed to know better. I sat back down in my chair, trying to act calm.

Finally, Dr. Sampson walked back into the room. He looked a little stressed, so I was guessing that his other patient wasn't doing well either.

"Sorry that took me so long," he opened with an apology. He ran his hand through his hair, trying to collect his thoughts.

"That's okay," I said. "I'm sure it was important."

He looked at me thoughtfully for a moment. "Yes, it was," he said softly. "Thank you for being so understanding." He seemed a little taken aback that a family member would consider another person's situation more important than their own. But I had been in his shoes, and I did understand.

"So, Mr. Sanford, how are you feeling?" he turned to the bed and reached to shake dad's hand. "Oh, I'm Dr. Sampson. We met in the ER briefly before you went to cath lab," he clarified. Dad must have looked confused, which can happen with those drugs.

"Oh right," dad said, recognition dawning on his face. "Well, I feel okay, really. Wish I could get out of bed."

Dr. Sampson smiled. "You don't seem like a guy who does much laying around," he said to dad. "Which is a good thing, it means you will recover quicker." Dr. Sampson looked around the room and saw an empty chair. He pulled it up next to the bed and sat in a circle with my mom and dad. I perched on the foot of the bed next to dad's legs to listen in.

"Mr. Sanford, we did the procedure like we had talked about," he started, looking at dad earnestly. "There was a blockage that we were able to open up. But you have what's called coronary artery disease. It affects the blood vessels on your heart so that enough blood can't get through to the heart muscle. If you have just one or two spots that are blocked off, we can usually open them up in a cath lab. But you have significant blockage in all three of the main arteries to your heart." He paused for a breath and looked from dad to mom.

"So, how do you fix that?" dad asked slowly. I was worried that he was jumping to the conclusion that since they didn't fix it, it couldn't be fixed. I wanted to reassure him, but I knew Dr. Sampson would clear things up in a few seconds.

"It's a surgery called coronary artery bypass grafting. We call it CABG for short," he explained. The acronym is pronounced just like the vegetable, and some families get pretty confused when the staff start talking about cabbage. "It's also called open heart surgery. A cardiovascular surgeon will open your chest through your sternum. Then he will take some blood vessels from your arms or legs and attach them to the heart, sort of in the same pattern as the vessels that are already there. This creates a bypass route for blood to get to the heart muscle."

Dr. Sampson stopped for a moment and looked closely at dad's face to see how he was processing all this. So far, he had only given a summary of what was involved. There was a lot more details dad needed to know before we went ahead with this. But it seemed he wanted to make sure my dad understood what he was saying.

I really liked this doctor. I had seen surgeons walk in, rattle off a lot of medical jargon and walk back out. Their patients had no idea what they were talking about, even as they were signing a paper agreeing to have the surgery done.

"So, I need to have this surgery then?" Dad looked at Dr. Sampson nervously.

"You do have the choice of deciding not to have the operation," Dr. Sampson explained. "But I have to be honest with you, your outlook is not very good if you don't. It's only a matter of time before you have another heart attack. If I were in your shoes, my choice would be to have the surgery."

Dad looked at him for a long moment. He had a way of judging a person's character based on just his gut feeling. It didn't usually take too long for him to decide, either. Today, he was a little under the influence. And this was about the biggest decision he had ever had to make.

"Doc, I trust you," he said firmly. Once dad makes up his mind about a person, he doesn't change it. He had decided Dr. Sampson was a good egg.

Dr. Sampson smiled. "Thank you," he said, sounding genuinely pleased at dad's approval. "I need to go through a little more detail on what the surgery involves. Are you up for that.?"

Dad nodded. Mom reached out and took his hand. She looked more nervous than he did.

"I'll just walk through the whole process," Dr. Sampson started. "They will take you to the pre-op area. They will shave off your hair on your chest, arms and legs. Then they will wash you with a special kind of soap. Another doctor, Dr. Kaine, will be your anesthesiologist. His job is to put you to sleep. He will have to put a breathing tube down your throat, but you won't be awake by that point.

"There will be two surgeons in the room. Dr. Weston is the heart surgeon who will be doing your surgery and Dr. Milya will be assisting him. They are both excellent. I would trust them with my own mother."

"Will you be there?" Dad asked.

"No, I wouldn't be much use to you in there," Dr. Sampson replied. "My area of expertise is in the cath lab, where we've already been. But I will see you every day while you are in the hospital. The surgeon and I work together on your care. And Dr. Weston will come in and meet you in a few minutes. You can give him the once over then." Dr. Sampson grinned at dad. His inspection process hadn't gone unnoticed.

"Okay," dad agreed. I hoped Dr. Weston knew the lead-in he was getting from Dr. Sampson. Those were some mighty big boots to fill.

Dr. Sampson continued the description of the surgery. "Once you're asleep, they will open your chest through your sternum." He gestured to his own chest as he talked.

"Once they have exposed the heart, they will put you on a heart-lung bypass machine. This will replace the function of your heart and lungs while we are doing the operation. While one team is doing this, another team will be getting the vessels to use for the bypass. They use either veins from your legs or an artery from your arm, whichever Dr. Weston feels is a better choice. Once they get the blood vessel out, Dr. Weston will cut it into lengths and suture it on to the heart." He paused for a moment.

"Are you okay?" he asked. Dad was looking a little pale. "I know it's a lot of information and it can be a little graphic. I just want to be honest with you about what will happen." Dad nodded slowly and grimly.

I had always been adamant that patients needed full disclosure of every detail of their care. I felt it was their body and their health and they had the right to know. I got frustrated with family members who wanted to brush over some details, or leave them out entirely. I thought they were infringing on the patient's rights.

But right then, I suddenly understood. I knew what the procedure involved, and I knew my dad needed it done. Dr. Sampson said it needed to be done and my dad agreed. Wasn't that enough? Why did we have to describe all the gory details? I just wanted to protect my dad from the fear that had to come with hearing a doctor talk about cutting open your leg and taking out veins. It sounded barbaric! Why would anyone agree to have that done?

But my dad needed this surgery to save his life. If I was going to stand by my principle that patients have the right to know everything, then I needed to let Dr. Sampson give all the gory details. Boy, this was an eye-opening experience. I wasn't too crazy about finding out I was a hypocrite.

Dad took a few deep breaths and once he looked a little better, Dr. Sampson continued.

"Once the bypass grafts are sewn on the heart, they take off the heart-lung machine and make sure your heart is getting good blood flow. Then they close the chest. They will leave a couple drainage tubes that come out from between your ribs for a few days. That way, any blood from the internal incisions drains out instead of pooling in your chest. Once you are all sewn up, they will bring back here to the ICU."

"How long will all that take?" mom asked.

"About 4 to 5 hours, if everything goes smoothly," Dr. Sampson replied. Mom's brow furrowed. I could tell she wasn't thrilled that he would be gone that long.

"Well, now, Betty, you don't want them rushin' things in there," dad said calmly. He squeezed her hand, trying to reassure her. I thought it was sweet that he was worried about her, even though he was the one going under the knife.

"Well, I know…" her voice trembled and trailed off. Her eyes were filling with tears and I think everything was just starting to catch up to her. I knew how she felt. I walked around the bed and put my arm around her shoulders.

"Mom, I'll stay right here with you the whole time," I promised her. "You won't be alone this time."

She sniffled and dabbed at her eyes with a tissue. She wasn't one to cry in public, so she was trying to hold it back.

"I know, Allison," she said. "I'll be ok. Really. Let's let the doctor finish what he has to say." She attempted to collect herself.

Just then, another man in a white jacket walked in. He was medium height with broad shoulders and a sturdy build. He had light brown hair cut very short and bright green eyes. Dr. Sampson stood up to shake his hand.

"Dr. Weston, how are you?" he asked the other man, who was already looking around the room and taking everything in.

"I'm good, I'm good," he said, nodding his head. "This must be Robert Sanford."

"Bob," dad said. Like me, he really didn't care for his full name. He thought it sounded stuffy.

"Well, Bob, I'm Jim Weston," he said, as he walked over to shake dad's hand. He turned to my mom next. "Ma'am," he said politely with a nod of his head. Mom looked completely embarrassed and she hadn't completely composed herself. He graciously didn't notice and moved back to dad.

"Dr. Sampson here tells me that you need to have some work done on your heart," he said, as he took a seat in the chair vacated by Dr. Sampson.

"Yeah, he told me the same thing," dad replied.

Dr. Weston smiled. "Well, as long as he's keeping his stories straight," he joked. I saw dad laugh and I knew Dr. Weston had passed muster as well.

"Did he explain what we were going to do?" he asked, looking around at all three of us.

"Well, mostly" dad said. "At least what happens in surgery."

"Do you have questions about any of it?" Dr Weston asked. He leaned back in the chair, looking comfortable and giving the impression he had all day to answer questions if needed. Dr. Sampson had done a great job explaining but it's so much information to process. It's easy to miss a few key pieces.

Dad hesitated for a moment, but Dr. Weston must have made him comfortable enough he didn't feel the need to bluff. "Yeah, a couple," he said.

Dr. Weston and dad spent the next 10 minutes discussing the details of the surgery. I tuned out, and just hung out in the corner. I trusted these doctors and I was glad my dad was comfortable asking questions. My brain needed to take a brief timeout.

"When you get back to the ICU, you'll still be on the ventilator," Dr. Weston was explaining. "We get that tube out as quickly as possible, we just have to make sure you wake up and you're stable. Then you'll spend the night here." He turned to my mom, who was looking like her usual self again. "Do you have any questions, ma'am?"

Something about the way he said 'ma'am' and his short haircut made me think he had some military in his background. He certainly had a physique for cranking out pushups.

"No, you've been very thorough," she said politely. "Thank you very much."

My mother would have been mortified to be blubbering in front of any stranger, much less her husband's heart surgeon. I don't know if Dr. Weston deliberately waited to talk to her until she had composed herself, or if it was a blessed coincidence. Either way, I was thankful for it.

"Well, if we have answered all your questions, we'll go ahead and get started," Dr. Weston said, as he stood up. "I know this is happening fast. The OR team will be here in about 20 minutes to get you." He shook dad's hand and squeezed my mom's shoulder. "I'll see you on the other side," he quipped, grinning at dad. Dad grinned back. Mom smiled feebly, but she never did have the same sense of humor as dad.

I had pretty much hung off to the side for most of this. The doctors were great, mom and dad had asked all the questions I couldn't answer and I was satisfied with the way things were going. All things considered, anyway. I didn't feel the need to play the 'I'm a nurse' card and it sometimes annoyed me when other people did it. So I just observed quietly.

Dr. Weston stepped over toward me, instead of walking out of the room. He reached his hand out in greeting and said "I don't believe we were introduced. I'm Jim Weston."

"Hi, I'm Allie," I said as I shook his hand. "I'm Bob's daughter."

"Are you a nurse?" he asked.

I was taken aback by his directness. "Yes, I am," I replied. "Dr. Sampson must have tipped you off that you had nurse in the family." I smiled warmly. Some family members require a forewarning from your co-workers. I've certainly met a few of them.

"Actually, no," he said. "You just seemed comfortable in the environment. Like it was familiar to you."

"Oh. Um, yeah, I guess so," I stammered. He was a very sharp and observant man. I didn't think he had even noticed me. Well, I was glad he was on dad's case then. I knew nothing would get by him.

"I promise to take good care of him," he assured me. I hadn't doubted him, but I felt honored that he went out of his way to make me that promise. Some doctors don't show much respect for nurses. We always notice the ones who do.

"Thank you," I said sincerely. He nodded and walked out of the room.

I walked back over to my dad's bed. This was happening so fast. I wanted to just sit with him and mom for a minute.

I knew when the OR crew arrived, he would be whisked off in a hurry.

"Well, dad, this has been an interesting day," I joked as I smiled at him. He nodded thoughtfully.

"I guess it was bound to happen," he said. "My dad had more than one heart attack. That's what killed him, actually." My grandpa Sanford had died when I was a teenager. I didn't remember how he had died. I was busy being a self-absorbed teenager. So now I knew we had a family history of heart disease.

Mom got up to get something out of her purse. Dad reached for me so I stepped up and sat in the chair. He took my hand and looked at me earnestly. "Watch over your mother," he implored. "Take care of her for me."

I really hoped he meant just while he was in the hospital. I didn't want to consider that he had a premonition of his death and he wanted to make sure I took care of mom after he died. I was just going to assume the best on this one.

"I will, Dad," I promised. He nodded appreciatively. Mom walked back over and sat in the other chair.

"What now, Allie?" she asked me.

"Let's just stay here until the OR team shows up," I said. "I guess can start up a cribbage game," I joked. Humor was a powerful tool for me, especially in stressful situations. Mom jerked her head up to look at me, and then realized I was joking. She didn't always get my sense of humor.

We sat around and made small talk. Dad seemed pretty calm, and mom seemed pretty nervous. I didn't even know how I felt at this point. I was relieved they had found the heart disease in time and that they had a way to fix it. I was worried about the surgery, but I knew he was in good hands. I also knew some things were beyond human control, and the best surgeons in the world still lost patients.

Dad must have heard the thoughts whirling through my head. "God is watching over me, Allie," he said calmly. "Don't you worry your pretty little head none."

I wanted to laugh out loud at that. I was the queen of worrying. Telling me not to worry is like telling a duck not to float on water. It just came naturally. But he was right. Worrying wasn't going to accomplish anything. I needed to just trust God.

Such an easy thing to say. And so terribly hard to actually do.

———∘∘◦)◉(◦∘∘———

Chapter 7

Faith and Chocolate

Our quiet family moment was interrupted abruptly by the privacy curtain being whisked open. A mid-30's male stepped into the room.

"Robert Sanford?" he asked, skipping right past 'hello'. Dad nodded.

"Sir, I need you to state your full name and date of birth, please," the man said. Dad recited off the requested information. "Ok, we're going to get you ready for the OR."

Then three more people bustled in to the room. They were all in blue scrubs, just like the first guy. They all had shoe covers and head covers on, and none of them had a smile. They descended on dad like a pack of crows, lifting his arm up to inspect his IV, checking his pulses, verifying his armband and disconnecting his monitor wires. Mom and I sort of got pushed into the corner, where we watched the flurry of activity in nervous silence.

Marcia came in the room and one of the blue people started asking her questions about which medications had been given. Another person was asking dad about dentures, glasses or hearing aids. I assumed they were nurses, but no one had introduced themselves to us and I couldn't see their name tags in all of the hustle and bustle.

"This is his wife and daughter," I heard Marcia say. She was talking to one of the staff, and the others briefly glanced over at us. The male who had come in first finally came over to talk to us.

"Hi, I'm Rusty," he said, shaking mom's hand and then mine. "I'm the lead nurse on the heart team here." Well, now we knew one of them. Rusty didn't seem like he cared much for socializing with family members, by the awkward way he was handling himself. But at least he was talking to us.

"How long before he leaves?" mom asked.

"We're going in about five minutes," Rusty replied calmly. I saw the color drain from my mom's face. This was really going to happen and it was going to happen now. I could tell she was not doing well with this.

"Will you please make sure she gets to say good-bye to him before you leave?" I asked Rusty. I had seen rushed OR teams whisk a patient out the door, leaving a distraught family member behind, wanting to just give him one more kiss or hug.

"Well, he's coming back here after surgery," Rusty started to say as an excuse for not needing to let her say good-bye. Then he caught a look in my eye and stopped. "Yes, we will," he promised.

"Okay, we're rolling," one person called out, unlocking the brake on the bed. Two of them started to pull the bed out of the room.

"Wait," Rusty said. "His wife needs to say good-bye."

They stopped moving the bed and stood there impatiently. One of them audibly sighed. I was so irritated that they would act like that in front of my mother. She stood there, looking terrified. I wrapped my arm around her shoulder and gently pushed her forward toward the bedside.

"Dad, good luck in there," I said. I couldn't really think of anything to say. I squeezed his hand and said, "I love you."

"I love you too, Allison," he said. He was using my full name to humor my mom, I'm sure. He looked over at her and reached for her hand.

"Betty, you behave while I'm gone," he joked. She smiled weakly and clutched to his hand. "I won't be gone long. Keep a pot of coffee on."

"Ok, hon," mom finally spoke. "You just make sure you get back here. Don't make me come looking for you."

Dad smiled and said "I will, I promise." Mom bent down and kissed him.

"I love you, Bob," she whispered.

"I love you too, Betty," he replied.

The OR team took that as their cue to move on, and the bed started to roll again. I pulled mom back into the corner with me and we watched dad get wheeled down the hall. Almost as an afterthought, Rusty looked over his shoulder at us and said, "We'll be back in four to five hours. Someone will update you partway through."

And then he was gone. Mom let out a long slow breath, and I realized I had been holding my breath as well. We stood there in the empty room, feeling helpless.

Marcia walked back in. "Boy, when they land, they don't waste time, do they?" she said. Mom and I nodded in agreement.

"Where should we wait until he gets out of surgery?" I asked Marcia. I figured the ICU Waiting Room was the obvious choice, but I just wanted to make sure the staff would know where we were when they needed to give us updates.

"Do you remember where the ICU waiting room is?" Marcia asked. I nodded, hoping that I could find it without tears this time. "That's where the OR nurse will go to give you updates. And there's a coffee shop farther down the hall, if you want coffee or something to eat."

I thanked her and we gathered up our stuff. Mom and I walked out in to the hall, and I made an effort to focus on which way we were headed. We walked to the waiting room in silence, though I'm sure her mind was racing as fast as mine was. We found the door and turned in to the room. There was now a few other people in there, family members of the other patients in the ICU. A couple of them were watching TV, one was texting while she sipped on a latte, and one was talking quietly on the phone. In the corner, there were about 5 people huddled, looking distraught. I wondered if they were the family of Marcia's other patient.

Mom and I found a sofa near the window and sat down. I was suddenly exhausted. I knew we needed to get something to eat and drink. It was going to be a long day. Dad wasn't even going to get back from surgery until 6 o'clock tonight.

"Mom, let's go find some food," I suggested.

"Oh, I want to stay here in case they need to find us," mom protested. I reminded her that he was still in pre-op, and they weren't going to have any updates for a while. I didn't think they would feel it necessary to inform us how the hair clipping went. We could just assume it was uneventful.

We walked back out of the waiting room and, to my relief, this time I remembered which way to go. We headed down the hall, following the delicious smell of fresh coffee. I hadn't been hungry two minutes ago, but suddenly I could definitely go for some lunch.

The coffee shop was tucked in an alcove and had a café feel to it. There were small wrought iron tables with chairs around them, plants along the windows and a rock sculpture with a waterfall running in the corner. They served sandwiches, soup and baked goods, as well as coffee. Classical music played in the background and the place smelled delightful. It was nice to have a break from the clinical setting.

Mom and I ordered a soup and sandwich combo. Mom had her perpetual bottle of water with her, and I ordered a latte. Then, I added on a cookie. They had a shelf full of those gooey chocolate chip cookies that are the size of a plate and they looked too good to pass up. I told myself I would only eat part of it, but I knew I was just kidding myself. Maybe I could convince mom to eat half of it for me.

We sat at a table by the window and ate. Mom was most of the way through her meal when she casually said, "What did Shelby and Andrew say about all this?"

I jumped in my chair, smacking my knee on the table. "I never called Andrew!" I cried. I had forgotten all about it.

"He doesn't know at all?!" Mom asked, distraught. I decided not to point out that she hadn't called either of them, so it wasn't fair for her to be upset that I hadn't.

"No, I called him in the car on the way here," I assured her. "But he doesn't know anything since then."

I pulled my phone out and hit his number. He answered on the second ring.

"Hey, sis" he said casually. I could tell he was trying to act calm. He had to be jumping out of his skin, though.

It had been over two hours since I had called him. I was pretty sure Shelby wouldn't have passed along the update I gave her.

"Hey, big bro," I said. "I'm so sorry I didn't call sooner. It's been hectic here." I had to pause for a moment and think of what part he already knew and where I needed to start.

"Dad went to cath lab and they found blockages in all three of the main arteries on his heart," I started. I was trying to remember to keep it in layman's terms. It was easy to slip back into medical jargon, but that was just going to make him more nervous.

"So, he needed to have open heart surgery," I continued. I heard Andrew take a sharp breath in. "They had an opening today, so they wanted to take him to OR right away. He's in surgery now."

There was a long pause. I admit it's a lot to process at once. Our dad had always been active and healthy, so this was foreign to us. He had never had any medical problems and I don't think he had been in the hospital since he was born.

"How long will he be in surgery?" Andrew finally asked. I think he had so many questions to ask, he didn't know where to start.

"About 4 hours," I said. "Then he'll come back to the ICU and spend the night there."

"How is mom doing?" he asked. We all knew this wasn't the kind of situation that our mom would handle well.

"Good," I replied. "We're having something to eat right now, while we wait." That answer let him know that mom was sitting next to me, so I couldn't say too much. "Do you want to talk to her?" I asked. I really wanted my family to start talking to each other instead of just going through me.

"Sure," he said, and I handed her the phone. They chatted while I finished my sandwich and now cold soup. I sipped my coffee while eyeing the cookie, trying to determine if I had enough self-control to only eat half of it. I realized the downside of letting mom use my phone is that now I didn't have a way to call Shelby. She should actually be getting here soon, although I hadn't gotten a text from her.

Mom and Andrew were talking about his girls and something they had done that day. Andrew and Nicole had 3-year-old twin girls that were adorable. Their names were Cassandra and Samantha, but they went by Cassie and Sammie. They had huge blue eyes and blonde ringlets and they were a little mischievous. So far, it was mostly cute when they got in to trouble. I'm sure when they are 13, it won't be as adorable.

They finished their conversation and mom handed the phone back to me. She looked more relaxed now that she had been distracted by something happy. She loved being a grandma. I pushed the cookie toward her, figuring some chocolate could only add to the happiness.

"Here, mom, let's split this," I said. She didn't argue, breaking off a piece and eating it. I needed to call Shelby, so I would distract myself with that until mom had eaten at least half of the cookie. That would leave less for me to devour.

Shelby didn't answer, so I left her a short message that dad was in surgery. Shelby liked to drive fast with the radio cranked up, so if she was on the road, she wouldn't hear the phone. I sent her a text, too, just in case. Sometimes I didn't trust cell service that much.

Mom had eaten half of the cookie and was now sitting with her chin on her hand, staring out the window. In my years of nursing, I had learned that quiet time is important and you don't always need to be saying something. I left her to her thoughts and savored every bite of the gooey cookie.

As I finished my coffee, mom broke out of her thoughts and looked around the café. She was starting to look a little tired. This had been a very draining day.

"Should we head back to the waiting room?" I asked her. It had only been an hour since he left, but I wanted to make sure we were back there before they came looking for us. Besides, this wrought iron chair was making my butt go numb. I was ready to move back to the couch.

She nodded and we stood up, gathering our things. We ambled slowly back down the hallway. I made note of the direction signs on the wall, telling us which way to go for the ER, cafeteria, gift shop, etc. I was trying to get some bearing of where we were in this large building. I knew they would have a desk at the front door with someone who could direct Shelby when she arrived. Which was good, because I was pretty sure I couldn't give her the right directions.

We got back to the waiting room and found a spot back on the couch. The group of worried people had left. I wondered if they were back in the ICU visiting now. The ICU usually had a visitor restriction of only two people at a time. The rooms were pretty crammed full of medical equipment and there wasn't much extra space.

I had a rough idea of what dad's room would look like when he got back. I wondered if I should try to forewarn mom. All he had when he left was a cardiac monitor and an IV pump. He would come back with a ventilator, chest tubes, a temporary pacemaker and a couple different monitoring devices stuck in him. It can be pretty overwhelming.

I decided to wait until a little closer to that time to bring it up. She looked somewhat calm for now. She actually looked like she wanted to take a nap. Which was how I felt as well. The couch was comfy and I laid my head back against it.

My phone vibrating in my pocket startled me. I grabbed it and looked to see that Shelby had texted me back. I read the message and it said she was 20 miles from Springfield. And obviously texting while she was driving. I smiled and shook my head. Ok, I had done it myself a time or two. I was supposed to know better than anyone, having seen the results of highway rollover accidents. But, like most people, I figured I was the exception to the rule.

I didn't reply because I didn't want her trying to read or respond to a text from me right now. I sent a quick prayer up asking God to keep her safe, because there was no way I could handle dad's surgery and Shelby being in a car accident at the same time. I would be in a padded room.

I told mom that Shelby was on her way. She nodded absently. We just relaxed on the couch for awhile. I was glad I could be here with her for this. My phone vibrated again, with Shelby calling.

"Where do I go?" she asked when I answered. I told her to go to the main hospital entrance and ask for directions to the ICU waiting room. I actually needed to move my car out of the ER parking lot at some point. After Shelby got here, I could do that. I didn't want to leave mom alone.

A few minutes later, Shelby came bursting into the waiting room. She looked around, saw us and rushed over to give mom a hug. Mom squeezed her tightly for a long time.

"I'm so glad you're here, honey," mom said, still holding her tight.

"How is dad doing?" Shelby asked, finally letting go of mom.

"Still in surgery," I said. "We haven't gotten an update yet."

"How long has he been in there?" she asked.

"Well, he left the ICU about an hour and a half ago," I replied. "But he had to go through pre-op, so he has probably only been in the actual OR for 30 minutes or so." Surgery is a much more timely process than most people realize. There is a lot of prep work to be done before the actual surgery starts.

"And how long until he's done?" she asked.

"They told us three to four hours," I told her. I knew there were a lot of variables with that, but it was the best estimate we had.

We settled back on the couch and made small talk for awhile. If nothing else, the family was getting caught up with each other. Shelby was entertaining us with stories about Snickers' adventures with the neighbor's pet goose. It seems that Snickers thought the goose was a great play toy. The goose didn't agree with that, so there were plenty of noisy romps around the yard, with the two animals taking turns chasing each other. We were laughing out loud by the time she was done.

About thirty minutes later, Rusty walked into the waiting room. He looked around until he saw us and then walked over to where we were sitting. He actually smiled when he walked up, so that was reassuring.

"Hey guys," he said, sitting down on the chair across from the couch. "How are you enjoying the waiting room?" he inquired.

"It's very nice," my mom replied, sitting up nervously.

"Yeah, they re-did this room a few years ago," he chatted nonchalantly. "It's really nice now."

I wanted to grab him around the throat and shake him, a la Homer Simpson, and scream 'How is my dad?!' but I restrained myself. He must have picked up on it though, because he stopped with the small talk.

"Bob is doing great," he said. "They have completed the vein removal and are now working on attaching the grafts. Everything is going very well so far."

I breathed a sigh of relief. Shelby was staring at Rusty with a horrified look on her face. I suddenly remembered that she hadn't heard the description of what the surgery involved. She didn't know why they would be removing veins from dad. But she glanced at me and saw that I looked relieved, so she figured out that whatever that meant, it wasn't as bad as it sounded.

"Any idea how much longer?" I asked.

"About another hour in the OR," he replied. "Then they take him over to ICU and get him settled in there. Once he's stable, they will come get you and take you in to see him. He won't be awake yet, though," he warned us.

"Thank you," I said to him. Rusty was growing on me a little. "So we should just hang out here?"

"Yes, this is where the ICU staff will come look for you," he replied. "You have a little time though, if you need to go get supper or a hotel room or anything."

We all thanked Rusty and he left. He had brought up another problem I hadn't thought of yet. Where were we all going to sleep? I had an overnight bag but mom didn't have anything, so we also needed to hit a store and get her a few things. It made more sense to do that now, since there was nothing else to do. But it felt wrong to drive off and leave dad there alone. It's not like we were doing anything to help him right now. He was unconscious. He didn't even know we were there. But I still felt like we shouldn't leave him. I could see by mom's face that she felt the same way.

I figured we had close to two hours of free time. I needed to move my car anyway, so I offered to go get a hotel room and stop off to get stuff for mom. I would be back within an hour. And that way, mom wouldn't have to leave dad.

Once we decided on the plan, I hugged mom and Shelby good-bye and headed back down the hall to the ER. It was strange how this place seemed so familiar to me already. I had never been here until a few hours ago.

I didn't know Springfield very well, so I wasn't sure where to get a hotel room. As I walked back through the ER waiting room, I glanced at the clerk's desk. A different clerk was sitting there now, and I paused, debating whether to ask her for help. She looked up and saw me standing there.

"Hi, can I help you?" she called out cheerfully. I walked over to the desk and she smiled at me with brilliant white teeth.

"My dad is in the ICU and I need to find a hotel room," I said. "I don't know which ones are close or decent."

"Oh, I can help you with that," she responded cheerily. I sneaked a glance at her nametag. It said 'Lacey' and I almost laughed out loud. Maybe there was a rule that if your name was Lacey, you had to be super nice and friendly. This Lacey also had long blond hair, but it was straight and pulled up in a high ponytail that swung around every time she moved her head.

Lacey handed me a printed piece of paper. It had names, addresses and phone numbers of several hotels, as well as a street map showing where they were.

"These places will give you a discount if you have a medical emergency," she said. "Just tell them your dad is in ICU. If you want a pool, the top two are the ones that have them."

A hot tub sounded nice and relaxing, but I was pretty sure none of us had a swim suit. I thanked her for the information.

"No problem!" she said. "I hope your dad is okay."

"Thanks," I replied. "Me too." I walked out to my car, still a little caught off guard. She was so nice, and such a stark contrast to the previous clerk. I'll bet the staff loved it when she was on duty.

I found a hotel that wasn't too far from the hospital. It was a national chain and all we really needed was beds and a shower. I booked the room and then they gave me directions to a Target where I could get a change of clothes and some toiletries for mom. I also grabbed some nuts, dried fruit and granola bars. If I was going to depend on the hospital café for snacks, I would end up eating a giant cookie every day. I needed some healthier snack options.

As I drove back to the hospital, the sunlight was starting to fade into evening. This day seemed to have been a month long. Getting up this morning was a distant memory. I pulled into the parking lot and found Shelby's car. I parked next to her and walked to the front door of the hospital.

When I walked in, the desk with an information clerk was to the right, just as I had figured it would be. She looked up at me and smiled. I walked over to get directions. I thought I could find it on my own, but I didn't want to waste time wandering around lost.

She gave me directions with a warm smile and I headed off down the hall. I noticed a door to the right with a stained glass window in the door. The sign beside the door said 'Chapel'. I pushed the door open a few inches and peeked in. No one was in there right now. There were three pews, a small altar with a kneeling bench and a large cross at the front of the room. A corner table held Bibles and other papers. A hymn was playing softly over the speaker.

I walked in and let the door shut behind me. It felt so calm and peaceful in there. Dad had told me I needed to trust God to take care of him. I wanted to just let go and trust God. But I was such a planner and a fixer, and so even as I claimed to be trusting God, I was still trying to figure out a solution inside my head.

I walked to the front pew and sat down, looking up at the cross. It was set in a recessed space and lighted from behind. I sat there in stillness for several minutes. No worrying or planning. I just sat there, feeling a peace fall over me.

After a few minutes, I got up to go find my family. I felt much calmer after that respite. I knew God was here with us. It was easy for me to forget that sometimes.

I headed back down the hall to the waiting room. Maybe someday I would be able to always just trust God and never worry.

And maybe someday I'll be able to resist giant chocolate chip cookies no matter how gooey and still warm they are.

No bets on which one of those might happen first.

Chapter 8

The Power of a Smile

I found mom and Shelby still in the waiting room. Mom was sitting on the end of the couch and Shelby was sitting next to her. She had her legs curled up underneath her and her head resting on mom's shoulder. Mom was flipping through a magazine and Shelby was reading over her shoulder.

I walked up and sat down in the chair across from them. They both looked up at me and smiled.

"We're all set," I said.

"Oh good," mom replied, looking relieved. "Thanks for taking care of all that."

"Did we get a hotel with a pool?" Shelby asked.

"Did you pack a swimming suit?" I asked her. I didn't know when she was planning on swimming anyway. I imagined we would be spending most of our time at the hospital.

"No," she replied, shrugging. "I just think pools are fun." She cracked me up sometimes. She was such a little kid at heart still.

"It actually does have a pool," I said, "but I picked it because it's close to the hospital. And I got you some stuff at the store, mom. I left it in the car for now."

Mom smiled at me. "You're such a good kid, Allison," she said fondly. "What would I ever do without you?"

"Yeah, someone should be the good kid," Shelby chimed in. "Good thing we have you, Lis." She smirked at me. I knew she was kidding though. She was more than happy to let me be the organizer. Shelby didn't do well with responsibility.

I sent a quick text to Andrew telling him dad was still in surgery and our update said everything was going well. I read through the other texts I had, but nothing was urgent. Of course, urgent had a whole new definition today.

I wondered when I should tell work I was out of town on a family emergency. I had the next few days off, so I wasn't missing any work. Would dad be stable enough for me to leave and go back to work? I decided to wait and see how he did after surgery. I kind of wanted to save my paid time off for after he went home. I wasn't sure how much help he would need or if mom would be able to handle it alone.

A girl in scrubs walked into the waiting room. "Sanford family?" she called out.

I jumped up. "Over here," I said. She smiled and walked over to us. I was really learning the power of a smile today.

"Hi, I'm Rachel," she introduced herself. "Your dad is back in the ICU and you can come in now." She must not have looked at mom too close, if she assumed we were all his daughters. Mom didn't seem to notice. We all gathered our things quickly and followed Rachel back down the hall.

"He hasn't woke up yet, but he's doing very well," Rachel explained as we walked. "He still has the breathing tube in, too."

I suddenly remembered that I was going to forewarn mom what dad would look like. I panicked briefly. Mom didn't handle situations like this well anyway.

We paused at the door while Rachel used her ID badge to access the ICU. "He's going to look really different," she continued. "They swell a lot at first with this surgery, and he'll have several tubes in him." She paused for a moment to finish what she had to say. We stopped and stood in the hallway with her.

"It can be a little frightening to see at first," she said, looking mostly at mom. "Please sit down if you feel lightheaded. And don't be embarrassed if that happens, it's pretty common. Just remember, he's doing well. Even if he doesn't look like it."

She turned then and led us in to the room. I stood close to mom's side, in case I had to catch her. I really appreciated Rachel giving her a heads up on what dad would look like.

We walked in a few steps and mom stopped. A tall, broad-shouldered male in scrubs was sitting in a chair with a computer station in front of him near the bed. He stood up when we came in.

"Hi, I'm Wade," he introduced himself. "I'm the nurse for the night."

Mom was just staring at dad, but she didn't look like she was going to faint.

"I'm Allie, I'm his daughter," I replied. "This is Betty, his wife, and Shelby, another daughter." I gestured toward them as I spoke. Shelby turned toward Wade and shot him an adorable smile.

Wade smiled back at her, then focused on mom. "Betty, you can come up here and touch his hand," he told her. "I can explain what everything is."

I gently nudged mom toward the bed, where I could see dad's hand resting by his side. I could see that his other hand had the blood pressure monitoring line in his wrist and his entire hand and wrist was wrapped in an immobilizer. This hand only had a sticker on one finger with a red light glowing in it. That was the monitor that read his oxygen level in his blood and we couldn't hurt anything there.

I reached out and squeezed his hand as a way of showing mom that it was ok to touch him. She followed my lead and wrapped her hand around his. When I touched him, he hadn't moved, since he was still under the effects of anesthesia. But I swear that when mom's hand touched his, he squeezed. It was like he somehow still knew she was there.

Wade started explaining the equipment starting at the top. Dad was covered in a sheet that hid his incisions and the drainage tubes coming out of his chest. I was thankful for that because I could see in the drainage container that they were draining blood, which is their purpose. But mom didn't care for the sight of blood.

"This is his breathing tube," Wade said, gesturing to the large plastic tube in dad's mouth. "It goes down to his lungs and this machine over here is breathing for him." He pointed to a large, noisy machine next to the bed that connected to dad with a long plastic tube. Dad's chest rose and fell with each whooshing noise the ventilator made.

"He's still wearing off the anesthesia, so that's why he needs that," Wade explained. I could see my mom was concerned about why dad couldn't breathe on his own. "Once he wakes up, we'll take that out."

He moved on to the device stuck in dad's neck. It looked like a very large IV, but it had more than one line running out of it.

"This is an introducer sheath," he continued. "This wire is a monitor that tells us how much blood his heart is pumping out." He pointed to a box that was sitting on the shelf behind the bed. It had a digital screen that had several numbers on it. The wire from dad's neck was connected to the machine. As we were watching it, the numbers changed.

"It reads continuously, so you'll see the numbers jump around," Wade explained. "He is doing very well, and has been since he got out of surgery." I knew a little bit about this monitor, but had never actually used one. It measured cardiac output, which was the volume of blood pumped out of the heart, measured in liters per minute. Dad's number was 5.1 right now. So dad's heart was pumping 5 liters of blood every minute. That seemed like a good amount.

Wade moved on to dad's far hand. "This is a monitor that is in the artery in his wrist. It reads his blood pressure continuously," he said, as he pointed up to the monitor above the bed. Dad's blood pressure was 123/62. I knew that was a good number. This monitor was familiar to me because we used them in the ER.

Wade looked at mom for a moment. "Are you doing okay?" he asked her. She nodded. I was impressed with how well she was doing.

Wade lifted up one of the long, rubbery drainage tubes that came out from under the sheet and connected to a box-type device. "These are his chest tubes. They are draining any extra blood out of his chest," he said. There was some blood in the tubing, but mom just looked at it calmly and nodded again.

Wade finished explaining the IV fluids, the pain medicine pump, the catheter and the rest of the numbers on the cardiac monitor. Shelby seemed transfixed with his explanation, but she could also just be fascinated with

Wade. He did have very nice green eyes and thick black hair. Maybe she could start dating a guy who had a steady job for a change.

Rachel stuck her head in the door and told Wade he had a phone call from a doctor. Wade excused himself and walked out. He stopped by the desk right outside the door and asked the nurse there to keep an eye on his patient. She looked up and into the room through the small window there. She nodded and Wade walked over to the main desk to answer the phone.

"Do you have any questions, mom?" I asked. I didn't know if I knew the answers, but I would try.

"No, he was very thorough," she replied. He had been very thorough, and I appreciated it.

"And cute," Shelby chimed in. I just laughed. Did I know my baby sister or what?

"How long do you think until he wakes up?" mom wondered aloud. As if on cue, dad started stirring in the bed.

Wade walked back in the room and saw dad moving. He walked over to the bed and leaned over dad's head.

"Mr. Sanford?" he called. He put his hand on dad's arm and shook him gently. Dad's eyes fluttered open. He looked around groggily and then fixed on Wade's face.

"Mr. Sanford, your surgery is all done and you're in the ICU," Wade assured him. Dad still seemed confused. He tried to sit up but couldn't. He furrowed his brow as if he was trying to figure out why.

"Mr. Sanford, your family is here," Wade said. "Come up here, Betty." He stepped back from dad's side and let my mom slide into the spot.

"Hi Bob," mom said, smiling down at him. His face lit up when he saw her. He tried to reach toward her, but all the tubes and wires kept him from moving much.

"It's ok, honey, don't move," mom reassured him calmly. "You're doing good. Just lay there and rest." She patted his hand and stroked his hair.

Who was this calm and collected lady? What had she done with my mother? I was astonished at her reaction. It's amazing how some people respond in a crisis.

"Oh, that was Dr. Weston on the phone," Wade said. "Sorry, I got distracted when he started waking up. Anyway, Dr. Weston apologized. He would normally have come to talk to you by now, but he had a family emergency. He said to tell you everything went well and he'll be here as soon as he can."

It actually hadn't occurred to me that a surgeon hadn't talked to us. Everyone else had been so informative and helpful. I felt a rush of sympathy for Dr. Weston. He must live with a pretty high stress level. Finishing an open heart surgery just to rush off to an emergency in your own family. I guess no matter how bad your day is, someone else is probably having a worse one.

Dad was trying to reach up to grab the breathing tube in his throat. Wade saw him and jumped to hold his hand back down.

"Don't pull that out, Mr. Sanford," he said. "You still need that to help you breathe for a little bit."

Dad scowled. I knew that those tubes were uncomfortable and most patients tried to pull them out. Wade picked up a package from a shelf and opened it. It had 2 foam cuffs, each connected to a couple long straps. I recognized those.

"Until he's ready to get the tube out, I'll have to put these on him," he said to my mom. "They're just a reminder for him not to pull things out." They are actually a wrist restraint, but that sounds a little mean. Tying patients down isn't a fun part of the job. But, once again, it's necessary and for their own good.

Wade wrapped the cuff around dad's wrist and then tied the strap to the frame of the bed. He left enough slack that dad could still move his arm some, just not all the way up to his tube. There is a nice way to tie restraints, and a not nice way to tie restraints. This was the nice way, and I suddenly like Wade even more. Some people cinched them down so tight the patient could barely wiggle their fingers.

"Mr. Sanford, these will just remind you not to pull on that tube," Wade explained to dad. "I'll take them off as soon as we get that tube out."

"You can call him Bob," I told Wade. "He's not much for formality. He would really prefer to be called Bob."

"Ok, Bob it is," Wade said. He looked at me and then at Shelby. He looked back to me and asked, "Are you the nurse?"

I nodded. "I work in the ER at Brighton County," I said. Obviously, the staff had been passing the tidbit about his daughter being a nurse along in report. I wondered if they had said anything else. We always got a little apprehensive when there was a medical professional in the family. Sometimes, they thought they knew more than they did. And sometimes they wanted to try to tell us how to do our job. And sometimes they criticized everything we did. I had tried very hard not to do any of those things.

Wade must have read my mind, because he laughed and said, "Don't worry, they said you were cool."

That was comforting. I had been in our ICU when the nurses were fighting over who had to take a certain patient, just because their family was so difficult to deal with. I didn't want to create that issue for my dad. For the most part, the staff had been really good to us.

I needed to make a bathroom break, so I stepped out in the hallway. I remembered seeing some public restrooms in the hall just outside the ICU. Rachel was pushing a linen cart down the hall stuffed full of dirty linens. She smiled at me and I smiled back. I glanced at her nametag and realized it said CNA. Curiosity got the best of me and I asked her, "You're a CNA?" I had assumed she was a nurse.

"Yep," she said.

"You knew so much about what was going on with my dad," I commented. After I said it out loud, I realized it sounded a little rude.

But Rachel just laughed and said, "I'm in nursing school. I have one semester left. So I'm trying to learn as much as I can on the job. Plus, the nurses tell me what I'm supposed to say, so I don't get something wrong. It's just that they can't leave the patient alone, so they send me to get families."

"Well, you did a great job," I told her. "Good luck with school."

"Thanks," she said. "I can't wait to be done." I remember that feeling. It was sort of a mix between eager to be out of school and terrified that I was now going to be on my own.

I walked out through the main ICU door and headed for the bathroom. I felt a lot more comfortable leaving mom alone now that she seemed to be handling everything so well.

On my way back, I stopped to look at a picture hanging in the hallway. It was an old black and white photo of a somber looking woman in a white dress and nurses' cap. According to the plaque, she was Dorothy Weinstein and she had been the director of nursing when this hospital first opened in 1931. It was amazing to think of all the changes nursing had gone through since she was here. I was most thankful that we didn't have to wear the cap.

I picked up the phone outside the ICU door and it rang to the desk inside.

"ICU, can I help you?" a cheerful voice answered.

"This is Allie," I said, out of habit. Then I realized that didn't mean anything to them. "I'm here for Bob Sanford."

"Ok, go ahead and come in," she replied and the door buzzed and then swung open. I hung up the phone and walked in. I concentrated on not looking into the other patients' rooms as I walked past. Mom had reminded me how important it was to respect their privacy. Which was something I knew to start with, I just got curious. I did notice the bustle of activity that seemed to be constant at the nurses' station. They were a busy unit. My work had its moments of mayhem, but they were broken up by spells of calm.

I got back to dad's room and saw that all was still status quo. Mom and Shelby were sitting in the corner and dad was asleep again. Wade had relocated to the desk outside the room now that dad was a little more stable. He could see in to the room through the window and he looked up periodically. I knew he was probably plowing through his charting. I'm sure there was a lot of paperwork involved with a patient like this.

"I'm hungry," Shelby suddenly announced. Mom and I hadn't eaten lunch until 2:00 p.m., so I wasn't really hungry yet. But I knew dad wouldn't wake up all the way for awhile, so going for some food would be a good way to pass the time.

"Mom, do you want to go grab some food?" I asked her. I was pretty sure of her answer, though.

"Oh, no, I don't want to leave him," she protested. I didn't argue with her. I was saving that for later when we had to drag her to the hotel room for the night.

"Well, how about if you stay here and Shelby and I will grab something," I offered. "We can bring something back for you."

She agreed, but insisted she wasn't hungry and didn't need anything. I figured we would just get her something anyway. She needed to keep her strength up.

I stopped to tell Wade what we were doing on our way out. I left him my cell number, just in case. Mom was notoriously bad about keeping her cell phone charged, so I was pretty sure it was dead by now. He promised he would call if anything happened. Shelby gave him another brilliant smile and then we headed out the door.

The sun had set and it was getting cool when we walked outside. It felt good to breathe fresh air. We walked over to where our cars were parked and got in my car. There was no need for discussion about which car to take. Shelby was a terrible driver. Plus, she didn't know where anything was here.

I drove back toward the hotel because I remembered seeing several restaurants along that street. Nothing sounded good, so I let Shelby pick. She decided on Mexican, and we pulled into the parking lot. As we walked in to the adobe building I decided maybe I could eat some supper after all. The place smelled fantastic.

We agreed to eat here and just take something back to mom afterward. I knew we couldn't eat in dad's room and I didn't want to try to eat out of a carryout container in the waiting room.

They seated us in a corner booth and brought as a basket of chips and salsa. Shelby tore into the chips with abandon. I started with slowly nibbling on one, reminding myself that I had eaten a late lunch. But pretty soon I was scooping up salsa and shoveling the chips in my mouth like Shelby.

The waitress came back to get our order and we had already emptied the basket of chips. We ordered dinners and she said she would bring us more chips.

"No!" I cried out. "Please don't!"

"Ok, ok," she said, laughing. "I'll tell them to rush your dinner, then."

The problem with chips and salsa is that I don't have to be hungry to eat them. They are there and they smell delicious and I just keep eating until they're gone.

I sipped my iced tea as I looked around at the colorful décor. There were sombreros on the wall and a piñata hanging in the corner. It was a very festive atmosphere.

I had been to Mexico on a missions trip a few years ago. The people I saw didn't seem like they had much to be festive about. They lived in tin shacks with dirt floors and struggled to find enough to eat. Of course, their Mexican food also wasn't covered in cheese and sour cream. It was mostly rice and beans, with occasional tortillas and bananas thrown in. I don't think that cuisine would bring in many customers.

The waitress returned with plates heaped with steaming food. Grilled chicken and shrimp mixed with peppers and onions sizzled temptingly. I was thankful to be in the U.S. eating some non-authentic Mexican food.

We dug in to our meals as if we hadn't just eaten a basket full of chips. I guess stress makes you hungry. I made it halfway through the plate before my stomach informed me I needed to stop. I was so full, I felt like I was going to pop.

Shelby made it through most of her dinner before she had to throw in the towel. The waitress came by to ask if we wanted dessert but then changed her mind and offered me a doggie bag instead. I actually would have loved to order some fried ice cream, but I had no idea where I would put it.

I packaged up the rest of my dinner to take back to mom. She probably wouldn't eat that much anyway. I also had the snacks I had gotten earlier that I could give her. I hoped dad woke up soon, because I was afraid we weren't going to get mom pried out of his room until he woke up and talked to her.

We walked down the street a few blocks and then back before we got in the car. I felt like if I sat down right away, something would burst. I needed my food to settle a little. Once I had digested a little, we got back to the car and drove back to the hospital.

We walked back in the front door. The clerk smiled at us but we knew where we were headed now. We walked back down toward the ICU. I stopped off in the waiting room to leave the food there. I didn't want to carry a container of food into the ICU. I wrote 'Sanford' on the lid, so people would know it wasn't just trash. I planned on bringing mom right back out to eat, and there was a microwave there for her to reheat it.

We called to be let in to the ICU and walked back to dad's room. He was still asleep and mom was half asleep in the chair in the corner. She looked up when we came in.

"How was supper?" she asked.

"Good. I ate too much," I replied. "We brought some back for you. Why don't you come out to the waiting room and eat?"

She started to protest but then looked at dad and realized he was still conked out.

"I can stay in here with dad," Shelby offered. "Go eat something, mom."

"Ok," mom said, getting out of the chair. I walked out of the room with her. Shelby settled into the chair and flipped on the TV.

We walked back out to the waiting room and found a spot at a table. I put the food in the microwave. There was a drinking fountain there and mom filled up her water bottle. I pulled the nuts and dried fruit out of my bag and set them on the table. I wasn't sure if mom liked her food as spicy as I did, so I wanted her to have other choices.

She either liked it, or was too hungry to care, because she ate the entire container. She also drank an entire bottle of water, so she must have been thirsty.

We got up and went back to the ICU. Dad was awake when we walked in, and Shelby was standing by his bed holding his hand. He kept trying to talk, not understanding that he couldn't talk with the tube in his throat.

Wade walked in the room behind us. "It looks like he's finally coming around," he said.

"He's a bit of a lightweight on sedation," I told him. "It takes him a while to sleep it off."

"Well, that explains why he took longer to wake up," Wade replied, nodding.

"I'm sorry, I should have told you that before," I said. Wade was probably worried that something was wrong.

"No problem," he said. He walked over to the bed and looked at dad. "Are you having pain, Bob?" he asked.

Dad shook his head 'no'. That must be quite the cocktail they have in that pain pump. I couldn't imagine it didn't hurt to have all that stuff stuck in you. Never mind what had gone on in surgery.

"We're going to try to get that tube out now, ok?" Wade told him. Dad nodded enthusiastically. Another lady walked in the room and introduced herself as the respiratory therapist. She was going to help with the extubation.

I had seen this procedure before and it was kind of gross. The tube came out covered with all kinds of goopy stuff and the patient sometimes coughed and gagged and turned purple for a few seconds.

"I think we'll step out for this," I said, motioning to mom and Shelby. They both looked at me and figured out they should leave with me. Wade smiled at me. I'm sure he was about to ask us to leave, because this wasn't something families needed to see.

"I'll call the waiting room as soon as we're done," Wade told me. I nodded and we walked back out the ICU door. I was relieved he was getting off the ventilator so quickly. I knew he would be a lot happier with that tube out of his throat.

After ten minutes, the phone in the waiting room rang. "Sanford family," I answered, figuring the call was for us. It was Wade, telling us to come back in. We walked back to the ICU and as we walked up to the door, it buzzed and swung open without us having to call in.

I glanced up and saw a closed circuit camera pointed down at where we were standing. They had seen us coming and buzzed open the door. I guess I should remember not to pick my nose while I was waiting for the door to open, since I was on camera. Not that I picked my nose anyway. But sometimes my undies got off kilter and I had to readjust them when I thought no one was looking. That would be embarrassing to have Wade see that.

We walked into dad's room and he was sitting up in the bed, looking much more like himself. Mom went straight to his side and he smiled at her.

"Betty," he croaked and then coughed. He grimaced with the coughing and mom looked concerned. Wade reassured her that this was normal and would get better over the next few days. I had seen the size of the tubes that I knew were stuck between his ribs and I'm sure they hurt when he coughed. Wade reminded dad to hug a pillow to his chest when he coughed to splint his chest incision.

"How are you feeling?" mom asked.

"Like I've been hit by a truck," he replied hoarsely. Apparently all the coughing had stirred up the pain he wasn't having earlier.

"A pickup or a semi?" Wade joked with him. I was glad dad had gotten a nurse with a sense of humor.

"Just a pickup, but he was going about 60," dad replied. "Was it a Ford or a Chevy?" My dad was a Ford man and would be until the day he died.

"I think it was a Chevy," Wade said.

Dad let his head sag back on to the pillow and closed his eyes. I heard him mutter, "Well then I hope it totaled the truck."

Chapter 9

Better Out Than In

It was now after 9:00 pm and I was fading fast. Mom was reassured that dad had woken up and talked to her, so I was pretty sure I could convince her to head to the hotel for the night. I didn't know what kind of visiting hours they had here. They had been pretty relaxed with us having three people in the room.

Shelby yawned, as if on cue. "I'm wiped out," she said. "Let's hit the hay."

Mom looked up at the clock and noticed what time it was. Since she didn't eat supper until almost 8 o'clock, she didn't realize how late it had gotten.

"I don't want Bob to be upset if we leave," mom protested.

"It's okay, he won't remember today at all," Wade assured her. "They never do."

"Really?" I asked. This was a pretty eventful day. The breathing tube issue alone seemed like it would leave a lasting impression.

"Nope," he said. "They get so much stuff in OR that it has an amnesia effect."

"So he won't know we were here at all?" Shelby asked.

"No, but I'll vouch for you," he grinned at her. She smiled back flirtatiously.

"Well, then let's all say good night to dad and go get some rest," I said, trying to redirect Shelby. She was such a shameless flirt.

We all filed past dad's bed and hugged and kissed him. The hugs were a little tricky, with all the stuff still stuck in him. But we knew the general intent.

"I'll still have my cell phone, if you need us," I told Wade. He assured me that he would call if anything happened. "I guess you'll be gone before we get back tomorrow," I said to him.

"Unless you're up before the sun," he said. "But Marcia is back tomorrow." I was relieved to hear that we would have a familiar face in the morning.

"Well, thank you for all you've done," I told him sincerely. I wasn't sure if we would end up seeing him again. Dad was only supposed to spend one night in the ICU.

"You're welcome," he replied. "It was nice to meet you."

We walked back down the hall and out the front door of the hospital. It was now very cool and I wished I had a sweatshirt. We headed back toward our cars. We decided to all go to the hotel in my car and just leave Shelby's car here.

I drove back down the street to the hotel on autopilot. Luckily, traffic was light that time of night. We parked and carried all our stuff into the hotel room. I had gotten a room with two queen beds. I figured Shelby and I could share a bed. I was so tired by then, I think I could have slept on the floor.

We took turns through the bathroom, washing faces and brushing teeth. Sanford women have pretty simple beauty routines. After a brief disagreement over who got how many pillows, we turned out the lights. I was asleep about thirty seconds later.

I woke up at 2 a.m. when Shelby kicked me. It turns out she is quite a restless sleeper. Or dreams of being a judo star. Either way, she throws a lot of kicks and punches in her sleep. I got up to get a drink of water. I climbed back in to bed but my brain started whirring and I couldn't fall back asleep. I looked at my phone on the charger. It didn't have any missed phone calls, so dad was obviously doing fine.

This is where being a nurse had a definite downside. I had seen all the things that could go wrong on a patient. Sometimes they were doing just fine, and then 30 minutes later, they were in critical condition. Things can change so fast. The rational part of my brain told me that if anything had changed, Wade would have called. The worry wart part of my brain wouldn't listen to the rational part of the brain. It almost never does.

I laid there, driving myself crazy for another 45 minutes. I usually try to distract myself when these worry sessions start. But I didn't want to wake up mom and Shelby, so I laid there in the dark, trying to turn off my brain. Suddenly, I remembered my dad saying, 'God is watching over me.' I was supposed to be trusting God, but, as usual, I was failing miserably. I said a silent prayer for my dad and a feeling of calm came over me. I closed my eyes and drifted off to sleep peacefully.

I woke up to the sound of someone slamming a door in the hallway. I really didn't like staying in hotels. They get noisy so early in the morning. I looked at the clock and saw it was 6:30. I sat up in bed and saw mom was getting up as well. Shelby was still conked out. She must be tired from all that kicking.

"Morning, mom," I said softly. She looked over at me and smiled.

"You must have heard the door, too," she said. I got my light sleeper trait from her.

"Yep," I said. "Do you want the shower first?" I asked.

"No, you go ahead," she said.

I grabbed some stuff from my bag and headed for the bathroom. A shower would start the wake up process and a cup of coffee would finish the job. I wondered what their continental breakfast looked like. I was a breakfast girl.

I finished up in the shower and got ready for the day, which doesn't take me too long. My hair was still wet but the blow dryer in the bathroom seemed to make a lot of noise without actually blowing any air. I figured it would air dry while I waited for mom and Shelby to get ready.

Mom headed for the shower next and I went down to grab some coffee. The continental breakfast had quite a few options. Unfortunately, they were doughnuts, biscuits and gravy, croissants and waffles. They did have some muffins, but they were huge. The cereal options weren't much better. I got my coffee and grabbed a banana from the small fruit bowl. I wasn't really hungry anyway, after my huge dinner last night.

I headed back up to the room. Mom was getting ready and Shelby was still asleep. I pulled back the covers and gave her a shove.

"Get up, we need to get going," I told her. She just grunted. I had a lot of experience waking Shelby up. She was not a morning person at all. I was not a patient person under good circumstances and today I wanted to get back to the hospital as quickly as possible.

"Shelby, if you don't get up right now, I'm leaving you here," I threatened. She groaned but still didn't move. She had her head buried under the pillow, so turning on the lights wouldn't work. I walked into the bathroom, got one of the plastic cups from by the sink and filled it with cold water. I walked back out to the bed. Mom was here, so I decided to try being nice.

"Last chance, Shelby," I said. She knew from past experience that I didn't make empty threats. She kept laying there, not moving. Maybe she thought I wouldn't use any of my usual tricks since mom was here. Oh, she was wrong. I dumped the glass of water right on top of her.

"Aahhh!!" she shrieked, jumping up. "I hate you!"

She didn't mean that, I'm sure of it. At least she was awake and upright now. And motivated to get in the shower, since her pajamas were soaking wet with cold water. She just glared at me and grabbed her bag. We had been down this road before. She would get over it, by lunchtime at the latest.

I looked over at mom, expecting a lecture on being nice to my sister. Instead, she was smiling to herself as she was tying on her shoes. I guess mom has a sense of humor after all.

I ate my banana and sipped my coffee while I waited for Shelby. It only took her 15 minutes to get ready, but it felt like forever. We finally got out of the room. Shelby stopped by the lobby for a cup of coffee to take in the car. Breakfast wasn't on her agenda.

We got in the car and headed back to the hospital. I parked by Shelby's car again. The lot was filling up fast. I suppose most visitors to the hospital come during the daytime. We got out and walked in the front door. I remembered how to get there from last night, so we headed straight for the ICU.

"Hey, look at that," mom said as we walked past the door to the chapel. She stopped and looked at the door for a minute. Then she opened it slightly and looked in. I peeked over her shoulder and saw a man kneeling at the prayer bench. Another lady was sitting on the bench in the middle row, crying softly.

I backed away and mom shut the door. It felt wrong to invade their moment. I wondered what their situation was. We were actually pretty lucky. Dad was going to recover and go home. Not everyone here was going to have that happy ending.

We walked on to the ICU in silence. We stopped at the door and picked up the phone to get buzzed into the unit. We walked in and went straight to dad's room. The unit was bustling again this morning. I don't think they ever had a slow day.

Dad was sitting up in the chair already. He had a breakfast tray in front of him, although he hadn't eaten much.

"Hi dad," I said cheerfully. I wasn't putting on a brave face, either. Seeing him up out of bed was very encouraging.

"Hey, gang," he smiled back at us. He still looked a little pale, and his voice was a little hoarse. I had heard that the breathing tube can make their throat pretty sore for a couple days. That was probably why he wasn't eating much, either.

Mom headed straight to his side and gave him a kiss. "Oh, Bob, you look great," she gushed. I could tell she was relieved as well to see him looking more like himself.

"Hi dad," Shelby chimed in. "Allie dumped cold water on me this morning," she tattled on me. She was daddy's girl, and she was hoping he would stand up for her.

Dad just grinned. I think he was still on some pain meds. I'm sure all those things stuck in him hurt, so pain meds were a good thing. If they made him a little goofy, that was okay. It was only for a few days. And it kept him from yelling at me for dumping water on Shelby.

Marcia came in the room with a cheery "Good morning," to all of us. She walked over to check on dad.

"Not hungry, Bob?" she asked with concern.

"My throat hurts," he replied. He had been drinking his coffee but the toast was untouched.

"That will happen," Marcia said, nodding understandingly. "How about some nice, cool Jell-O instead?"

"That sounds good," dad said. Marcia said she would bring some in with his morning medications, and walked back out.

"How was the night?" mom asked dad. I wondered if he remembered any of it.

"Good, I guess," he replied. "I think I slept all night."

Now I knew he didn't remember it. ICU patients get woke up about every hour or so. It is one of the most common complaints we hear from patients. Some of them are too sick to notice, but once they start feeling better, they start complaining about the lack of sleep.

I'm sure it's hard to sleep in there. Everything makes noise and the nurse is in and out all the time. The blood pressure cuff inflates every hour and any time the patient moves too much, the monitor starts dinging away. The bed can't be that comfortable either. But, I guess people don't go to the ICU because they need sleep.

Mom had pulled a chair up by the recliner and was sitting there, holding dad's hand. It seemed she had found her spot for the day. Shelby flopped on the now empty bed and turned on the TV. I wandered around the room looking at all the various equipment.

"Good morning," a deep voice called out, and Dr. Weston walked in the room. "Bob, you look great," he said. "How do you feel?"

"Not too bad," dad said. "A little rough, maybe." Dad was not one to complain, so I knew he wouldn't be honest about how he felt.

"Well, you should feel like you got hit by a truck," Dr. Weston said, grinning.

"That might be a good description," dad replied, smiling back. That was the description dad had used last night, but obviously he didn't remember that. Apparently, it was an accurate description of how it felt after open heart surgery.

"Every day gets a little better," Dr. Weston promised dad. "Today, we'll take out a couple of those tubes and move you out of the ICU to the cardiac stepdown unit."

"Isn't that a little soon?" mom asked with a worried look on her face. They had told us ahead of time that dad would only spend one night in the ICU, but it still seemed pretty quick.

"He's doing great," Dr. Weston assured her. "We like our heart patients to get up and move, and all this stuff," he gestured to the tangle of tubes and wires, "makes it hard to move."

Mom nodded but still had a furrow in her brow. I knew these people had a lot of experience with open heart patients and they knew what they were doing. Mom didn't seem so sure.

"The unit he is going to is specifically for open heart patients," Dr. Weston informed her. "The nurses are trained cardiac nurses, and he'll still be on a heart monitor, just a portable one."

Mom looked a little less worried then. The nurses had been great so far, so she really didn't have a reason to be concerned. Maybe she was just finally getting familiar with this scene and anxious about moving in general.

Dr. Weston leaned against the counter, as if he had plenty of time to sit and chat. I really liked that about him.

"Sorry I couldn't get here last night," he apologized. Dad just looked at him, puzzled.

"That's okay," I spoke up, since I knew dad didn't remember that the doctor didn't come by last night. "Wade said you had a family emergency. I hope everything is okay."

"Thank you," Dr. Weston replied sincerely. "I appreciate your concern."

"What happened?" Mom asked. I cringed inwardly. It was not appropriate to ask him something so personal. I think she was just being kind, but it still came out as nosy.

Dr. Weston didn't seem to feel that way though. He replied, "My ten-year-old son has epilepsy and he had a couple seizures at his soccer game. They took him to the ER and he had another seizure there."

I just stood there in shock. He said it so matter of factly. It had to be scary to watch your kid have a seizure, especially when you are powerless to stop it.

"Is he okay?" mom asked.

"He's still in the hospital," Dr. Weston replied. "He hit his head pretty hard when he fell with the first one. And the third seizure was almost two minutes long, so he has some muscle soreness from that. The neurologist increased the dosage on his medications and we're hoping that does the trick. He hadn't had one in over a year."

So, Dr. Weston had his son in the hospital and yet he was here chatting with us as if we were the most important thing in his day. Impressive. I don't think I could have done that.

But he knew that dad was the most important thing in our day, so he took the time to visit with us. I appreciated his sacrifice and admired his attitude toward his patients.

"Well, you should go be with him," mom said earnestly. "We won't take up any more of your time."

Dr. Weston smiled. "I just came from there, actually," he replied. "He's doing pretty good. His whole soccer team had come to visit, so old dad was just in the way anyway."

Dad smiled at that. Apparently, he remembered a time or two that his teenage kids didn't want him around. Well, I was a full grown adult now, and I wanted my dad around as much as possible for a long time.

Marcia came back in with the Jell-O and pills. "Well, hello Dr. Weston," she said, as she walked past. I could tell by her friendly tone that she actually liked Dr. Weston and wasn't just being professional and polite.

"Good morning, Marcia," he replied. "You're doing a fantastic job with Bob here. You have him nearly good as new."

Marcia grinned at dad. "He's quite the trouper," she said. "I can't take too much of the credit."

"I'll go ahead and write the transfer orders," Dr. Weston told her. He turned to dad and said, "I'll come see you on the fifth floor later today."

Dad nodded and Dr. Weston walked out. Marcia started opening pill packets as she explained each one to dad. This would be interesting. My dad had never taken any medications. I could tell by the look on his face that he wasn't thrilled about the cup full of pills she was handing him. Luckily, as she explained each one, she said what it was going to do for him. Mostly, she emphasized how it would help prevent another heart attack. That was the selling point for dad. He didn't like taking pills, but he didn't like being in the hospital even more.

Dad swallowed the pills with a grimace. Then he started eating his Jell-O. It must have felt good on his sore throat, because the cup was gone in seconds.

"That hit the spot, huh?" Marcia asked, laughing. "I'll get you another one and maybe a popsicle too."

We spent the morning just hanging out in the room. The plan was to transfer to the stepdown unit after lunch, so we had time to kill. I felt antsy, like I should be doing something, but I don't know what. I wish the waiting room had a treadmill. I could burn off some nervous energy.

We called Andrew and let him talk to dad. Cassie and Sammie got on the phone and chattered away to 'Papa'. They are tough to understand over the phone, but I don't think dad cared. He just loved listening to their voices.

Marcia came back in after awhile. "I'm so sorry I didn't get back in here sooner," she apologized. "We had a little trouble down the hall."

"Oh, we've been fine," I said, quickly, before mom could ask anything inappropriate. I wasn't sure if mom understood that medical staff aren't allowed to talk about other patients. I have had a lot of people in the ER ask me about the patient next door. Some were genuinely concerned and some were just being nosy, but either way, it was a violation of privacy laws if we said anything.

"Well, I'm going to take out a few of those lines," she said to dad. She turned to mom and added, "You'll probably want to step out for a few minutes."

I smiled. She sounded so polite and kind when she said that, but I knew that she wasn't offering an option. Some things are just better done without an audience. I had heard that taking out the chest tube was pretty painful. And one of the tubes to come out was the urinary catheter, so Shelby and I definitely didn't need to be there for that.

"Let's go grab a snack at the café," I suggested. It was late morning and my banana and coffee breakfast was not holding me. We gathered our stuff, told Marcia we would just come back in 20 minutes and headed out the door.

We headed down the hall toward the coffee shop. I smelled the enticing aroma of the coffee and almost drooled. I knew too much caffeine wasn't good for me and I had had a cup of coffee already. I rationalized that if I got a latte it would be mostly milk, which was good for me. I could always use some calcium. Didn't want to get weak bones and break a hip. That justified a latte in my mind. Now I had to avoid the cookie, because I didn't have a justification for that.

We all ordered a drink and I got a yogurt to go with the granola bar I had stashed in my purse. Luckily, it was early enough they hadn't put out the sweet treats for the day yet. Apparently, chocolate chip cookies were not considered a breakfast food.

We sat at a table by the waterfall. This place was a nice little getaway from the hospital setting. It was relaxing to listen to the waterfall gurgle and the espresso machine hiss. It was a lot better than the constant beeping in the ICU. I knew all those machines were necessary, but I wasn't going to miss their noisy chirping when we left.

We wandered back down the hall to the ICU after we figured we had given Marcia enough time to complete her tasks. We called and got buzzed through the door, and walked back into dad's room. He was back in the bed and looked a little grim.

"Is everything ok, dad?" I asked.

"Yeah, I'm fine" he said, but his face didn't match his words. I felt a nervous flutter go through my stomach. We hadn't had any complications so far and I was optimistic that we wouldn't. But suddenly dad didn't look so good.

"Dad, you don't look fine," I told him.

"Well, that one tube stung a little on the way out," he confessed. "And the other one downright felt like getting kicked by a mule."

Technically, my dad has never been kicked by a mule. But he has been kicked by a couple horses and a cantankerous heifer. I'm sure a mule can't feel much different. I was really glad we didn't stay in the room. Mom would have passed out. Shelby probably would have punched the nurse for hurting her daddy.

I knew what Marcia had done was necessary, and I'm sure she did it as carefully as she could. I've certainly been in her shoes, having to do something necessary but painful to a patient. As much as my brain understood what she had to do, my heart still felt a sharp pang of sympathy for my dad. He looked pretty miserable.

Marcia walked back in with a white pill cup. "Here's the pain pills, Bob," she said as she handed them to him.

"Thank you," he said with a grimace. "I shoulda listened to you before."

Marcia laughed. "That's okay, honey. You weren't the first and you won't be the last. These should help you feel better."

I was surprised to see my dad taking pain pills, although he obviously needed them. Marcia turned to us to explain.

"We usually give some morphine before we pull the chest tube, since it's so painful," she said. "Bob said he didn't want to take it and he would just tough it out. I tried to persuade him but I failed. So we took it out without pain medicine."

Dad shuddered at the memory of that. "Well, I won't ever argue with you again, I guarantee that, missy," he said.

She smiled at him. I'm sure she has had her share of stubborn patients. Sometimes it's pointless to argue with them. They eventually learn that the nurse has their best interests at heart.

"Those should start to help in about twenty minutes," Marcia told him. "I'll check back on you in a bit."

Mom pulled a chair up next to dad's bed and sat there holding his hand and looking worried. Shelby hopped into the recliner dad had been sitting in earlier. I ended up standing, which was starting to become a pattern. Maybe the next room would have more chairs.

"I'm okay, Betty," he assured mom. "Nothin' a coupla aspirin won't fix."

I was pretty sure the pills in that cup weren't aspirin, but I didn't correct him. This situation called for something a little stronger than usual. I knew that if he was in pain, he wouldn't want to get up and walk, or take deep breaths. Both of those things were important for a quick recovery, so pain medicine was going to be essential for a few days.

We just hung out for the next half hour. Dad gradually relaxed and even dozed off as the pain pills kicked in. Shelby was flipping through channels but not finding much worth watching. I wandered around the small room aimlessly, still feeling restless. I wasn't a person who sat still much.

Just before noon, Marcia came back in. "Bob, are you ready to get up in the chair?" she asked.

Dad opened his eyes and looked around the room for a minute like he wasn't sure where he was at. Then he saw mom and smiled. He looked a little bit looped.

"Bob, it's time for lunch," Marcia gently prodded him. "Let's get up in the chair and eat."

"Sure," dad said. He threw back the blanket and tried to swing his legs over the edge of the bed. He was promptly stopped by the compression cuffs on his calves.

"Hold on a second, you're still connected to everything," Marcia said. She disconnected his leg cuffs. He tried to sit up again and this time he got hung up on his oxygen tubing. Marcia was trying to get all his lines adjusted as quickly as she could, but dad was moving too fast for her.

He finally got to the edge of the bed and stood up to walk to the recliner.

"Bob, wait! Your IV pump," mom cried out. Dad was walking away and his IV tubing was stretched tight to the pump on the other side of the bed. Marcia was still frantically trying to get his remaining chest tube container around the bed.

"Boy, you sure don't pokey diddle around, do you Bob?" Marcia asked, laughing. I was pretty sure they wouldn't have too much trouble getting my dad to get up and move. He was used to being on the go and he didn't move slowly. I jumped in to help with the IV pump while Marcia got the chest tube and then the monitor wires. We got dad settled in the recliner with a sigh of relief.

"I ordered some chicken noodle soup and mashed potatoes for you," Marcia said. "And some more Jell-O, of course. That should feel better on your throat."

She brought the tray in and set it up on the table in front of dad. Dad had to be getting hungry at some point. He hadn't eaten anything but Jell-O for a day and a half now. I wanted to see him eating some protein to help heal his incisions.

Dad took a few bites and swallowed gingerly. The warm, soft food must have been okay, because he started eating heartily. Smelling the food and seeing the mountain of mashed potatoes covered in gravy made my stomach growl. Sheesh. Why was I so hungry? It wasn't like I was doing anything strenuous.

"Let's go get lunch," Shelby piped up suddenly. I guess the food had the same effect on her.

I was hungry and I was also ready for a breath of fresh air. I needed more of a break than just the café down the hall.

"Mom, do you want to come with us?" I asked. "We're going to go find something to eat."

"No, you go ahead," she said. "I'll stay here with Bob." She was in her usual position in a chair right next to dad.

"Ok, we'll bring something back," I told her as Shelby and grabbed our things and headed out the door.

We walked out the front door of the hospital to a warm, sunny day. It felt fantastic to be outside for a while. We got in the car and drove out of the parking lot with the windows down. I remembered seeing a chain restaurant that was known for its fantastic bread. They served it with sandwiches, soups and salads, which would be a better option than a burger and fries. I just had to avoid the dessert menu.

We pulled up and saw they had a patio for additional seating. Perfect. I could sit outside and enjoy the weather even longer. We went in and ordered and then took our food back outside. I ate my salad and warm, chewy breadstick and sipped my iced tea. I was feeling very virtuous that I had resisted the cookies. Shelby devoured her sandwich in record time. Of course, she hadn't eaten breakfast. She said she would go back in and order a sandwich for mom while I finished.

I had finished and carried my trash over to the trash can when Shelby walked out with a to go bag of food. We got in the car to head back to the hospital.

"I got mom a turkey and swiss," she said. "Oh, and I bought you a cookie. I know chocolate chip is your favorite." She grinned at me.

Brat.

Chapter 10

Don't Be Mean, Eileen

When we got back to dad's room, he was sitting in a wheelchair and all his stuff was packed up in bags and sitting on a cart. Mom was standing off to the side while a young man rearranged all of dad's remaining tubes so they wouldn't get pulled on. Marcia came back in the room with some papers.

"Oh, hi girls," she said, a little breathlessly. "Sorry for the rush but we have a critical patient coming in so we need to get Bob moved out." She handed the papers to the man who tucked them in a pocket on the back of the wheelchair.

"I'm Tyrone," the young man introduced himself. "I'll be moving Bob up to the fifth floor."

Marcia stopped for a moment and rested her hand on dad's shoulder. "Good luck, Bob," she said, sincerely, looking down at him with compassion. She looked up at the rest of us and added, "It was very nice to meet all of you." Then she rushed out the door.

"Can we help with anything?" I asked Tyrone. They seemed to be moving quickly.

"If you don't mind bringing that cart with all his belongings," he said, "I can push the wheelchair."

I grabbed the cart and did a quick scan around the room to see if we had left anything behind. I looked like they had been very thorough. Tyrone pushed dad out the door in the wheelchair and we all followed along behind.

As our little caravan made its way down the hall to the elevators, Tyrone chatted with dad. It seems they had some sports team in common. I didn't follow sports much. Or at all. It was nice that dad had some male bonding time. It made things feel more like they were getting back to normal.

We all crammed into the elevator and headed up to the fifth floor. As we came down the hallway to dad's new unit, I noticed it was as bustling as the ICU had been. It seemed this hospital was always busy. Tyrone wheeled dad into his room and we followed. I was relieved to see that it was much more spacious than the ICU room. Or maybe it was that there was less stuff in it. There were extra chairs lined up by the window, so I would get to sit down, at least.

Dad was thrilled to see that there was an actual bathroom and asked if he could go in there right away. I guess he wasn't too enthused about the methods they used in the ICU. Tyrone helped him up and carried his chest tube container in with him.

I started unloading the cart of dad's belongings. Most of them were hospital-acquired. He hadn't come in with much more than his clothes. I placed the clothes in the closet in the corner of the room. I arranged dad's water bottle and other items on the bedside table. I just felt like I should be doing something useful, and that was all I could find to do.

As dad was coming back out of the bathroom, a nurse came striding into the room.

"You must be Robert Sanford," she said to dad.

"Call me Bob," dad replied as he made his way toward the recliner, with Tyrone following carrying the chest tube container.

"Don't sit down!" she said sharply. "There has to be a blanket on that."

It makes sense that you wouldn't want the patient's bare backside against the vinyl covering. I didn't think she needed to be quite so harsh about it. She opened a cupboard that was apparently supposed to have linens in it.

"Great. Just great," she muttered, as she slammed the cupboard shut. "I guess no one decided to stock this room." She scowled and shook her head as she marched out of the room. We all stood there looking at each other, not sure what to do.

"I think she went to get the blanket," Tyrone offered helpfully. That was my guess as well, but after five minutes we were all still standing there. Dad was starting to look a little tired.

"How about if you just sit on the edge of the bed for now?" Tyrone asked dad. He agreed and they made their way over to the bed so dad could sit.

"That feels better," dad sighed. Tyrone connected the drainage container to a suction tube from the wall.

"Whenever you get up, you need someone to disconnect that," he instructed dad. "Don't just get up and take off."

Dad nodded in agreement. He didn't look like he was taking off anywhere too quickly for awhile. Tyrone gathered the wheelchair and cart and headed for the door.

"Good luck, Bob," he said as he left. I was kind of bummed to see him go. He actually took care of dad, and so far, our nurse hadn't returned.

As if on cue, the lady came rushing back in the room with an armful of linen. She saw dad sitting on the bed and scowled again.

"So, you want to get in the bed now?" she asked, with the same sharp tone.

"Well, I was getting tired standing up, so I needed to sit down," dad explained. I bit my tongue to keep from pointing out that she was gone for ten minutes to get a blanket.

"We're slammed here today, and someone called in sick, so I have to take extra patients," she said, impatiently. "I have about five different things I'm doing right now."

She shoved the linens in the cupboard and shut it, then turned to look at all of us. Her name tag said 'Eileen, RN'. She walked over to dad and started looking at his dressings and chest tube. She wasn't being all that gentle either. When she yanked on the gown to see the chest tube site, I saw dad wince in pain.

"Does that hurt, dad?" I said clearly. I would try the polite route first.

"It's a little tender," dad said, tightly, as she kept pushing on his side.

"Well, it hurts to have open heart surgery," Eileen replied without sympathy. "You got some pain pills earlier, that should help." She had finished attacking him and stepped back from the bed. I looked over at Shelby and she looked like she wanted to punch the nurse. I felt the same way, and I suddenly longed to be back in the ICU with the kind nurses. Even if it was full of beeping noises.

"I'll go look at your orders and see what I have to do," Eileen said, and turned and walked out of the room. I stood there, stunned, for a moment. She hadn't even introduced herself to us. She hadn't given dad the call light, or offered to help him to the chair, or even filled his water pitcher. Ok, none of those things were critical, but we did them for patients in the ER with a sprained ankle. It seemed like she should do them for the patient who had open heart surgery yesterday.

"Dad, do you want to sit in the chair or get into bed?" I asked him. I guess I was going to have to be the nurse.

"The chair," he replied. He wasn't one to lay around in bed, I knew that. I took a blanket from the now stocked cupboard and put it over the recliner. I helped him stand up and walk the few steps to the chair, keeping an eye on his chest tube drain. There was enough slack on the suction tubing that I could just move the container over by him. He sat down carefully and I helped him raise up the foot rest. His ankles and feet were still swollen from all the fluid he got in surgery. Marcia had assured us that was normal and would go away, but to elevate his feet whenever possible.

I looked at all the wires coming out of the wall above the bed and located the call light. I set it on the chair next to him. I don't know that it would be necessary, because mom probably wouldn't leave his room now. It was hard enough for her when we had a good nurse. She had already pulled a chair up right next to the recliner to sit in.

Shelby followed my lead and grabbed dad's water pitcher. "I'll go find some ice water, daddy," she said and headed out the door.

I couldn't think of anything else to do for dad, so I grabbed a seat in one of the chairs. I felt tired all of the sudden.

Shelby came back after a few minutes, and I could tell by her face that something was wrong. I didn't have time to ask before she burst out,

"This place sucks! How long do we have to stay here?"

"What happened?" I asked, avoiding the question. Dad had to be here for several days.

"I found the little kitchen with the ice machine," she started, "and I was filling daddy's pitcher and that mean old snit came in and yelled at me that only staff were allowed in there." She was talking loudly and gesturing wildly, so I knew she was really upset.

"So, I informed her that I had to go in there since no staff had bothered to fill my dad's water pitcher," she continued. "And she just made the same excuse about being busy. So, fine. You're busy. Got it. But don't yell at me because I'm doing your job." I didn't try to interrupt her rant, because I completely agreed with her. I was proud of her for standing up to the 'mean old snit.' Unfortunately, now we had to worry that the nurse was mad at us and would take it out on dad.

That was the double-edged sword of complaining about your nurse. You still had to have them as your nurse for at least the rest of the shift. And if they weren't very nice to you to start with, it wasn't going to get better after they got their butt chewed by their manager.

We only had 4 more hours of this nurse's shift. I prayed we got a good nurse for the night shift and we could request a different nurse tomorrow.

Eileen walked back in the room, saw dad in the chair, and scowled. It seemed to be her favorite facial expression.

"You can't get up without help," she scolded him. "You have that tube in your side."

"I helped him with that," I said. I didn't care for her talking to my dad like that.

She turned to me and said, "You can't do that. You don't know what to do if it comes apart."

"Actually, I do," I replied. "I'm a nurse. I've worked with chest tubes before."

She stood there for a moment, and I could see her wheels were turning. She realized now that she may have gotten herself in a little trouble. Another nurse would recognize all the things she had done wrong.

"Oh, really. Where do you work?" she asked, suddenly saccharin sweet.

"Brighton County Hospital. In the ER," I replied. I wasn't buying her fake-nice routine. But if having a nurse in the family meant she would be nicer to my dad, I would gladly play the nurse card.

"That must be very exciting," she said, awkwardly. I don't think friendly conversation came naturally to her.

"It certainly has its moments," I replied. I never know how to respond to those comments. My job doesn't look at all like the Hollywood depiction. I still love it, though, even on the mundane days.

Eileen looked around for anything else she needed to do. She already knew he had ice water and she saw the call light by dad.

"Call if you need anything," she said. She half-smiled and then walked back out of the room.

"Yeah, right," Shelby muttered under her breath. I agreed. It would take something pretty serious before I would ask for that nurse to come back in the room.

We all relaxed and just chatted. It was amazing how much had happened since this time yesterday. Dad kept dozing off in the chair, which I'm sure was a side effect of the pain meds. At least he was comfortable.

An aide came in after a while and checked dad's blood pressure. She asked if we needed anything, and then left.

About 6 o'clock, the aide reappeared with a supper tray for dad. At the sight of food, I was suddenly starving. I didn't want to leave dad alone, though. Not with this crabby nurse. Although she hadn't been back in the room. I couldn't decide if that was good or bad.

I helped dad sit up in the chair to eat. He still wasn't eating too much, since his throat was still sore. But he did polish off his cup of ice cream in quick fashion.

Eileen came in with a pill cup that had a couple pills in it. She handed it to dad.

"Here's your pills, Bob," she said, politely. I guess she was going to be on good behavior now.

"What are these?" dad asked. He probably figured he had taken enough pills this morning to last him the whole day.

"They're your pills," Eileen repeated.

"I know, but what are they?" dad pressed her. I was glad he didn't just take them without questioning her. It's a good idea to know what something is before you put it in your body.

"It's your metoprolol and docusate," she said bluntly. As if dad would have any idea what that meant. She just stood there, looking at him impatiently.

"Dad, the metoprolol is for your heart," I explained, since Eileen wasn't going to, apparently. "The docusate is to keep you from getting constipated while you're on the pain meds."

Dad looked at me and figured it was okay to take them if I knew what they were for. He swallowed the pills with his water, grimacing slightly when he swallowed.

Eileen looked down at his tray that was mostly untouched, except for the ice cream cup.

"Only having dessert tonight?" she said, a little tartly.

"My throat is sore," dad replied. "The ice cream made it feel better."

Eileen half smiled at that and then cleared dad's tray out of the room. She didn't offer him anything else to eat. I remembered Marcia and her generous offerings of Jell-O and popsicles. Why couldn't all the nurses be as awesome as her?

About 7o'clock, there was an increase in people and activity at the nurses' desk. I knew that shift change was then, and I was praying we got a good nurse. Dad was looking tired and mom was starting to fade too. I wanted to get dad tucked in with a nice nurse and head to the hotel.

We heard a deep, booming voice in the hallway, talking to another person. I was sitting there, nervously watching the door, when Santa Claus walked in.

Well, it wasn't actually Santa Claus, but he was tall with a white beard and a potbelly. He was wearing blue scrubs, though, not a red suit.

"Bob," he boomed. I almost expected him to say 'Ho, ho, ho.' He really looked like Santa Claus. "I'm Randy, your nurse for the night."

He walked over to dad and shook his hand firmly. Dad smiled as he shook his hand. I could tell him liked Randy already.

Randy turned and shook mom's hand as well. "How are you, ma'am?" he asked by way of introduction. "I'm Randy."

"I'm Betty," mom replied warmly. "These are our daughters, Allison and Shelby." She gestured to each of us as she said our name.

Randy smiled at us from under his thick, white beard. Then he turned his attention back to dad.

"Bob, I hear you didn't eat very much supper," he said, looking concerned.

"My throat is still sore," dad explained. He was probably starting to feel like a kid who didn't clean his plate, the way everyone kept bugging him about not eating.

Randy nodded, understandingly. "That breathing tube is a bugger, isn't it?" he said. "Well, I have an idea. How about if I get the kitchen to make you a milkshake. They put protein powder in it so you get some protein to help you heal. But it goes down a lot smoother than a steak."

My stomach growled with all this talk about steaks and milkshakes. At least we had a good nurse, so I could go get supper soon.

Dad agreed to the milkshake. Randy went about assessing dad, listening to dad's heart and lungs, checking all his lines and dressings, and looking at his chest tube. But, unlike Eileen, he was gentle about it. He also kept talking to dad, asking him how he was feeling and if certain things were hurting him. I liked this guy more and more.

"So, how did you end up being a nurse?" dad asked. Randy didn't look like the typical nursing student, and he would have gone to nursing school 30 years ago.

"I was a corpsman in the Navy," Randy replied. "I loved it, and when I got out, the best way to keep doing it was become a nurse."

"You must have stood out in nursing school," dad said. Randy laughed at that.

"They didn't even have a uniform for me to wear. All they had were dresses, so I had to get a shirt and pants made. I was the first male at that school. I had to share a bathroom with the janitor," he chuckled. "Nobody was sure what to do with me."

Randy must have been quite the sight in nursing school. He was well over six feet tall. But appearances don't mean much, and he was a great nurse. I was glad he toughed it out.

Randy told dad that he would be back in a little bit with the milkshake. He asked if he could get us anything else. I told him we were going to head to the hotel room soon and he nodded.

"Bob will probably go to bed early, anyway," he said. "It's been a big day for him."

We all went past dad and gave him hugs. I was comfortable leaving him here now that Randy was on shift. If we had gotten someone like Eileen, I may have set up camp in the recliner for the night, just to be on watch.

We walked back out to my car. The evening air was cooling off. After a brief discussion on where we should eat supper, we headed for a Japanese restaurant. Randy's comment about steak had me hungry for a juicy New York strip, but I didn't need to eat a huge steak with all the trimmings. All I was doing after dinner was going to bed.

After dinner, we headed back to the hotel. I figured I should bite the bullet and bring up the sticky topic of when I would leave.

"So, mom, I have to go back to work in a couple days," I started out. It was Wednesday now, and I had to work the weekend. I knew dad would be in the hospital until probably Monday.

"Ok, sweetie," mom said calmly.

"I go back to work on Saturday, too," Shelby chimed in. "I guess I can call in."

"Well, dad will be here until Monday, I think," I said. "We should try to get back and work while he's still here with a nurse to take care of him. That way, if he needs help after he gets home, we'll still have vacation time to use."

"That makes sense," mom said. I was always the practical one of us kids. Now came the sticky part.

"Mom, you need to get home to get a vehicle," I told her. She stared at me blankly for a moment and then it dawned on her that she didn't have a way to drive dad home when he got discharged. She looked at me anxiously.

"How am I going to do that?" she asked.

"Well," I started cautiously, "I could drive you home tomorrow and you could get your car."

"Oh no! I can't leave Bob," she cried out. "He would be here all alone!" She looked stricken at the thought of this.

"Mom, if we go tomorrow, Shelby can stay with dad until you get back," I offered. "You would only be gone part of one day."

"Shouldn't you stay with dad, since you're a nurse?" Shelby pointed out.

"No, you should stay with dad because you're a terrible driver," I reminded her. She just shrugged in agreement. She knew I was right.

"It's only for a little bit," I reassured both of them. "We can get back to Madison, mom can pack stuff for her and dad, and drive back here in six hours."

Mom still looked uneasy. I knew it would take her a little while to agree to it. That was why I was starting now. We really needed to go tomorrow, so I was hoping by 9 a.m. she had come around.

Shelby's comment about me being there reminded me, though, that I had forgot to ask for a different nurse for tomorrow. I needed to call and give that message to Randy. I started looking through all of the stuff we had gotten from the hospital, looking for a phone number. I finally found the main hospital number. I hoped the switchboard could get me to the right place.

"Springfield Memorial Hospital, how may I help you?" a pleasant voice answered.

"I need to speak to Randy," I said, then realized that made no sense. "I mean, my dad is a patient there, and I need to speak to his nurse," I rushed to explain. "He's on the fifth floor. Robert Sanford. That's the patient. Randy is his nurse." I finally stopped babbling, because even I was getting confused.

There was a long pause. "Your father is Robert Sanford, and he is a patient here?" she asked politely.

"Yes," I replied.

"Ok, I have him in Room 509. And you said you want to speak to his nurse, not the patient, correct?" she asked.

"Yes, please," I said, hoping that politeness would make up for my disorganization.

"Ok, I will transfer you to that nurses' station," she answered and transferred my call.

"Smooth," Shelby said, sarcastically. I tried to smack her but she jumped out of my reach. I was using the hotel phone so I was attached to a wall.

"Cardiac stepdown, can I help you?" a female voice answered.

"Could I speak to Randy, please?" I asked, my professional air returning.

"Who may I say is calling?" she asked.

"Allie Sanford. Bob is my dad. Robert Sanford. His patient in room 509," I started babbling again. It was like I had never talked on a phone before.

"Ok, one moment," she said, and hold music came on. She must have figured out what I meant from that jumble of words.

"This is Randy, can I help you?" his deep, booming voice came over the phone.

"Randy, this is Allie Sanford. Bob's daughter," I said. "I just forget to ask you one thing."

"No, Allie, I am not single," he said, with teasing in his voice. "I appreciate you asking, but I'm spoken for." I busted out laughing. This guy had my kind of a sense of humor.

"Well, I guess you're not too broken hearted," he said laughing. "What can I do for you?"

"The nurse today, Eileen, was pretty mean to dad," I said. I didn't feel the need to sugar coat it. "Can we request to have a different nurse tomorrow?"

Randy chuckled. "She's a mean one, that Eileen. See? It even rhymes. Mean Eileen. And she doesn't work tomorrow, so you're in luck."

I was relieved to hear that. I'm sure some people would say it was unprofessional for Randy to joke around with me about his coworker. But it made me feel like Randy and I were on the same team, and that was what I wanted.

"I will handpick my replacement from the crew coming in tomorrow morning for you, how's that?" Randy asked.

"That sounds great," I said, smiling. Dad was going to love having Randy as a nurse. I said good night to Randy and hung up the phone.

We had gotten back to the hotel a little earlier tonight, so we sat around and chatted. I called Andrew and gave him the latest update. I left out the details about the crabby nurse and just told him that dad had moved to the stepdown unit and had Santa Claus for a nurse.

I decided to wander around the hotel, just to move around for a bit. I cruised past the pool, where a group of kids were playing rambunctiously. Their moms were all sitting in the lounge chairs, periodically yelling at them to stop something they were doing. I wondered when in life you hit the point that you no longer got in the pool and played, and just sat in the lounge chair instead. I think Shelby would still be playing in the pool.

I wandered through the hotel gift shop with its grossly overpriced toiletries and snacks. I guess if you needed a toothbrush bad enough, you would be willing to pay $8 for it.

There was a small workout room in the hall behind the front desk. No one was in it at this time of night. I didn't have any workout clothes with me anyway, so I kept wandering. Finally, I had run out of stuff to look at and I was starting to look like a creep, wandering up and down the stairs and halls. I headed back to the room.

Shelby was flipping channels and mom was stretched out on the bed, reading. I decided I should eat some of the snacks I had bought the first day. The fish and seaweed salad from supper wasn't sticking with me. I pulled out some almonds and dried fruit mix.

"Hey, give me some of that," Shelby said, in true sibling fashion. I guess she was hungry again too. We munched on snacks and watched nothing at all on TV. Finally, I decided I should go to bed, if I was going to be this unproductive. Not that there was anything for me to do. I just wasn't used to sitting around. I must have gotten that from my dad.

I slept through the night without a problem. Shelby kept to her side of the bed, which was good. If she kicked me again, I was going to start retaliating.

But, once again, I was awakened shortly after 6 a.m. by a door slamming and some guy yelling down the hall to his wife who forgot her coat. Part of the problem with hotels is a lack of soundproofing. But a bigger part of the problem is inconsiderate guests.

I got up and hit the shower. I was hungry this morning, even with the bedtime snack. I dressed and headed down to breakfast. As if they had read my mind, today they had some healthier options on the counter. There was fruit, yogurt and oatmeal. I had some of each of them as well as my cup of coffee. I was still sitting there eating when mom came down. She grabbed some oatmeal and a banana and joined me.

"Shelby is in the shower," she informed me. So I wouldn't need to use any of my cruel methods of getting her out of bed this morning.

I was trying to figure out how to bring up the trip home again. Mom beat me to the punch.

"I guess we should go get my car today," she said. She didn't look too thrilled about it, but there wasn't really much choice. If Shelby and I both left, she wouldn't have any way to get around. Since we didn't know for sure which day dad would get discharged, there was no guarantee that Shelby or I would be free to come pick them up, either. Joe's could probably cover one of Shelby's shifts. My job wasn't one you could just call in at the last minute. Working short staffed in a medical setting could have serious consequences.

"Shelby will be with dad while we're gone," I reassured her. "We'll get back as quick as we can."

She nodded. "What time should we leave?" she asked.

"Let's go see dad," I replied. "If he looks good, we can take off right after that. That way you won't have to drive after dark."

Mom nodded. Driving at dusk was risky in our rural area. There were wild animals that liked to try to commit suicide on the front of your car. I never did understand what they were so depressed about. Or why they stood there and waited until just the right time to run out in front of you.

We headed back up to the room. Shelby was finishing getting ready. I grabbed all my stuff and packed it back in my bag. When I left here, I would be going home for the weekend of work.

"Shelby, where are your car keys?" I asked her. She hadn't had to use them in two days, so there was a good chance she had lost them. She started digging through her pockets and overnight bag. She finally found them at the bottom of her purse. She didn't ask me why I wanted to know. She knew I was making sure she had them before I drove off and left her there alone.

We headed out to the car and drove back to the hospital. We were walking down the hallway to the elevators when I saw a doorway for the stairwell.

"Hey, let's take the stairs up," I suggested.

Shelby just stared at me. "Are you nuts?" she exclaimed. "That's five flights!"

Technically, it's only four. I didn't think that was going to convince her. Mom thought it was a great idea though, and pushed open the door. Shelby glared at me and then headed up the stairs as well.

By the second floor, Shelby was sighing loudly and deliberately breathing hard. She wasn't a morning person and she wasn't one to go looking for exercise either. In spite of being sisters, she managed to stay slim without any effort at all. Which is so unfair, it should be illegal.

We had a not-very-nice great uncle who used to say that I got the brains and Shelby got the looks. I thought that was pretty offensive to both of us, but we were definitely two very different people.

The tough question was- if I had the choice, would I want to trade?

Chapter 11

Back to the Salt Mine

We got to the fifth floor without Shelby going into respiratory arrest and walked down the hall to dad's room. He was sitting up in the chair already, and a breakfast tray was in front of him. It had oatmeal, yogurt and a protein shake. He was actually eating, which was good to see. I was grateful for Randy and his idea of the protein shakes to help with dad's nutrition.

"Good morning, dad," I said as we walked in. He looked up at us and smiled. Mom walked over to give him a kiss.

"Hi daddy," Shelby said. "Allie made me walk up all the stairs and I nearly died." She loved to tattle on me.

"It's good for you," dad replied. "Keep you from ending up in here with a heart attack."

Shelby didn't look too happy with his reply. She was used to dad being on her side. Now I had an ally in my efforts to keep my family living healthy.

"How was the night, dad?" I asked.

"Good," he replied. "That Randy was a hoot. I didn't get too much sleep, though. Everytime I rolled over, this thing stabbed me." He gestured to his chest tube. That would make it hard to sleep. Dad was normally a side sleeper, so he probably kept trying to roll onto his side. Unfortunately, all the medical equipment pretty much mandated that he sleep on his back.

I was about to ask who his nurse for the day was when Wade walked into the room.

"Hello, again, Sanford family," he said cheerfully. He smiled an extra few seconds at Shelby, who promptly forgot she was pouting and lit up with a smile.

"You're dad's nurse?" I asked.

"They had a sick call, so they asked me to cover," he explained. "I work this unit sometimes when they are short staffed."

I was really happy to see him. Maybe not as happy as Shelby, but still happy. I knew he was a great nurse, and I could trust him when mom and I had to leave.

"Randy told me that you had requested me," Wade said, grinning.

That wasn't exactly what I had asked, but it had worked out perfectly. "The nurse yesterday was not so great," I said. "So I asked to have someone different."

Wade laughed. "I've heard that about her before," he said. "It's too bad, really. People shouldn't be scared of their nurse."

I agreed wholeheartedly. It was funny the contrast between the nurses we had met. Some were so fantastic and seemed to love what they did. Others seemed like they were permanently pissed off and the patients were just a bother to them. I wondered what made that difference in people. And I wondered which nurse I was. I hoped it was the good one.

We filled dad in on the plan for me to take mom home so she could get the car. He agreed that this was the best plan. He, of course, insisted he didn't need Shelby to stay with him and he was fine. He didn't like to create a fuss.

Shelby was more than happy to stay now that she knew Wade was here. I told her we would call her when we got to Madison and again when mom left to come back to Springfield. Mom and I hugged dad goodbye and headed for the car.

We got on the highway and settled in for the drive. We had almost two hours of car time ahead of us.

"How are you doing with all of this, mom?" I asked. She had held up really well, considering. But since I wasn't going to be there to offer support, I wanted to make sure she was doing okay before I dropped her off.

She sighed and answered, "I don't even know. Everything has happened so fast." She stared out the window at the country passing by for a few minutes.

"I really thought I might lose him for a little while," she finally said, softly. Her voice caught on the last word. "I couldn't even imagine what I would do if I did."

I almost cried when I heard her say that. My parents had been married for close to 40 years and they went together like mac and cheese. I didn't want to think about the possibility of one of them dying and the other one being all alone. I knew the reality was that it would happen someday. But I couldn't think about it today. Someday was years down the road, I was just sure of it. I would be better prepared by then.

We talked about everything that had happened with dad. I explained the medical stuff that she had been too nervous to ask about at the time it was happening. She wondered why this happened so suddenly, and I explained how heart disease builds up silently over years. It wasn't actually sudden, we just didn't know about it until now.

She wondered what she could do to help dad, so we talked about diet changes. Dad's favorite fried strip steaks were going to be a rare treat. Mom was going to have to get skilled with vegetables and grilled chicken.

"Your dad is not going to be happy if he doesn't get bacon for breakfast," mom warned me. "I'm not sure that will fly."

"Well, tell him if he eats bacon he'll have another heart attack," I countered. "That should keep him on the straight and narrow."

Mom laughed. "I'm sure he doesn't want to repeat any of this week!" she said.

"Besides, mom," I continued, "he can still have it once a week or so. Just not every day. That should make him a little happier."

We chatted as the miles flew by and soon we were turning off the highway at Brighton to head west to Madison. Suddenly, I longed to be home. I didn't realize you can get homesick, even when you don't have anyone at home. But my quiet little house with all my stuff in it sounded delightful. However, I still had to drive to Madison to drop mom off and then drive back.

The winding road to Madison was a little more scenic. I guess I should get used to this drive. It looked like I would be making it a lot more often after dad got home from the hospital.

I gave mom the rundown on what she should pack for herself as well as for dad. I knew the razors in the hospital were terrible, and the deodorant and toothpaste weren't much better. Dad would appreciate having his own stuff to use. I reminded her to take her cell phone charger and keep her phone charged so I could get ahold of her. I had written down the number of the hospital, just in case. If mom wasn't answering her phone, I could at least call dad's room for updates.

By the time we reached the house, mom had a list of what to pack and she was ready to go. I asked if she wanted me to come in and help her, but she said she would be fine. It wouldn't take more than 20 minutes to pack and she would be headed back out.

"Drive safe," I told her. "You want to make it back there in one piece."

Mom smiled at me. "Aren't I supposed to be the one who tells you to drive safe?" she asked. The role reversal was ironic. I guess that meant I was an adult now.

I gave her a hug and got in the car to head back home. My brain started whirring with all the stuff I needed to do when I got home. I had an extra day off since I didn't go back to work until Saturday. But I had to get mom home to a car today, since Shelby needed to come home tomorrow. I knew mom only agreed to come home because Shelby would be able to stay with dad.

I got home and saw my mailbox was stuffed full with mail. I hadn't thought to ask someone to come get my mail for me. I opened the door to a raunchy smell that reminded me I hadn't taken the trash out when I left. I hadn't had time to think of those things. I grabbed the trash bag and hauled it out, then opened windows and lit some candles to air out the place.

The clothes I had left in the washer now smelled like mildew, so I dumped more soap in and restarted the washer. It was close to lunchtime and I wondered what food I had that was still good. I had actually only been gone for two days. It seemed like a lifetime, though.

I grabbed some crackers and hummus to snack on and went to turn on the laptop to check my e-mail. It was still on, however, since I hadn't remembered to turn it off before I left. I clicked on my inbox and I had 27 new messages. I sighed and started plowing through them. Nothing was really that urgent, but I figured I might as well deal with it now. I didn't have energy to do much else.

I had sent text messages to some friends during the hospital adventure to let them know what was happening, so I shot out some quick messages to let them know dad was doing well and I was back home.

I called Shelby to see how dad was doing. She said he was doing great and had walked in the hallway already. She also mentioned that Wade had been very nice and he was in the room a lot to check on dad. I wondered if that was because dad needed the attention or if he was making excuses to come in and talk to Shelby. I was glad we had a nurse who was attentive to dad, either way.

I unpacked my bag and put all my stuff away. I was still hungry, so I opened a can of chicken rice soup, dumped it in a bowl and stuck it in the microwave. I really wanted to go get a burger at Joe's, but I had eaten out enough in the last few days.

A knock on my front door startled me. I opened the door to see my neighbor, Cathy standing there. She had a concerned look on her face.

"Allie, is everything ok?" she asked.

"Yeah, why?" I asked, puzzled.

"You disappeared and you normally tell us when you're leaving town," she said. "I was worried something bad had happened."

"Oh, my dad had a heart attack," I explained. "He had to have open heart surgery and he's in the hospital in Springfield."

Cathy gasped and clapped her hand to her chest. "Oh no!" she cried. "Is he okay?"

I realized at that point how it would sound to someone else to hear the news. I had gotten used to the news and said it nonchalantly. He was fine, now, but it did seem odd to consider having open heart surgery as 'being okay'.

"He's doing great," I rushed to assure her. "He's in the stepdown unit and will come home early next week."

"Well, that's good," she replied. "I got nervous when I realized I hadn't seen you in two days and your mail wasn't picked up. I didn't want to be nosy, but..." she trailed off.

"That's fine, Cathy, you can be nosy all you want," I told her, smiling. "It's nice to know I have someone looking out for me."

Cathy smiled back at me. Her kids were almost my age and they had all moved away. It was fine with me if she wanted to play substitute mom for me.

We once had an elderly lady come in to the ER in the ambulance. She was a widow and had no family or close friends in town. Apparently, she spent most of her time alone. One day, the mailman realized that she had three days worth of mail still stuck in her mailbox, which was unusual for her. He started looking in her windows and saw her laying on the floor. She had fallen and broken her hip and couldn't get up or get to the phone to call for help. And since no one ever called her or came over, no one noticed that she was 'missing' for three days. That made me so incredibly sad, to think about being that alone. I was glad to know that someone noticed when I was 'missing'.

"Well, I'm so glad that everyone is okay," Cathy said. "Do you need anything? Can I do anything to help?" she asked.

"Thank you," I replied, "but I'm good for now. I probably will be out of town more once dad gets home. I'll let you know when I'm leaving, if you could keep an eye on my house."

"I would be happy to," she said. "Just let me know."

I thanked Cathy again and went to eat my soup. It wasn't the best soup I had ever eaten, but it wasn't the worst either. The worst soup I have ever eaten was a detox soup that had lots of green vegetables and was supposed to make you feel great. I like green vegetables, but the combination of celery, cucumbers, kale, spinach and onions did not end up being tasty. And I did not feel great afterward. I can see how it would help you lose weight, because I barely choked down half of it before I decided I wasn't really that hungry anyway.

I spent the afternoon doing laundry and mowing the lawn. Towards supper, I called mom's cell phone to see if she had made it back. She answered, so she must have gotten the phone charged.

"How's dad doing?" I asked her.

"Oh, he's doing great," she replied enthusiastically. "He walked three times today and ate all of his lunch. He's starting to look pink again and his legs are a lot less swollen."

I was glad to hear that he was doing so well. I was about to ask to talk to him but mom spoke first, "Hold on, Shelby wants to talk to you."

"Hey, Lis," Shelby said when mom handed her the phone. "I have a question- is it okay if I give my number to Wade? Or is that against some nursing rule?"

"Did he ask for your number?" I asked her. They had certainly seemed interested in each other. But that was still a bit forward.

"No, not yet," she said. "But I didn't know if it was ok, since he's dad's nurse and all."

"Well, it probably is against some policy for him to ask you," I told her. "Since he is your dad's nurse, you might feel like you had to give him your number or he wouldn't be good to your dad, or something like that. But it would be fine if you just gave it to him. Then he can call if he wants to."

"So, how do I go about doing that?" she asked. "Just write it down and hand it to him?" I almost laughed. Shelby was asking me for advice on how to pick up guys? She got way more dates than I did, she should be the pro at this.

"I guess," I said. "I would wait until shift change, just in case it gets awkward after that. At least then you don't have to see him again." I had never really thought about the intricacies of getting a date while at work.

"All right, that's what I'll do," she decided. I wasn't sure when she would go on a date with him, since she was coming home tomorrow and they lived 100 miles apart. But I never got too concerned about Shelby's dating life. I had enough things to worry about.

I made some chicken and pasta for supper and followed it up with an ice cream bar. I firmly believed that a meal should end with dessert. I just had to keep it to a small dessert, which was hard to do some days.

I vegged out on the couch and flipped through channels. I was watching a fairly interesting murder mystery show until they got to the autopsy scene. Seeing that body with its chest cut open was just a bit too much, even though I knew it was fake. I wondered if my dad looked like that while he was in surgery. Well, minus the blue skin. I flipped the channel and tried not to think about it.

Finally, I decided to go to bed. I normally turned my phone off at night so I didn't get woken up, but I wanted to be reached if anything happened with dad. So I put the phone on the charger with the ringer on high and set it on the bedside table. Then I snuggled down into my soft sheets and sighed with satisfaction. There was nothing like sleeping in your own bed.

I was startled awake by the extremely loud ringing of the phone. It took me a second to register what the noise was, and then I panicked that something was wrong. The clock said 5:30 and that was no time for social calls.

"Hello?" I answered breathlessly, without even looking to see who was calling. My heart was pounding.

"Hi, Allie," a female voice said. It took me a moment to place the voice, since I was expecting mom or Shelby. It was Connie from work.

"Sorry to wake you up," she continued, "but we had a sick call and we desperately need a nurse for today. Would you be able to come in?"

I pondered for a moment, while my heart rate returned to normal. I tried to help out whenever I could, because working short-staffed was no picnic. And work would give me nice distraction from worrying about my dad.

"Ok, I can," I told her. "I need to hit the shower but I should be there by seven."

"Oh, thank you so much!" she exclaimed. "I really appreciate it."

I hung up the phone and crawled out of bed. I was certainly wide awake after that wake up call. I hopped in the shower and then got dressed. I made some oatmeal for breakfast and grabbed an apple and a yogurt for a snack. I ate lunch at the hospital cafeteria, but twelve hours was a long time, so I usually ate a couple snacks as well.

I headed to work, trying to get my brain back into ER nurse mode. I still felt a little out of sorts.

I walked into work and went straight for my cup of coffee. The adrenaline rush had faded and now I was going to need some perking up.

"Thank you for coming in," Connie said as I walked up to the desk. "You're a lifesaver."

"No problem" I replied. "I could use a distraction today, anyway."

"What's wrong?" she asked.

"My dad had a heart attack on Tuesday and got life flighted to Springfield. He had to have open heart surgery," I said, calmly. I had gotten used to saying it as if it were no big deal.

"Oh, no! Is he okay?" she cried. There was that question again. How do I answer? He's going to live and come home next week. That's the plus side. But he's sitting in the hospital with tubes still stuck between his ribs and he now has wires holding his sternum together. Did that really qualify as 'okay'?

"He's doing well," I answered. Which was true, considering what he had been through.

"He's in cardiac stepdown now and he will probably come home next week."

"Are you sure you want to come back to work?" Connie asked. It did seem weird to go about my life as usual with dad in the hospital. But there was nothing for me to do that would help him right now.

"Yeah, I'm fine," I replied. "I might take time off after he gets home if my mom needs help."

She nodded. That did make the most sense and as nurses, we all knew that. Things just changed a little bit when it was your own family.

I got report from the night shift, which was fairly uneventful. My pal, Lacey, wasn't working today, since she had classes. It was always more fun to work when she was there. The doctor today was Dr. Wallace, so I hoped we had a calm day. Dr. Wallace didn't handle stressful situations very well. He reminded me of that cartoon guy who gets really mad and his face turns red until steam blows out his ears. Somedays, I honestly was waiting for the steam to show up.

The clerk called for a triage. Looked like we had our first customer for the day. I went up to the window to see a plump woman sitting there with her husband.

"How can I help you?" I asked her.

"Oh, my stomach is just hurting and I can't take it anymore," she said, dramatically. "I have been sick for weeks and I've been to the doctor over and over and I just can't do it. I have pain all the time and the pain gets worse sometimes and I feel sick and it's just terrible. I have to get some help. I just can't take it anymore."

"Ok, we'll get you checked in and get you to a room so we can check you out," I told her. I think she would have gone on even longer, but it was better to get her in a room to start assessing her. Her husband sat there in silence, with a look of infinite patience on his face. I imagine she did most of the talking in their marriage.

The clerk took down the necessary information and then directed the patient to the room. Her name was Judy Walkins and she was 76 years old. She had been to a doctor or clinic every week for the last two months.

I went in to start the assessment. I started with the usual questions about when it had started, how long it lasted, what made it worse, etc. I got about a five minute long answer to every question and I was starting to get impatient. This was going to take forever.

I had her lay back so I could feel her stomach. I had barely touched her and she let out a howl.

"Ooohh, that hurts!" she cried. I tried to press gently to feel for abnormalities.

"Oh, oh, oh, oh," she wailed with each touch. "That hurts, that hurts so much!" At that point, I wasn't even touching her, but she continued to wail as if I were driving spikes into her.

I wasn't really in the mood for this. My dad had open heart surgery and he didn't wail like this. She had some vague abdominal pain that she had had for weeks and she was acting like she was dying in agony. I didn't want to deal with her histrionics when my own dad was in the hospital and a lot sicker than this.

But then I remembered Dr. Weston standing there, giving all his attention to my dad, even though his own son was in the hospital. Mrs. Walkins didn't care if my dad was sick. She cared that she was sick, and she was here at the emergency room to get some help. I took a deep breath and reminded myself 'everyone is fighting some kind of battle.' I couldn't remember offhand which extremely wise person said that, but it was an admonition to 'be kinder than necessary', and I needed to use that logic right now.

"Would a warm blanket make it feel better?" I asked her. Warm blankets really have no healing or therapeutic properties. But they make people feel better anyway, so I was happy to use them.

She stopped wailing and answered, "Well, it might help."

"I'll go get one and be right back," I told her. "The doctor will be in in a minute to see you." I walked to the blanket warmer and got out a couple toasty warm blankets. I took them back in the room and wrapped her up in them.

"Oh, thank you, honey," she gushed. "That feels so good."

Such a simple thing, just like a cup of Jell-O. Almost no effort on my part, but it made such a difference to the patient.

I filled Dr. Wallace in on what I knew about the patient and he went in to see her. He seemed fairly cheerful today, so I was thankful for that.

He came back out after a few minutes and gave some orders for an IV, some pain meds and a CT scan of her abdomen. That was pretty standard for abdominal pain.

I went back in to start the IV. Mrs. Walkins informed me that she was terrified of needles and 'they always had a hard time getting an IV in her'. She said it almost proudly, like it was an accomplishment. I would hate being someone who was tough to get an IV. That meant you had to get poked more times.

I put the tourniquet on and started looking at her veins. She was right, she didn't have much to choose from for veins. She was pretty pudgy, so her veins were all buried under the extra padding. Luckily, deep veins were my specialty. I just had to be able to feel one.

I found a good possibility on the inside of her elbow. There's a vein in the center of the elbow crease called the median cubital vein. It's used frequently for lab draws. Hers took a sharp curve though, so an IV wouldn't go into it. There's another vein farther inside the elbow crease called the basilic vein. It was nice and straight and usually pretty big. It's just deeper than the median cubital.

I was cleaning the area with a disinfectant swab, getting ready to place the IV.

"I've never had an IV there before," she said. She seemed concerned that the IV wouldn't work in that spot.

"I have pretty good luck with this vein," I assured her. "I'll be as careful as possible."

"Well, you better," she said sharply. "And you better get it on the first try and no digging around."

I assured her I would do my best. I'm never sure what people hope to accomplish by making threatening statements like that. Making the person with the needle nervous isn't going to help things go better.

But after years in this field, I was used to it. I was also pretty good at IVs, and I slid the needle right in. She didn't even jump.

I drew the blood and connected the IV tubing. I taped everything down and stood up to leave.

"You're all done?" she asked, incredulously. She looked down at her arm in disbelief. "That didn't even hurt!"

I smiled at her and told her that I was going to send the tubes of blood to the lab. She had definitely calmed down since she first arrived. I told her I would be right back with the pain medicine the doctor had ordered.

I got the morphine and walked back in to the room. She was chattering away at her husband, still going on about how she couldn't believe that I got the IV so easily. He still had that same calm smile, and he didn't really have to contribute to the conversation. I hadn't actually heard him speak a word since they had arrived.

I injected the morphine slowly while she watched me closely. She wasn't complaining of pain like she had been when she arrived, but we still wanted to treat her pain. After I gave the morphine, I told her I would be back in a bit to check on her. I gave her the call light and told her to call me if she needed anything. And I gave the remote to her husband, who looked grateful for it. He immediately turned on a basketball game.

I walked back out into the hallway to hear a commotion in the room next door. Linda, the other nurse on duty, had a confused, combative lady that wasn't too keen on being examined by the doctor. She was a tiny little thing, about 90 years old, and had severe dementia. She was convinced that the doctor was 'doing funny stuff' to her and she was kicking and biting and yelling at the top of her lungs. Linda was trying to assure her that the doctor just needed to look at her, but having no success. The lady let out a string of colorful words in the direction of both of them and grabbed for Dr. Wallace's stethoscope. She yanked it partway from around his neck, just as I jumped in to help. A stethoscope can be a painful weapon if someone is inclined to use it that way.

I caught her arm that was pulling the stethoscope and got it out of her hand. She glared at me and reached to slap me. I ducked out of the way just in time.

Linda was still trying to convince the lady that we weren't going to hurt her when the clerk announced that her son was here. We breathed a sigh of relief. Someone that she knew would have a much better chance of persuading her to let the doctor examine her.

Her son walked in and seemed quite familiar with the situation. I imagine he had been through this before.

"Mom, you need to let them help you," he told her patiently. "You're sick, remember?"

She stared at him for a moment. "Mom, I promise you, they won't hurt you," he continued. "Can you let the doctor look at you?"

She pondered for a moment and we thought we had won an easy victory. We were wrong. She looked at Dr. Wallace and snapped, "He's too fat to be a doctor!"

I swear, I could hear a steam whistle.

Chapter 12

According to Plan

O nce Dr. Wallace calmed down a little, we convinced the patient to let him examine her. Her name was Dorothy Renkin and she came from an Alzheimer's unit. She wasn't getting enough fluids, so she had developed a urinary tract infection. I'm sure the staff had their hands full trying to get her to eat and drink. She seemed to do what she wanted and only that. Of course, with advanced dementia, she couldn't understand why it was so important to drink water.

Now Linda had the fun job of putting in an IV. I went in to help hold the patient's arm for her.

"Dorothy, we need to put an IV in your arm," Linda started to explain. There's no easy way to go about that explanation. Usually, you're kind of hoping the patient won't understand what you're saying. Then they're more likely to cooperate.

Her son, Mike, was standing by the bed. "Mom, I'll sit right here and hold your hand," he promised her. Linda got everything ready and then placed the tourniquet on Dorothy's arm.

"Ouch! That's tight!" she yelped. She tried to reach and pull it off, but Mike caught her hand.

"It's only for a moment," I promised her. "Then we'll take it back off." I held her other arm at the elbow and wrist.

I wasn't sure how to distract her while Linda started the IV. I didn't think singing was going to work.

"Dorothy, how many kids do you have?" I asked pleasantly. I was trying to pick a conversation that she could follow.

"Don't be nosy!" she snapped at me. "You think I'm a hussy 'cause I have lots of kids. Well, there ain't nothing wrong with that!"

I was taken aback. That tactic failed. Most women love to talk about their kids. I tried bribery next.

"Would you like to have some ice cream as soon as we get this done?" I asked her. She certainly could use the calories. Even though they were the little tiny cups and only came in chocolate or vanilla, it was still pretty good ice cream. I had snitched them once or twice.

"Why, so I can get fat?" she replied. I was really striking out here. Linda was having trouble finding a vein that was big enough to get an IV in.

Mike, her son, came to the rescue. "Mom, we can turn on the TV," he said, grabbing the remote. He flipped to a channel with a show about tattoo artists. I saw a shot of a woman wearing very little clothing and a whole lot of ink. Dorothy's face lit up.

"Yes! I love this show," she said, and sat transfixed, looking at the TV. She didn't even flinch when Linda got the IV in. I almost giggled. At least she wasn't fighting us, and we could get some fluids and antibiotics in her. I was glad Mike stepped in when he did. I never would have thought of using a tattoo show as a distraction.

Once Linda had the IV secured, I stepped out and went back in to Mrs. Walkins room. She was dozing, so I assumed her pain was better and I didn't wake her up. Mr. Walkins looked at me and smiled, then went back to his game. The CT tech would come get her shortly for her exam.

"Hey, I need a nurse!" I heard Kim, the front desk clerk call out, with a touch of panic in her voice. I ran to the front to see a man at the window, leaning on his friend. His left hand was wrapped in a dirty t-shirt that was soaked in blood. The man had a lot of grease on his clothes and face, but even under the black smears, he was looking pretty pale. Some of the black on his clothes looked more like blood instead of grease. I grabbed a wheelchair and sat him in it and headed for the suture room.

"What happened?" I asked, as we wheeled in.

The patient was leaning over and groaning. His friend answered, "He had an accident at the shop. A pulley broke and an engine block fell on his hand."

I looked at him in shock for a second. "How did you get it back off?" I asked incredulously. Those things were heavy.

"Me and another guy grabbed it and flipped it off," he answered. "I don't know how we did it. That thing weighs 600 pounds." He seemed a little awed by it as well.

I snapped back to ER nurse mode and called for Dr. Wallace to come in right away. We didn't need to bother with getting a medical history first. This guy needed checked out now and probably needed to get to surgery.

I helped him on to the gurney as Dr. Wallace walked in. We both grabbed a pair of gloves since there was blood and grease everywhere. I grabbed a couple clean towels as Dr. Wallace carefully pulled back the bloody t-shirt.

His hand and wrist were pretty mangled, and he still had blood oozing from the artery in his wrist. I wasn't even sure where to start. I grabbed some gauze and held pressure against the artery, as I called out to Linda for help. This guy would need an IV right away and I didn't have four hands. Some days, I almost wish I did.

I looked up to see if I was causing him pain with the pressure, but he had his head laid back and his eyes closed. He had been watching when Dr. Wallace uncovered his hand, so he may very well have passed out. That was okay for right now.

Linda came in and I asked her to start an IV. She grabbed the stuff quickly and got an IV in his right arm without any trouble. The guy had great veins, unlike the last IV start. Dr. Wallace ordered some pain meds and went out to call the surgeon.

Nikki, the CNA, came in to get vital signs. I could pretty much predict that his blood pressure would be low and his heart rate would be high.

Since I was stuck there holding pressure, I started asking his friend questions. His name was Daniel White and he was 28 years old. Mike, his friend, didn't know much else about him.

"Does he have a wife or somebody we can call?" I asked him. We needed some medical information, and I'm sure his family would want to be here in this situation.

Mike grabbed Danny's cell phone out of his shirt pocket. Danny was starting to stir and moan again and Linda was coming in with the morphine just in time. Mike found a number and was calling someone.

"Hey, Alison?" I heard him say. "Uh, Danny is in the ER. He got hurt at the shop." I could hear her cry out "What?!" from across the room.

"The pulley broke and an engine block fell on his hand," he started to explain. I interrupted him, because we could explain the accident later. I needed her here as soon as possible.

"Ask her to come here right away," I instructed him. He nodded.

"Hey, you need to come here right away," Mike told her. There was a pause and then he disconnected.

"She's on her way," he said. I hoped she wasn't too panicked and drove safe. That's tough to do when someone you love is in ER. I knew that firsthand now.

Danny was a little more alert, so I tried asking him the major questions. He wasn't allergic to any medications, which was good to know for surgery. He didn't take any medications either. Most people in their twenties have a short health history. He didn't know when his last tetanus shot was, which meant we would be giving him one. He gave us his birth date, so the clerk could get him registered.

Dr. Wallace came back in and informed us that Dr. Anderson, the orthopedic surgeon, was on his way now. We didn't want to do too much with the hand while we were waiting, in case we did more damage. Danny looked as comfortable as he could be for now. He actually looked pretty shell-shocked. But he wasn't complaining of pain. I kept holding pressure on the artery, to prevent any more blood loss.

Linda came in to tell me that my other patient was going to CT scan now. I hoped it went smoothly. It got a little tricky when you were stuck in one room and your other patient needed something. Luckily, we had pretty good teamwork and covered for each other.

"Alison should be here soon," Mike said. "They only live about a mile away."

When I heard him say her name, I realized that I hadn't introduced myself. "I'm Allison, too," I told him. "But I go by Allie. Sorry I didn't introduce myself earlier."

Mike smiled. "That's okay, you were busy," he said. That was certainly true. It was still nice to at least get the name of the person taking care of you.

"Allie, his wife is here," Kim said. "Is it okay if she comes in?"

"Yes, she can come in," I said. A slender woman with long black hair walked in. She got about two steps inside the door and stopped. Her face turned pale and I was worried she was going to pass out on me. I couldn't really let go of what I was doing to catch her either.

"Mike, will you grab her?" I asked him. He jumped up and grabbed her arm to help her to the chair. She slid into the chair, tears streaming down her face. I glanced down at Danny and realized he was laying back with his eyes closed, not moving. She didn't know details of the accident and probably thought he was near death.

"He's going to be okay," I assured her. "He just needs to go to surgery and get his hand fixed."

She looked at me for a moment, as she processed what I had said.

"He's just resting now because we gave him some morphine," I continued. She nodded and carefully stood up to walk over to the side of the gurney.

"Danny, Alison is here," I said, and he groggily opened his eyes. He looked at me and then turned his head and looked at his wife. He tried to smile at her, but it didn't really work.

"You can touch his hand over there," I told her. She carefully took his hand in hers. She was being sure not to look down at his other hand. I'm sure she would have passed out if she did.

"We are waiting for the surgeon to come look at his hand," I explained to her. "I'm holding pressure because he was bleeding from his artery."

She nodded that she understood. She glanced at my nametag and asked "Your name is Allie?"

I really had to get better at introducing myself. "Well, it's actually Allison, but I go by Allie," I said.

She laughed. "That's funny, his nurse has the same name as his wife," she said. "As long as he doesn't get us mixed up."

"I guess that depends which one of us he likes better," I replied. "He might like me more if he thinks I'm his wife."

"You have the morphine," she said. "I'll bet he likes you more right now." It was such a relief that she could joke around, even in this situation. Humor can be a powerful tool in coping. There were a lot of times I laughed because otherwise I would cry.

Dr. Anderson strode into the room. He is a tall man, about 6' 4", with crystal blue eyes and white hair. His hair was covered with a surgical cap and he was dressed in blue scrubs. He must have been in the operating room down the hall when we called him. He had a commanding presence, but he was an excellent surgeon, and I was glad to see him.

"Dr. Anderson, this is Daniel White," I nodded toward the man on the gurney. "This is his wife, Alison," I continued, nodding my head in her direction. My hands were still occupied.

He strode over to Alison and shook her hand firmly. "Jim Anderson. I'm the surgeon. I'm here to look at his hand." He turned toward me.

"Alison, you might not want to watch," I told her. We were about to uncover the mangled hand again. She nodded vigorously and walked over to where Mike was sitting. He stood up and gave her the chair.

I removed the gauze covering the hand. The blood was oozing from the artery still. That was actually a good sign, it meant he still had blood flow to the area. The hand itself was disfigured but the skin was mostly intact. The wrist had a large gash and the bones were visible. One of them was obviously broken, since one end of it was sticking out of his skin. This would be a major operation and there was no guarantee they could save his hand.

Dr. Anderson put on some gloves and started pushing on Danny's fingers. Danny yelped in pain.

"Good, good," Dr. Anderson said. This meant the nerves were intact, if he still felt pain.

"Can you move your fingers at all?" he asked Danny. Danny grimaced and tried.

"That really hurts," he gasped.

"I know it does, I just need you to move them a little," Dr. Anderson told him. Danny gritted his teeth and tried again. His thumb and pinky finger both twitched. Dr. Anderson watched, nodding silently.

"Ok, that's good," he said and Danny relaxed back on the gurney. Dr. Anderson turned toward me and gave me orders for an IV antibiotic and to get the patient ready to go to OR.

He stopped by Alison to explain that they were going to OR immediately. He was hopeful they could save the hand but would know more once they got in there. She nodded, looking a little frightened. Dr. Anderson patted her shoulder and walked out of the room.

I wrapped a gauze dressing around Danny's wrist. The oozing had slowed enough I could take pressure off for a few minutes. I went out to the station to get the IV stuff

I needed, as well as the antibiotic dose and some more morphine. We needed to get all of Danny's clothes off before he went in to OR and that might hurt.

I grabbed Nikki to help me and went back in to the room. Danny said his pain was ok for now, so we each grabbed a pair of scissors and started cutting his shirt away. We tried to move his arm as little as possible. Once we had his shirt out of the way, we put a hospital gown on him. He didn't look thrilled with the gown, but it was necessary since we were about to take his pants.

We took off his work boots and socks and then carefully slid his jeans off without jostling him too much. I gave the jeans and boots to Alison. The shirt was trash. I checked all the pockets to make sure they were empty and then threw it away.

"I need to put another IV in," I told Danny. He looked at me, puzzled.

"Another IV?" he asked. He looked down at his good arm and realized there was an IV already in it. I guess he really had been passed out when Linda started the IV.

"You need to have two IV sites when you go to OR," I told him. He was going to get a lot of IV fluid and possibly a blood transfusion. I started another IV easily, and hung up the antibiotic bag. I saw a group of people in blue at the nurses' station looking at a chart and I knew they were here for him.

"It looks like the OR crew is here," I said to Alison. "Do you want to come say goodbye and good luck to him?"

She walked up to the gurney and took his hand. I wanted to give her a minute with him before he went to OR. I walked out to the desk to see if they OR nurse had any questions for me.

"I just hung the antibiotic," I told Cindy, the lead nurse. "He had two IV sites in and I'm about to give him some more morphine."

"Don't forget the tetanus shot!" Dr. Wallace barked out. Of course, Dr. Wallace had forgotten to give me an order to give a tetanus shot. But I wasn't going to point that out. I grabbed the vial and a syringe and needle and walked back in the room.

"Danny, I need to give you a tetanus shot," I told him. He just nodded grimly. This was going to be the least painful part of the day. I gave the injection in his right shoulder. I figured his left arm would be sore enough.

"Danny, they're going to have to move you a little bit when you get to OR," I started. He grimaced at the thought of that. "I'm going to give you some more morphine to help with that, ok?"

"Yeah, that would be great," he said. I was pushing the morphine in when Cindy walked in the room. She walked over and introduced herself to Alison and then came over to the bed.

"Hi, Daniel, I'm Cindy and I'm with the surgery crew," she said. "We're going to take you to surgery now." She had already told Alison when and where they would come find her. She unlocked the brake on the bed and started pulling it toward the door. She stopped just before the door, where Alison was standing.

"Wanna say goodbye?" she asked Alison. I was happy to see that. I liked knowing that my coworkers were considerate like that. Unlike the crew in Springfield. All right, there were probably considerate OR nurses in Springfield Regional Hospital. Just not on the crew that my dad got.

Alison kissed Danny goodbye and they wheeled him out of the room. I walked Alison and Mike down to the surgery waiting room, where the OR team would come find them with updates on Danny's case.

"Thank you so much," Alison said, as I showed them the room. "You were really great." I smiled at her, feeling happy that, at least for today, I was one of the good nurses.

I got back to ER and saw Mrs. Walkins was back from CT scan. I went in to check on her. She didn't look too happy and I didn't even have time to ask her what was wrong.

"That was terrible!" she cried out. "That room is freezing and the table was very uncomfortable. I had to lay there forever! They were very rough, just jerking on me without even telling me they were going to. I am already in pain and they were making it worse!" She was getting more wound up as she went.

I couldn't really disagree with her either. Some of the radiology techs were pretty rough with the patients. And the CT room was freezing, I had spent plenty of time in there.

"I'm sorry about that," I said. "Can I get you a couple more warm blankets?"

"Yes, that would be nice," she replied. I told her I would be right back and went to the warmer. I came back into the room and got her all wrapped up.

"My mouth is terribly dry," she said. "Could I get a glass of water?"

"We don't want to put anything in your stomach until the doctor makes sure it's ok," I informed her. She scowled at that. Most patients do. "I can get you some swabs to wet your mouth, though," I offered her. She agreed to that. I got a cup with some water in it and stuck a foam swab in it. I set it on her bedside table so she could wet her mouth whenever she needed to.

I had heard the radio going off that the ambulance was on their way in, so I knew we might be getting another busy patient. Unfortunately, patients like Mrs. Walkins had to be put on the back burner, since their condition wasn't as serious. She might be waiting for a little while and I wanted her to stay comfortable.

"What happens now?" she asked me. I told her that the doctor would look at the results of the CT scan and see if he could identify the problem. Then he would decide if we needed more testing or if there was something we could do to help it.

"Well, I've had four of these in the last month, and none of them have showed anything," she said, sounding irritated.

"You've had four CT scans in a month?" I asked her.

"Yes," she replied. "One at every hospital I've gone to. I've been going to different towns trying to find a doctor who can figure out what's wrong with me."

That would explain why we didn't show a record that she had just had a scan done. I wish she would have told us beforehand, though. That was a lot of radiation exposure, and if four CT scans were all negative, I'm sure ours would be too. We could have gotten a record from one of the other hospitals and started looking for a different problem then.

This was a common problem in the ER. Patients with chronic problems came in hoping for a quick answer. Our staff didn't specialize in chronic problems, though. We specialized in medical emergencies. It was like going to a fast food restaurant looking for a gourmet meal. Yes, they have food, but it's not the food you're looking for. She would have been much better off going to a gastrointestinal specialist.

I told her I would let her know as soon as we knew anything. I went back to the desk to inform Dr. Wallace about what the patient had just told me.

"Four?!" he asked, incredulously. "She's had four scans?" He understood as well the excessive radiation exposure. There was a lot of risk with having that many scans. And repeating the same negative scan over and over made it a very unnecessary risk. Unfortunately, we had no way of knowing about them until she told us.

The ambulance pulled in the bay just then. Linda had taken report on the patient, so I had no idea what was rolling in. The crew came in with a very thin woman, sitting up on the cart with an oxygen mask on her face. She was gasping for every breath and looked very anxious.

I felt a momentary twinge of disappointment that Jake wasn't on the crew. I reminded myself I wasn't supposed to care and went to help get the patient settled in a room.

The patient was Lenora Sherman and she had a lung disease called COPD. She had been a dedicated smoker for forty years and she was paying the price now. We saw her in the ER frequently. She was on oxygen and inhalers at home, but sometimes the disease still got ahead of her. She would come in to the hospital for a few days of IV steroids to get her through.

We slid her over to our gurney, still sitting up. People with respiratory problems can't handle laying down. She was really struggling to breathe. It was exhausting just to watch her. We attached the monitor and her oxygen level was only 86%, even with the oxygen mask on.

Kim was already calling respiratory therapy to come down and give her some nebulizer treatments. We all knew what to do for Lenora by now. Unfortunately, our bag of tricks didn't have anything that would actually fix her. It was really sad because she was only 67 years old and just the nicest lady.

Once I had helped settle Lenora in, I went back to the desk to start the charting on Danny. I had jotted down a few things on a piece of paper, but now I needed to fill out all the official forms.

My stomach growled, telling me my oatmeal was long gone. I ducked in to the break room to get my yogurt and ate it while I was charting. I always read in fitness and health magazines that you shouldn't eat while you are doing other things. Well, some days, if I didn't eat while I worked, I wouldn't eat at all.

I was just finishing the paperwork when Dr. Wallace told me that he thought Mrs. Walkins abdominal pain was probably her gallbladder. That was something that wouldn't necessarily show up on a CT scan. There was a specific test for gallbladder function that she could schedule to have done later this week. It wasn't a test that needed to be done in the ER.

He went in to talk to Mrs. Walkins and then came out to write discharge orders. I went in to check vital signs and take out the IV. She was disappointed that she didn't have a for sure answer today, but pacified that she was getting checked out more. She said the other hospitals just told her nothing was wrong with her and sent her home.

She was still pretty mellow from the pain medicine. I helped her get dressed and got a wheelchair to take her to the car. Mr. Walkins went out to pull the car up to the door. I still hadn't heard him say a single word.

I was caught up for the moment and Linda was too. I told her I was going to step outside and make a quick phone call. When I took Mrs. Walkins to her car, it was already warm and sunny, so I was anxious to spend a few minutes in the balmy weather. I wanted to call and check on my dad.

Mom's cell phone went to voice mail so I tried Shelby's next. She answered on the second ring.

"Hey, Lis," she said cheerily. "What's up?"

"Just calling to see how dad is doing today," I replied.

"Sheesh, are you just getting up?" she asked. It was almost 11 o'clock.

"No, work was short so I came in for an extra shift," I explained. "I'm on my break."

"Gotcha," she said. There was a long pause.

"So.... How is dad?" I asked. I'm pretty sure I had said that was the reason I'm calling. Even though it was obvious that was why I was calling.

"Oh, he's fine," she replied glibly. I really wanted to strangle her through the phone. I took a deep breath and reminded myself the family shouldn't fight. And there was no possible way to strangle her through the phone anyway.

"Anything new?" I asked, still trying to keep a handle on my patience.

"They took another one of those tubes out of his side," she replied. "Now he just has one left. And they took that big IV thingie out of his neck."

"That's awesome!" I said. "Did Dr Weston say when he thought dad would go home?"

"He said if it stays like this, he'll go home Monday," she said. That was when I had been planning on him going home. But planning didn't always mean it happened that way in the medical field. 'Best laid plans o' mice and men', and all that.

"That's good news," I said. "Anything else?"

"Yeah, I went out to dinner with Wade last night," she said nonchalantly. "Well, mom came too, but it was fun."

"So, the phone number trick worked?" I asked.

"I gave him my number and he asked what I was doing after he got off work," she told me. "Mom and I hadn't eaten supper yet and he was hungry so we all went out for Thai food. Wade knew this awesome little place downtown."

"And mom went with you on your first date," I chuckled. Shelby was twenty-six years old and still had her mom as a chaperone.

"Well, she didn't want to go," Shelby said. "She said she would just go back to the hotel and eat some crackers or something. But I told her no way, she had to go with us or I wouldn't go. And she loved it! She had never even tried Thai food before."

I knew Madison didn't have a Thai restaurant and my parents weren't usually adventurous eaters anyway. I was relieved that Shelby had insisted mom eat with them instead of ditching her at the hotel to go on a date. Maybe my little sister was maturing some after all.

"Are you headed home today?" I asked. She had said she worked tomorrow.

"Yep, right after lunch," she said. "Wade has today off and we're going out for lunch."

Wow, it looked like Wade and Shelby were really hitting it off. He was a huge step up from her usual choice in boyfriends, so I was happy as a clam if it worked out.

I told Shelby to hug mom and dad for me, drive safe and call me when she got home. I headed back in to make sure Linda was doing okay.

"How's dad?" Linda asked. Things were calm for now and she was drinking a cup of coffee at the desk.

"Good," I replied. "He'll probably come home Monday. Got another chest tube out."

"That's good," Linda said.

"And Shelby had a date with his nurse last night," I continued. "He was a really nice guy and they're going out again today."

"Well, maybe she'll finally find a good man and settle down," Linda said. My co-workers had heard plenty about Shelby's dysfunctional dating life.

It would be fantastic if my sister settled down with a great guy. The only downside would be all the jokes about me being an old maid because my little sister got married before I did. I mentally groaned at the thought of enduring all those comments with a smile. The wedding day would probably require a Valium.

Then I realized I would have to be a bridesmaid and wear some fancy satin number and heels. At that thought, I groaned out loud.

Chapter 13

Serious as a Heart Attack

By Saturday morning, I was starting to feel a little more back to my normal routine. I headed in to work feeling relaxed. I got to work with Lacey today, which was always a good time. I knew my dad was doing well and would be coming home in a few days. All was good in the world of Allie.

Saturday mornings always started out slow and then got pretty busy by about noon. We saw a lot of people who couldn't get to the doctor's office during the week because of work. They came to the ER on the weekend, but their problems usually weren't too urgent. Rashes and coughs and back pain. It wasn't too stressful but it made the day go by quickly. The warm sunny weather had people outside playing, so by the afternoon, we usually got a couple minor accidents showing up. People were always doing something that ended with a fall and an injury. I was frequently one of them, but today I was stuck inside at work, so I was safe. The days I got on the mountain bike, I was much less safe.

Lacey and I spent some time catching up. I filled her in on everything that had happened with my dad. I was feeling much calmer now that everything was going so well.

We had our usual morning trickle of non-emergent cases. About 11 o'clock, I heard Tracy call out "Chest pain" which was the way they notified us when anyone came to the window with chest pain. That meant we would skip past all the usual check-in steps and go straight to a room with them, so I grabbed a wheelchair and headed for the front. A couple was standing at the window, looking about in their sixties. The lady was slim and average height with short, curly blond hair. The man was about six feet tall with salt and pepper gray hair. He had broad shoulders and a bit of a belly hanging over his jeans. And his face was as gray as his hair. I hurried to his side with the wheelchair, but he just looked at it and shook his head. He didn't seem to be able to speak, but he was still refusing to sit in a wheelchair. Ah, stubborn people.

"I need to get you to a room right away," I told him. His wife looked exasperated. I'm sure she had dealt with his stubbornness before.

"Dave, sit in the chair," she said tersely. He shook his head again.

"I can walk," he gasped.

"Sorry, it's the rules," I fibbed. I really wanted this guy in a room right away. He did not look good. I took his arm and firmly guided him toward the chair. He resisted a little, but he had to know something was really wrong. He relented and sat in the chair so I could get him to a cardiac monitoring room.

I helped him transfer to the gurney and take off his shirt. Lacey came in and started placing monitor wires. We had a protocol we followed with any patient who had chest pain, so we all knew what to do.

Jesse was the other nurse on for the day. He didn't seem to like to actually work very much. He liked to spend a lot of time looking at stuff on his phone. He occasionally took a break from that to read a magazine.

He didn't usually go looking for any extra work to do, but he had seen the patient go by and knew this was serious. Some of the patients that come in with chest pain turn out to have something wrong besides their heart. This guy looked like he was the real deal.

The goal on a chest pain patient was to get all of the initial steps completed in ten minutes. Lacey had started the vital signs and was attaching wires to his chest for an ECG. I was listening to his heart and lungs and trying to ask questions. Dave was having trouble speaking, so I was asking his wife, Nancy. Jesse was starting the IV and getting a blood sample drawn.

The pain had started about an hour ago, while he was outside raking leaves in the yard. She said he had been pale and sweating, even though it wasn't that hot. He had tried to insist that nothing was wrong, that it was just dehydration. Then he decided it was indigestion. Heart attack patients usually try to convince themselves they aren't having a heart attack.

However, the ECG had the trademark signs of a heart attack. Jesse was starting a blood test that would confirm the diagnosis. Dr. Wallace came in the room and got the story from Nancy as well. As he was talking to her, I went to get the aspirin and nitroglycerin I knew we would be giving.

As soon as I returned, Dr. Wallace gave me the order to give the medications. I instructed Dave to chew the aspirin before he swallowed them. He looked at me oddly, so I explained that they would be absorbed into his bloodstream much quicker if they were chewed up. Technically, they are flavored, but I've tried them and they still don't taste very good. He made a face as he chewed them that told me he felt the same way. I gave him some water to wash them down and then instructed him on how to place a nitroglycerin tab under his tongue and let it dissolve.

We waited for five minutes and Dave was still having chest pain. He said it was better than before, but not completely gone. I gave him another nitro tab to put under his tongue. Dr. Wallace was already talking to a cardiologist in Springfield about transferring the patient there emergently. We didn't have the services to fix Dave's heart, so he needed to get to them as quickly as possible.

After another five minutes, Dave still had a little bit of chest pain. He also had a headache, which is a common side effect of the nitro tabs. I needed to give him a third dose, but he didn't want to take it.

"I have a horrible headache from the last one," he argued. "I would rather have a little chest pain than have this headache."

"The nitroglycerin opens up the arteries on your heart," I reminded him. "We need to make sure that enough blood flow gets through." He still looked skeptical, so I phrased it a little more bluntly.

"The headache isn't going to kill you. The chest pain might," I said.

He pondered that for a moment and his wife sighed. "Dave, take the pill, for crying out loud," she said with frustration.

He begrudgingly agreed and took the third dose of nitro. I got him an ice pack for his forehead, which would help the headache. Like all medications, nitro went throughout the whole body. So it opened the arteries on the heart, which is what we wanted. But it also opened the arteries in the brain, which caused a migraine-like headache.

Dr. Wallace came back in to inform Dave and Nancy that the blood test confirmed that Dave was having a heart attack and needed to get to Springfield right away. Dave didn't look too thrilled and Nancy looked nervous. I imagine this is about how my parents looked in the ER in Madison.

Even though Springfield was only 100 miles away, it was still faster to have the helicopter come get Dave than it was to send him up the road in an ambulance. Dave, it turned out, was terrified of flying. Since his chest now felt much better, he was starting to insist he didn't need to go to Springfield at all. Definitely not in a helicopter.

Dr. Wallace wasn't really diplomatic. Usually his abrupt manner of speaking was offensive to patients. Today, it turned out to be what was really needed, because Dave wasn't going to listen to polite persuasion.

"If you get up and walk out of this hospital, you'll be dead before tomorrow," Dr. Wallace snapped at him. "I don't send people on a helicopter unless they really need it."

Dave seemed to understand that. The helicopter was already on its way. I asked Nancy if she needed to call anyone before they left.

"I better call our kids," she said. She pulled out a cell phone and dialed a number. I went back to the desk to make sure all my charting and other paperwork were in order. When the flight crew landed, they didn't waste too much time getting the patient loaded and getting back in the air.

The crew was there about ten minutes later. I gave them report on Dave and they loaded him on their cart.

For safety, the patient has to be strapped to the cart pretty securely. From the look on Dave's face, I would say he was claustrophobic as well. The flight paramedic noticed it too, so he left Dave's arms outside the chest strap. That way he could move some, but still couldn't fall off the cart.

They had Dave prepared and loaded him and Nancy in the helicopter in less than fifteen minutes. And then they were off. There was a sudden quietness in the ER after having 45 minutes of non-stop action.

I helped Lacey clean up the room and then told Jesse I was going to step outside and make a phone call. I was sure my dad was still doing fine, but I suddenly wanted to talk to him.

I stepped out the back door and dialed mom's cell phone. She answered on the second ring.

"Hey mom" I said. "How's it going?"

"It's ok," she said, but her voice didn't sound right.

"Are you sure?" I asked. "You don't sound ok."

"Well," she hedged, "I'm worried about your dad."

My heart started pounding. "Why? What's wrong?" I cried out.

"I'm not sure, really," she answered. "He just looks different today. He isn't as pink and he said he doesn't feel good."

It wasn't uncommon to have a slump day a few days after surgery. I tried to stay calm. He had open heart surgery, after all. It would be normal to not feel well after that.

"He said his leg hurts," she continued. "And one of the dressings looks funny."

"What do you mean by 'funny'?" I asked her.

"It was just white before," she replied. "They all were. But now the one that hurts him has some colored liquid soaking through."

"What color is it?" I asked. I was hoping she said pink. Or yellow.

"It's kind of tan," she replied. Rats. That's not a good color.

"What did the nurse say about it?" I asked her.

There was a long pause. "She hasn't looked at it," mom replied, hesitantly. "She said she's too busy right now and I shouldn't worry about it."

Sounds like we had Eileen back. Or her evil twin sister. Mom wouldn't be as gutsy as Shelby about standing up to a bad nurse.

"I take it we didn't get a good nurse today?" I asked.

"She's not as mean," mom replied. "But she's really busy and she hasn't been in here very much. She said they're short-staffed again."

Argh. This was so frustrating. And I was miles away and powerless.

"What did Dr. Weston say?" I asked. Surely our awesome surgeon would look at it.

"He didn't come today," mom replied. "He's off for the weekend and another doctor is covering for him."

"Did that doctor look at it?" I asked.

"No," mom said. "The doctor came through early this morning. Bob didn't tell me about it hurting until a couple hours ago. But I knew something was wrong as soon as I showed up this morning. He just doesn't look right."

My mom wasn't one who went looking for stuff to be wrong. So if she said dad didn't look right, I knew something was wrong. I had to decide how wrong it was and if I should use an emergency family day to go back to Springfield tomorrow or wait until my day off on Monday.

It was irritating to me to hear the nurses say they were short-staffed as a reason for not giving good care to my dad. So I didn't want to bolt and leave my co-workers here in the same situation. Getting someone to work on short notice on a weekend was hard to do.

As if she read my thoughts, mom said, "It will be fine, you don't need to come back."

Dad echoed that in the background. I knew they didn't want to be a bother to me. I sighed with resignation.

"Will you ask the nurse to look at it?" I asked mom. Maybe it was just some old blood seeping through the dressing and nothing to worry about. Dad was probably skipping his pain pills, since he didn't like to take them. That would explain the increased pain, which would make anyone look and feel crappy.

"I will," mom promised. She handed the phone to my dad so I could chat with him. He insisted he was fine and mom was just being a worrywart. He was adamant that I did not need to come back. I wanted to believe him, even though I had this tiny nagging doubt in the back of my head. But since I was the queen of worrying, I tried to convince myself I was overreacting.

I went back in to work. Not much was happening right now so Jesse went to lunch. I told Lacey about the phone call.

"What do you think it is?" she asked me. Lacey knew me well enough to know that I was already diagnosing my dad from a hundred miles away.

"One of his leg incisions could be infected," I said. "That would explain the tan drainage and the increased pain." I didn't know what his temperature or heart rate were, but I knew they would be elevated with an infection.

Lacey tried to reassure me that my dad was an overall healthy guy so he would certainly heal up without problems. I appreciated the effort, but I don't know how successful it was.

The rest of the shift was a typical Saturday afternoon. A sprained wrist from a jungle gym fall, a dislocated knee from a soccer game and a middle-aged man who fell off a ladder trying to get a Frisbee off the roof. Sprinkled with the usual back pains and stomach aches, it was busy enough to keep me distracted.

I gave report to the night shift, since Jesse had already gotten his stuff and left. I had taken most of the patients anyway. All Jesse could have told them was what text messages he got. That was about all he did all day. Usually it annoyed me to work with him and do most of the work. Today I was thankful to be busy. I don't know how Jesse got away with being so lazy. I think he was friends with the manager. He never seemed to get in trouble.

I headed home, suddenly tired and hungry. I looked through the fridge and cupboards while I called mom. I needed some reassurance that my dad was doing ok still.

Mom answered and she sounded a little better.

"Hi, Allison," she said. "You didn't have to call again." Right. Like I wasn't going to call again. She knew me better than that.

"How's it going now?" I asked.

"He's feeling better," she said. "He finally took a pain pill a few hours ago and he said it's not hurting as bad. He's kind of dozing off in the chair now."

Dad got looped pretty easily on pain meds, so I wasn't worried that he was dozing. Under normal circumstances, my dad was never one to sleep during the day. But this was far from normal circumstances.

"What did the nurse say about his leg?" I asked.

"She just looked at the dressing and said it was fine," mom answered. "I guess I was worried for nothing."

"Did she change the dressing?" I asked.

"No, she said it was fine and maybe they would change it tomorrow," mom replied. That set off a little alarm in my head. Why wouldn't she change a dressing that had suspicious drainage on it? How do you know what's underneath it if you don't take it off?

"Did we get Randy back for the night shift?" I asked. I knew their nurses worked three shifts a week, just like I did. I was hoping it was Randy's weekend to work.

"No," mom replied. "It's another guy, but he's younger. His name is Jesse."

I cringed. Hopefully, their Jesse was better than ours.

"Will you ask him to look at the dressing?" I asked mom. I just needed a second opinion, and I wanted it from someone who actually looked at the incision.

"I will," she promised. "But I'm sure it's fine."

"Call me if anything is wrong," I told her. "I'll leave my phone on all night. Don't worry about waking me up. Just call me. Ok?"

Mom agreed. I knew I was being bossy but they were always so worried about waking me up. I didn't want her to wait to tell me if something was wrong.

I had hit the grocery store last night after work, so the fridge looked pretty good. I made a turkey and avocado sandwich and ate it with some grapes. Then I ate one of the chocolate macadamia cookies that had somehow ended up in my cart last night. Grocery shopping when you are tired and stressed is dangerous on the willpower.

I read for awhile, trying to unwind for bed. Mom hadn't called and it was after nine, so I figured the dressing change was uneventful. I put my phone on the charger and crawled in to bed.

I slept fitfully and had weird dreams most of the night. I woke up with the alarm, already feeling exhausted. I sighed and headed for the shower. It was going to be a long day. I hoped it was fairly busy again, that would help keep me awake.

I started with a cup of coffee as always. After years of saying coffee was bad for us, the health experts had decided it was good for us again. Which was great, because I never stopped drinking it anyway. But now I could say I was being healthy when I did.

The morning started out slow. Jesse was texting and Dr. Wallace was hanging out in the doctor room, watching some Civil War show. Lacey and I chatted about how school was going for her. She only had a couple weeks left and she was getting nervous. I knew she was going to be fine. It was a lot of testing. You took all your finals and then had to take state nursing board exams shortly after. You couldn't even really enjoy your graduation party, because you still had boards looming over you.

About 10:30, the ambulance radio went off. An elderly lady had collapsed in the Methodist church.

"Maybe the Holy Spirit came over her," Jesse joked. I'm sure it caused quite a disturbance in the sermon.

The voice that answered back over the radio made my heart skip a beat. Jake was on the rig that was going to pick her up. Once again, I tried to convince myself that it didn't matter. Jake was just a paramedic, doing his job. It wasn't like he was coming to the ER just to see me.

I paced around the nurses' station, trying to act busy while I waited for the ambulance crew to call with report. The Methodist church was 80 years old and huge. It was not very handicapped accessible, so the crew was probably having a time trying to get the cart in to the patient.

The radio finally crackled with report. It was Kent, Jake's partner, calling report. Mrs. Mildred Wilton had been feeling poorly for a few days, it seemed. Ever a devout parishioner, though, she bucked up and made it to church this morning. But while standing through one of the pastor's extremely long prayers, she got lightheaded and went down. She hadn't really hurt anything, but she was eighty-six years old and weak, so they thought she should get checked out. Which wasn't a bad idea.

They rolled in a few minutes later. Mildred was laying on the cart looking tired and a little pale. I think the good Lord would have understood if she had missed services today. My grandmother was the same way, though. If it was Sunday, you went to church, or you weren't a good Christian. She was horrified that I had a job that required me to work on Sundays sometimes. I couldn't make her understand that the hospital couldn't close its doors on Sunday so I could go to church. I went to church on the Sundays that I didn't work. For her, that wasn't good enough. Must be something that generation was taught.

Jesse was trying to sit at the desk and be his usual lazy self. His plan failed because Mildred was friends with his grandma. She saw him and her face lit up.

"Oh, do you get to be my nurse?" she said, excitedly. As excited as she could get, anyway. Jesse was stuck taking the patient. She had personally requested him. I helped transfer her on to the gurney and then left Jesse to do the questions and assessment. She was a pleasant lady and wouldn't be a difficult patient. Jesse just didn't like to work.

Kent was sitting at the EMS desk filling out the ambulance report. Jake wandered back over to the nurses' station where I was standing.

"Hi, Miss Allie," he said, his fantastic blue eyes twinkling. "How have you been?"

"Good," I replied. That wasn't true, but it was just a polite question and didn't need the full twenty minute answer.

"I haven't seen you for awhile," he said. "I was worried you might have run off and got married or something."

I laughed. "Nope," I said.

"Good," he replied softly. I didn't let myself think about what that might mean.

"I've been in Springfield," I explained to Jake. "My dad had a heart attack and had to have open heart surgery."

Jake looked concerned and put his hand on my shoulder. "Is he okay?" he asked. "Are you okay?"

His hand was strong and warm and very distracting. I focused on my dad and answered his questions.

"He's going to be fine," I told him. "He's in the cardiac stepdown unit and will probably go home tomorrow."

"And how are you doing?" Jake asked.

"Well, it's a little stressful," I said. "My dad had never been sick, so this is new to me. Some of his nurses were really great but some were horrible. I felt really helpless, being there but not being able to help him. And now that I'm back here, I feel even more helpless." I wasn't sure why I was pouring my heart out to Jake, but he was listening intently. Maybe I wasn't coping as well as I thought I was.

Jake nodded thoughtfully. "He's lucky he has you in his corner," he said. "But it is hard. I went through that when my dad had his hip surgery. It took them four sticks to get an IV in. I wanted to rip the needle out of the nurse's hands and do it myself."

I chuckled at that. It was nice to have someone that understood how I felt. Jake had moved his hand off my shoulder, but was still standing close enough beside me that I could feel the heat from his arm. I looked at his strong chest and broad shoulders and wondered briefly how it would feel to have him wrap me in his arms. Just the thought made me feel safe and secure. There would be advantages to being married and having someone for support. I could be there for my mom and dad, but who was there for me when I needed someone to just hold me?

I shook my head to clear those thoughts before I got too wallowed down in feeling sorry for myself. I was used to being on my own and having to be strong. This was nothing new for me.

Jake was playing with the end of my ponytail, which was distracting me, but not in the right direction. I knew he was just being goofy.

"Well, I hope it all comes out ok," he said, sincerely.

"Me too," I said, nodding. It was hard to think of the right things to say sometimes in situations like this.

"Thanks for listening to me babble," I said to him. He just smiled.

"No problemo, bonita," he replied. "Call me anytime you need an ear."

"Just ring you up on the EMS radio?" I asked him, teasingly.

"Oh, yeah, I guess you don't have my number," he laughed. "Hold on a sec." He grabbed a pen and a piece of paper off the desk and wrote his phone number on it. He started to hand it to me then pulled it back.

"Wait, I better put my name on this," he said, writing 'Jake' across the top of the paper. "I don't want you to get it mixed up with all the other phone numbers you get." He smiled at me with those killer dimples.

I had to laugh at that. I wasn't the girl guys usually fell over. That was Shelby. She was petite with long, blond curls and big, blue eyes. I was average build with shoulder length caramel-colored hair that was usually up in a ponytail. I had pretty green eyes and straight teeth. That was the extent of my attractive features. I was usually dressed in scrubs or jeans, and my beauty routine was best described as 'low maintenance'.

Jake handed me the piece of paper with a smile. "When you get to your phone, send me a text message so I'll have your number too," he said. Well, there. I already had a reason to text him. I knew he was being kind and this didn't mean anything. It would still be nice to have someone outside the family to talk to about all this. Someone else in the medical field who would understand my point of view.

Kent was done with his report so they were headed back out the door. Jake waved goodbye with a reminder to text him my number. Lacey overheard that and her eyebrows about hit her hairline. She had been in the patient's room when I was talking to Jake, so she missed the whole thing.

"Did Jake tell you to text him?" she whispered to me.

"Yeah, he gave me his number if I needed someone to talk to," I told her. I tried to sound nonchalant.

"Uh huh. Talk. That's what I would want to do," she said, laughing.

"He was really understanding when I was talking to him about my dad," I told her. "He's just being nice."

"Good," Lacey said. "You need a chance to decompress sometimes." She was right about that. She was good at listening to me, but she was a lot younger than me and hadn't been through any of this yet. Her parents were in their late forties and healthy. Plus, no one was expecting her to handle everything because she was a nurse herself. That would change in a few months.

Mildred's call light came on and Jesse was off somewhere. I went in to see what she needed. She was cold and wanted some more warm blankets. I went to the warmer and got her a couple. I wrapped her up good, making sure to tuck her cold feet in. She was looking a little better now that she had some IV fluid in her. She was probably just dehydrated. That happens easily with the elderly.

"How about that young man on the ambulance?" she said to me, grinning. "A gal could get used to looking at that." I tried not to laugh out loud. Jake really could woo any woman, without even trying.

"I tell you what," she continued, "if he's gonna be the one picking me up, I'll fall down in church every week!"

Chapter 14

Is There a Doctor in the House?

It was about lunchtime, so I told Jesse I was going on break. I was getting hungry, but I was more concerned about calling my mom. I was sure that she would tell me everything was back to normal and dad was doing great again.

I pulled my phone out of my bag to see that I had three missed calls from my mom already. My heart was in my throat instantly. She hadn't left a message, so I just called her immediately. I was still in the hallway, where I wasn't supposed to be on my personal cell phone, but right then, I didn't care.

Mom answered right away. "Allison, I've been trying to call you," she said, sounding distressed.

"What's wrong?" I asked. My mind was already racing a mile a minute.

"His leg is looking worse," mom started. "And he feels terrible today. He thinks it's just from taking the pain pills, but he looks pale. Something is wrong, I just know it." She sounded like she was going to cry.

I took a deep breath to calm myself down. "Ok, first the leg. Did the nurse look at it last night?" I asked.

"He said he was going to when I left," mom replied. "But Bob doesn't think he ever did. The other doctor was here this morning and he took the dressing part way off. It looks terrible under there. It's all red and swollen and part of it has opened back up. There's slimy, brown stuff on the gauze."

My heart was sinking. "What did the doctor say?" I asked. Surely he had something to say about the leg incision that was obviously infected.

"He said it didn't look good," she started, "but he was going to let Dr. Weston handle it tomorrow."

"What?!" I cried out. I couldn't believe he would just ignore it.

"He wasn't very nice," mom said. "He kept interrupting me when I tried to ask questions. And he was pushing on Bob and really hurting him. He was rough. I finally just wanted him to leave so he would stop hurting Bob."

I wanted to scream. How did these horrible people end up in the medical field? Weren't you supposed to be kind and caring and want to help others? Why were they inflicting more pain on my dad but not bothering to treat him?

"Is it the same nurse today as yesterday?" I asked mom. I was afraid of the answer.

"Yes," mom said dejectedly. Well, we weren't going to get very far with her. She had ignored the leg yesterday. But now the dressing was off and it was obviously infected. She had to realize that was a problem, right?

"Did she changed the dressing yet?" I asked mom.

"No, she said she would when she gets a chance," mom replied.

"Let me guess- they're short-staffed," I said bitterly.

"Yes," mom said. "Although they're sitting down at the desk a lot. It looks like they had a potluck, everyone is eating."

I was getting angrier. Working short was a raw deal, but if you have time to sit and eat, then you have time to take care of your patient. Of course, on weekends, there are no managers around to notice poor behavior. Staff can get away with a lot.

"Mom, please ask the nurse to change the dressing," I said, emphatically. "It's really important."

"Ok, honey," mom replied, less than enthusiastically. "I'll ask her again."

Again. So mom had asked her already and it still wasn't done. I did not feel good about this at all.

"I'll call you later, ok?" I said as I got off the phone. I needed to call in backup and my lunch break was only thirty minutes long.

Shelby was at work so her phone went to voice mail. I left a short but urgent message that dad was not doing well. I hoped she could head back to Springfield when she got off work at 2 o'clock. I wouldn't be done until 7:30 this evening and I didn't want to wait that long.

I grabbed my lunch and shoveled it in during the remaining ten minutes of my lunch break. I didn't even taste it. I could have eaten cardboard and not noticed.

I walked back up to the desk so Jesse could go to lunch. My mind was not on work anymore. Lacey could tell something was wrong by the look on my face.

"Uh oh," she said. "That's not a happy look."

I filled her in on what was happening with my dad. She was shocked as well that the nurses were being so lazy.

"Are you going to go back there tonight or tomorrow?" she asked. She already knew I was going back. That wasn't even a question.

"I left a message for Shelby," I answered. "She can leave before I can. But I'll go as soon as I can."

Of course, by the time I got off work, got home and packed a bag and drove it Springfield, it would be almost 10 o'clock at night. My common sense side said to let Shelby go today, and I could drive up in the morning. But it was losing the argument to my worried daughter side. There was no way I could sleep until I had seen my dad.

I had my cell phone stashed in my scrub pocket. We weren't supposed to have them on us at work, but today I was making an exception to the rule. I didn't want to miss a call from mom or Shelby. Besides, it wasn't like Jesse could turn me in for breaking the rule. He had his on all the time.

I saw the paper with Jake's number on it and remembered I was supposed to send him a text. That was a momentary distraction. What do I say? Should I send an actual message? The point of the text was just so he would have my number. Should I come up with something cute or witty to say? I finally gave up and just texted 'Hi'. I made sure the phone was on vibrate so it didn't ring while I was in a patient's room and stuck it back in my pocket.

My pocket buzzed a few minutes later, startling me. I looked at the screen to see Jake had texted back. 'Hi yourself. I hope someone falls down so I get to come back and see you.' I laughed at that. 'Be careful what you wish for', I texted back. I really hoped we didn't have anything too serious this afternoon because I was not focused on work.

Shelby called me back about forty-five minutes later. I ducked in to the staff bathroom to talk to her.

"What's going on?" she asked, panicked. I told her about the infected incision and the nurses not changing the dressing. I told her the doctor wasn't doing much either and mom needed someone to stand up to the staff for her.

"And you thought of me!" Shelby said, laughing. We both knew she was a spitfire when she needed to be.

"I can't get there until almost 10 o'clock tonight," I told her. "I was hoping you could go sooner."

"Sure," she said. "I'll tell them I need to leave right now." The advantage of a waitress job is you can just leave like that. As a nurse, it was illegal to walk out in the middle of a shift. Not to mention unethical.

"Call me when you get there," I told her. "I have my phone in my pocket."

She promised she would and got off the phone. I went back up to the desk, at least a little relieved that mom would have backup in a couple hours. Shelby was probably going to piss off some nurses, but by this point, I didn't care. I would stay in dad's room around the clock if I had to.

The rest of the shift was quite dull, which was a good thing from my point of view. I thanked the Lord for that, because Sunday afternoons can get pretty crazy some weeks. I didn't have the concentration to handle that today.

About 5 o'clock, I was counting down the minutes until I could leave, when my pocket buzzed with a phone call. I jumped up and darted into the nearest private place, which happened to be a supply room.

It was Shelby calling me. She should have gotten to Springfield over an hour ago, but I figured she had just forgotten to call me. I wasn't too worried about that, as long as she was there with mom.

"What's going on?" I asked her, in lieu of hello. I didn't have patience for small talk.

"He looks terrible," she said bluntly. "He's pale and his leg looks awful. He didn't want me to look at it because it's the part at the top, up by his..." she trailed off.

"Groin. The word you want is groin," I told her. I knew where the incision went to and I'm sure our very modest father would not want his daughter looking at that area.

"Yeah. Groin," she continued. "But mom kept the gown over him so I could see the spot and it's all red and nasty. There's this gross stuff on the gauze and it doesn't smell very good. I was trying to hold my breath." She paused for a moment. "I thought maybe dad farted. It was really stinky."

I wanted to laugh at that comment, but I was too distracted by the fact that dad's incision was obviously infected. I couldn't understand why no one there was worried about this.

"Did the nurse come change the dressing?" I asked.

"Yeah, after I asked her three times," Shelby snorted. "Then she was so rough ripping the tape off, I was sorry I asked."

My stomach clenched at the thought of more people hurting my dad. This song was getting very old. I was glad someone finally changed the dressing but there was no need to be rough about it.

"It's not Eileen, is it?" I asked.

"No, this chick is fat," Shelby replied. "But she's just as mean." Shelby didn't really have a filter when she spoke.

"What did she say about the incision?" I asked. It was pointless, she obviously hadn't said 'this is infected, let's call the doctor and wash it up'. Which is what she should have said.

"She said it was no big deal and she would let the doctor know in the morning," Shelby replied, flatly. She was obviously as unimpressed with that as I was.

"How does dad feel?" I asked. I was pretty sure I didn't want to hear the answer to that question.

"He keeps saying he's fine, but he's not," she said. "He looks terrible. He's ready to go to bed already, and it's not even supper time."

Now I really had alarm bells clanging. My dad didn't go to bed early the day after his open heart surgery. In fact, the last time my dad laid down at 5 o'clock in the evening, he was having a heart attack. Something was really wrong. I couldn't exactly put my finger on it but there were a half dozen red flags on this situation.

"I'm leaving as soon as possible," I promised her. "I'll see if night shift can come in early for me."

"Ok," she said. "Keep me posted. And drive safe."

Drive safe? Did my kid sister just tell me to drive safe?

—∘∘❈∘∘—

I called Connie, who was scheduled to come in to work tonight at 7 o'clock. I filled her in on the situation and she said she would be happy to come in early so I could get on the road. She said she could get here by a little after six. I thanked her heartily and went to update Lacey.

I went through the rooms, making sure everything was cleaned and stocked. Since Connie was doing me a favor, I didn't want to leave her a bunch of extra work to do. Besides, I needed some busy work to occupy me.

I had all my stuff in my bag sitting at the desk by six. I didn't have any patients to hand off, so I was bolting as soon as Connie walked in. We actually had three patients in the ER at the time. Jesse had overheard enough of my conversations to know that my dad wasn't doing well and

I was leaving early. He had just stepped up and taken each patient when they came in, so I could leave sooner. I guess he had his decent moments.

Connie came bustling in and told me to get going and good luck with everything. I thanked her again and headed for my car. I was almost to my house when my pocket buzzed again. I saw it was Shelby and tried to answer while I was turning on to my street. I almost hit a kid on his bike. I guess that's why they say it's dangerous to use your cell phone while you're driving, huh?

I managed to answer without any damage done. Shelby jumped straight past hello, just like I had.

"When are you getting here?" she demanded. Not a good start to the conversation.

"I'm just getting to my house now," I answered. "What happened?" I parked, grabbed my bag and ran in to the house while she talked.

"Dad was getting back in the bed and he felt something kind of pop," she said breathlessly. "Suddenly, his leg had blood running down it. He got on the bed and we rang the call light, but no one came in. Mom was holding the gauze against the part that was bleeding, like she had seen you do before. It was like ten minutes and still no nurse! So I walked out in the hall and there's three people just sitting at the desk. I say we need a nurse right now and they just stare at me and ask what for. I pretty much yelled that my dad was bleeding and needed help and the fatty finally got out of her chair to come look at him."

Shelby was getting louder and louder as she talked. I wondered where she was standing and who could overhear her. Although I didn't really care, anymore. I was beyond worrying about upsetting the nursing staff.

"So, she gets in the room and mom's holding his leg to stop the bleeding, and she says 'What did you do?' to her! Like mom did it to him!" Shelby was livid.

"I told her it popped open when he was getting back to bed and she says, all snotty, that he's not supposed to get back to bed by himself," she rattled on. "I say, 'oh, so he should ring the CALL LIGHT?' and she looks at me with this nasty glare. His call light is still going off and no one is even looking up at it.

"She looked at the leg and part of the incision is popped open now and bleeding. She tells mom 'hold pressure right there' and then walks back out of the room! She goes and gets some gauze and finally comes back in with another nurse. They shove mom to the side like she's in their way. Never mind that she is doing their job for them. So, they finally changed his dressing. Except now the dressing keeps getting soaked with blood."

Shelby finally stopped for a breath. I was shaking, I was so furious. I was already in the house and shoving stuff in my overnight bag. I couldn't get there fast enough. I was starting to worry they were going to get my dad killed off before I could get there to protect him.

"I'm leaving here in five minutes," I told her. "I'll have my phone on so call if anything new comes up."

She promised she would. They would have shift change in less than an hour and I was praying that we would get a good nurse. I didn't know much about Jesse from last night except that he had also ignored the soiled dressing.

I pulled on the highway and tried to keep from gunning the car to 100 mph. I didn't need to get in a car wreck. Or get a ticket either. I remembered talking to God on this stretch of road, not even a week ago. He was getting an earful again tonight. I don't know which lesson I was failing this time. I was definitely not trusting God instead of worrying. And my patience was long gone. I was pretty sure that as soon as I saw a nurse, they were going to get a butt-chewing. So, trust, patience, kindness- what else was I failing at?

Grandma would probably say it's because I didn't go to church today.

———∘∘∘ᴥ∘∘∘———

I pulled in to Springfield only fifteen minutes earlier than I would have gotten there doing the speed limit. I headed for the hospital and made my way from the parking lot to dad's room without getting lost. It felt like a long time since I had left here.

I walked in to dad's room and saw Randy standing by the bed. I almost cried, I was so happy to see him. Randy didn't look happy, though. He was looking at dad's incision and scowling. He looked up and saw me standing there.

"Allie," he boomed out, "come look at this." I walked over to his side, grateful that he was so willing to involve me. Dad had apparently gotten used to having his daughters look at the wound because he didn't protest. Or maybe he thought I was different, because I was a nurse. Actually, now that I looked at dad a little closer, I think he felt too tough to argue. Shelby was right, he looked terrible.

The incision was gaping open for about 7 cm in the middle of his thigh. The whole incision from there up to his groin was very red and angry. There was thick tan drainage oozing from the upper portion and it was dried and crusted on the edges of the incision.

My stomach rolled over at the sight of it. I was used to seeing gross things, but this was my dad, and I suddenly could see how bad his leg was. This did not happen just today. This had been getting infected for a couple days, at least.

"Dad, when did they change the dressing last?" I asked him.

"Wade did it," he replied weakly. That was on Thursday. "He said it was a little red and he told the next nurse to keep an eye on it."

A little redness was common around an incision. The body's immune system could fight off a few bacteria and the redness would go away and the incision would heal right up.

But a hospital was teeming with bacteria, and they weren't just your garden variety bugs. Some were resistant to antibiotics and could cause serious problems. Either way, dad's leg never should have gotten this bad before someone noticed it.

Randy was washing the incision with some disinfectant soap. Dad was cringing slightly, even though Randy was being very gentle. That incision had to hurt. After he was done, he put a clean gauze dressing over the leg.

"I'm worried about more than the leg," Randy said quietly to me. "His heart rate is up in the 120's and his temp is 100 degrees." Technically, it wasn't considered a fever until it was over 101. But coupled with the high heart rate, it looked like the infection might have spread to his bloodstream.

"I'm going to call the doctor as soon as I'm done here," he said. I was so grateful we had Randy back on duty. I guess I should have trusted God like I was supposed to. I walked over to give mom a hug. She didn't look too hot herself. I could tell she had been crying. Shelby was standing next to her, still steaming.

"Thanks for coming earlier," I told Shelby. I was so glad she was here when dad's leg started bleeding. Otherwise, my poor mom might still be standing there holding pressure.

She nodded. I knew she was thinking the same thing I was. I couldn't believe how quickly we had gone from fantastic nurses to horrible nurses. And dad's condition had followed right along with the nursing care. As the care got worse, so did his health.

I stepped out to get a bottle of water and a granola bar from the vending machine. I was suddenly starving, now that I had seen my dad. Randy was at the desk, on the phone. As I walked back toward dad's room, I heard him saying "I really think you need to come look at it now," with some insistence. He listened to the phone and the furrow in his brow deepened.

I paused to eavesdrop on the conversation, since I knew they were talking about my dad. Randy kept trying to speak, but the other person obviously kept cutting him off. I figured it was the doctor from earlier that kept interrupting my mother. That was a bad sign. Interrupting is annoying and rude in any setting. But a doctor needed to listen to his patients, as well as their families and nurses. Anyone who was interrupting wasn't listening.

Randy finally hung up in exasperation. He saw me standing there and walked over to talk to me in the hallway.

"Dr. Weston is out of town for the weekend," he said. "Dr. Malik is covering and that's who I called." He paused and took a deep breath. "Dr. Malik doesn't think it's a cause for concern, and he wants to just leave it up to Dr. Weston in the morning."

I could see that Randy was frustrated by this. The sooner we started treating the infection, the better. But if the doctor refused to come in or give an order for antibiotics, the nurse's hands were tied. We can't do much without a doctor's order.

"I'm sorry, Allie," he continued. "I don't know what else to do."

"I know," I assured him. "I'm just glad you're here. Let's hope dad turns the corner during the night."

He nodded gravely, but neither of us truly believed that was going to happen.

"I'll keep calling him if I have to," Randy promised me. I nodded and headed back to dad's room. We finally had a good nurse but still had a bad doctor.

I walked back in the room and went to sit by mom. Now that we had a good nurse on, there was really no reason for the three of us to set up a bedside vigil. It seemed wrong to go off and leave him, though. I was torn about what to do, and I wasn't sure I was going to convince mom to leave anyway. I didn't want her getting too run down, or she would end up sick as well.

"So, what's the plan, Lis?" Shelby asked.

I sighed. "The doctor on call wants to let Dr. Weston handle it in the morning," I told them. They could tell from my face that I wasn't happy with that plan.

Randy walked in the room just then. "Did Allie fill you in?" he asked mom. She nodded. "I'm sorry," he continued. "I really tried to get him to come in tonight."

"Well, I appreciate you trying," mom said. "I guess he knows what's best."

I stifled a scream. No, he did not know what was best. He was just being lazy and my dad was suffering because of it. I could tell by Randy's expression that he was as angry about it as I was. Santa did not look too jolly right then.

"I think we'll hang out for a little bit," I said to the room in general. "Then if he's staying stable we can go catch a little sleep."

Everyone agreed that that sounded like a good plan. I was really hoping that dad didn't get any worse before Dr. Weston came in the morning. He would treat the infection and dad would heal right up. We had thought we were going home tomorrow, but that plan wasn't working out.

Dad slept and we sat around, not saying much. The general mood was pretty grim. Randy came back in a little before 10 o'clock. He checked dad's heart rate and blood pressure. They were about the same as before and he still had a low grade temp. He wasn't any better, but he wasn't any worse.

I decided we should try to get some rest ourselves. Mom reluctantly agreed and we all whispered good night to dad. He didn't really wake up, but I figured he needed the sleep. We headed out to the parking lot where we now had three cars parked. Mom had kept the same hotel room that we used last week. I suddenly realized that it was charged to my credit card. They just kept adding days each day that mom told them she wasn't checking out. That was going to be a hefty bill.

We went to the hotel in my car and left mom's and Shelby's car at the hospital. There was still not much conversation as we all got ready for bed. I made sure my phone was on the charger right by the bed with the ringer turned up high. I had given Randy the number before we left and told him to call with anything, no matter what it was.

I crawled into bed and curled up on my side. I tried to say a silent prayer, but it came out more like a lecture. What is the point of all this, God? Why is my dad getting sick?

Can't he just get better and go home like a normal patient? I didn't really feel at peace and I laid there, fuming at God for about an hour. I was exhausted but I still couldn't quite fall asleep.

I couldn't even think about the possibility of dad not making it through. I would dissolve in a pile on the floor if I did. Mom and Shelby were looking to me to be the strong one. I had to keep it together for them. But I wasn't as strong as I acted. Even with Shelby sleeping in the same bed with me, I still felt incredibly alone. In the darkness, I felt the hot tears slide out of my eyes and down to the pillow.

Chapter 15

A Shocking Experience

I woke up every couple of hours all night. I would check my phone and see that there were no missed calls. Then I would lay down and try to fall back asleep. I wasn't going to be very rested tomorrow. I hoped my mom was sleeping a little better.

At 4 o'clock, I woke up abruptly. Something was wrong, I could feel it. My stomach was cramping and I felt sweaty. This must be what a panic attack feels like, I thought.

Suddenly, my phone rang. I jumped about two feet of the bed and answered on the first ring. There was only one person who would be calling me.

"Allie, it's Randy," he said, skipping right past the pleasantries. "Bob took a turn for the worse and we're transferring him to the ICU."

My blood ran cold. This wasn't good news. "What happened?" I asked, while I was shoving on Shelby to wake her up. We were going back to the hospital right now and she wasn't easy to wake up.

"He did okay until midnight," Randy said. "Then his blood pressure started dropping and his temp went up.

I called Dr. Malik, who still didn't want to do anything except give some IV fluids. By four, he had gotten a liter of fluid but his blood pressure was still 90/40 and his heart rate was 130. And he hasn't peed since yesterday evening. I called Dr. Malik again and he told me to transfer him to the ICU."

By now, Shelby was awake and I was shaking my mom to get her up. I gestured that she needed to get dressed.

"The good news," Randy continued, "is now an intensivist will see Bob right away. They are on duty around the clock. So he'll get some treatment finally."

That was a small relief. If Dr. Malik just would have treated this on Saturday, we could have prevented the whole mess. I thanked Randy for calling me and told him we were headed to the hospital now. We already knew how to get to the ICU.

I hung up and yanked on my clothes. Shelby and mom were already dressed and waiting. I repeated what Randy had said as I got dressed and we walked down the hall.

"Why does it matter that he didn't pee?" Shelby asked.

"It means his kidneys aren't working," I explained. "That can happen when your blood pressure is too low."

"Well, he didn't really drink much yesterday," mom interjected. "He wouldn't have any urine." My mother would never say the word 'pee'.

"They gave him a liter of IV fluid, though," I reminded her. "That should have made him go."

"Oh," she replied. A liter was a lot of fluid to put in and not get anything back out.

We got in the car and headed down the street. The traffic lights were all flashing and there weren't many other cars on the road.

We parked and walked quickly into the hospital. I wanted to break out in a dead run, but that wouldn't get me there that much quicker. I was the only runner of the three of us, so I was pretty sure mom and Shelby wouldn't agree with that idea.

We walked to the ICU and I picked up the phone. I wondered what we looked like on the security camera. I hadn't even looked in the mirror before I left the hotel room. The nurse buzzed us in right away and told us he was in room 8. He had been in room 6 before and I probably would have walked right back there if she hadn't said something. That would have been awkward for the patient that was in there now.

Dad was back on the cardiac monitor and I could see his heart rate was still 130. The automatic blood pressure cuff was reading 87/38. Dad was laying with his eyes closed and he was taking fast, shallow breaths. Mom rushed over to his side and took his hand. He opened his eyes weakly and tried to smile at her.

"Bob, are you okay?" she cried. That was a silly question. He was nowhere close to okay. He looked pale and clammy. He had a catheter back in, which I'm sure he hated. Although, at that point, I think he was beyond caring. I could see that there was only a little bit of urine in the bag and it was amber colored. I knew that wasn't a good sign, either.

A young, athletic looking woman in her twenties walked into the room briskly, her ponytail swinging as she walked.

"Hi, I'm Lana," she said as she walked up to the IV pole and started messing with a bag of medicine and the IV tubing. "I'm his nurse."

Mom and Shelby just stood there, so I spoke up. "Hi, I'm Allie, his daughter," I told her. "This is Betty, his wife, and Shelby, his other daughter." She smiled at us briefly and looked back at the IV pump. She was working with it while she talked to us. I got the impression she didn't have the luxury of free time right now to chat.

"His blood pressure is still too low," she started out. "We are going to start an IV medication that will help bring it up. And we gave him an antibiotic." She finished programming the IV pump and pressed 'start'.

A tall, lanky man about thirty years old walked in the room. He had dark hair and eyes and olive skin. His hair was cut very short and he had a five o'clock shadow on his face.

"Dr. Ghanda," he said as way of introduction. He looked very serious.

"Betty, his wife, Allie and Shelby, daughters," I said as I gestured to each of us. I didn't want a long conversation, I wanted to cut to the chase.

"His leg is infected," he said bluntly. "And the infection has spread to his blood and he is going in to septic shock."

I nearly collapsed. Part of me knew that was what was happening. I recognized all the signs- the high heart rate, low blood pressure, fever, decreased urine. But I was effectively in denial until I heard the doctor say it in no uncertain terms.

"How bad is that?" mom asked. He paused before answering.

"Worst case scenario- it's fatal," he said. I wanted to slap him. Why did he start with that? Mom turned pale and Shelby gasped.

"But I think we caught it in time," he continued. "We gave antibiotics for the infection and we are giving some Levophed for the blood pressure. He should be fine."

'Fine' was a subjective term. He was back in the ICU five days after open heart surgery with an infection that could be fatal. 'Fine' was not the word I would use.

I wasn't thrilled with his bedside manner, but Dr. Ghanda was treating my dad correctly, and that was more important.

"When does Dr. Weston round?" I asked.

"He's usually here by about six," Dr. Ghanda replied. "I called Dr. Malik and talked to him. He didn't want to add anything. I'll update Dr. Weston when he rounds."

I'm sure Dr. Malik didn't have anything to add. He was probably thrilled to have someone else taking care of his work now.

It was not quite five, so we had over an hour to kill. I asked Lana if there was any place to get coffee this time of the night. She told me the cafeteria had a coffee station and some vending machines if we were hungry. I hadn't eaten anything but a granola bar last night, but I still wasn't hungry. I was too upset.

Mom didn't want to leave dad's room, so Shelby and I headed to the cafeteria. Part of me didn't want to leave dad's room either, but I needed a breather. If I sat in there, staring at the monitor flashing a low blood pressure, knowing this could have been prevented- I was going to lose it.

The cafeteria was eerily quiet. The sign said they didn't start serving breakfast until 6:30 and it seemed the kitchen crew hadn't started cooking yet. We found the coffee machine and each got a cup. We wandered over to the vending machines and I got some almonds and a bottle of juice for mom. Shelby got a candy bar that had almonds in it. She justified that made it healthy.

"Let's just sit for a bit," I said to Shelby. We sat at a table by the window, even though it was still completely dark outside. I looked at our reflection in the window and was glad to see my hair was at least laying flat.

"So...." Shelby drug out the word. "Is dad going to be okay? For real, Lis." She looked a little terrified when she asked.

"Yeah, he should," I told her. "It's a treatable condition, he just needs to get the treatment." There were always those freak cases when someone died anyway, but I didn't need to tell her that. I didn't even need to think about that.

"How did this happen?" she asked. Good question. Three people in thirty-six hours had a chance to catch this and fix it. They all dropped the ball.

"No one caught on that dad's leg was getting infected," I said. "Even when they did realize it, the doctor didn't want to deal with it. So the infection got out of control."

"What is septic shock?" she asked next. Hoo boy. That was going to be tougher to explain. The definition of shock was 'inadequate end organ perfusion'. That wasn't going to make sense to Shelby. Neither was 'circulatory compromise' or 'metabolic acidosis'.

Shock was actually pretty scary stuff. The longer it went on, the worse the chances for recovery. The kidneys shutting down was especially a red flag. Dad had started going in to shock probably fourteen hours ago.

"Sepsis is an infection in the bloodstream," I started out. "Shock is when the circulation doesn't work properly because of it. The cells don't get enough oxygen."

"How does it kill him?" she asked.

"It's not going to kill him!" I cried out. I wasn't even going to think about that possibility.

"Sheesh, I'm just asking," she said. "The doctor said it was fatal."

"It CAN be fatal," I emphasized. "And usually it is not." I could choke Dr. Ghanda for that comment. I wondered if my mom had misunderstood that as well, and was sitting up there thinking dad was going to die.

I decided we needed to get back to dad's room. My coffee was already gone. I didn't waste any time when it came to drinking coffee. I grabbed mom's almonds and juice and we headed down the hall.

When we got back in the ICU, I saw a middle-aged man standing at the desk outside dad's room. He had on rumpled hospital scrubs and his hair was sticking up in the back. He had apparently been sleeping and had gotten up quickly.

He was looking at dad's chart and shaking his head. "Jim is going to explode," he muttered. "This is not good." I assumed he was talking about Dr. Jim Weston and I was sure he was going to be upset when he saw what had happened while he was gone.

Lana walked up to hand him some more papers. She looked a little irritated as she said, "Here's the labs, Dr. Malik."

So this was the infamous and lazy Dr. Malik. He had finally dragged himself in to see the patient. I didn't feel the need to introduce myself. As soon as Dr. Weston got here, Dr. Malik would be just a bad memory. I walked back in the room to check on mom. She was still sitting by the bed, holding dad's hand. Everything else looked about the same.

I walked over and crouched down by mom. I had to make sure she knew dad was going to make it.

"Mom, what Dr. Ghanda said about septic shock- you know he didn't mean dad, right?" I asked. She looked at me blankly for a moment. "He's not going to die from it," I said.

"How do you know for sure?" she asked. Well, she had me there. We didn't have any guarantees in this world, especially in the medical field.

"I mean, his condition isn't that severe," I clarified. "He's getting treatment and he'll get better."

She nodded. I wasn't sure if I had made things better or worse.

We heard a commotion in the hallway and a distinct, deep voice demanded "Why is Bob Sanford in here?!" I glanced out the glass door and saw Dr. Weston standing at the desk, looking freshly showered and clean shaven. He was wearing a button down shirt and tie, with a white coat over it. He apparently was starting rounds for the day.

Dr. Malik was standing there, looking disheveled and a little frightened. Dr. Weston had his chest out and his chin jutted forward and his face was about two inches away from Dr. Malik's. I could definitely see that he had been in the military.

Dr. Malik was trying to string together an explanation but he wasn't getting it done quick enough for Dr. Weston's liking. Dr. Weston turned and strode in to dad's room. Dr. Malik followed him, still trying to explain.

Dr. Weston pretty much ignored him. "Bob," he said, putting his hand on dad's shoulder. Dad opened his eyes and smiled weakly.

"Hi doc," he said. "How ya doing?"

"Terrible!" Dr. Weston replied. "I don't like seeing my patients get sick."

"I'm sorry," dad started to apologize. Dr. Weston instantly softened.

"Bob, you didn't do this," he assured him. "You don't need to be sorry. I'm just unhappy to see you here." He smiled over at mom. "How are you holding up, Betty?" he asked.

"Fine," mom answered softly. Her face told a different story.

Dr. Weston turned back to Dr. Malik to hear the rest of his explanation. I hadn't been listening to the first part when they first walked in the room.

"It really came on very sudden," Dr. Malik was saying in a self-righteous tone. "I didn't even know about it until late last night."

And that was when I lost it. Outright, blew a cork, steam coming out of my ears, lost it.

"That is not true!" I yelled. "No one even checked the dressing on Saturday and you SAW the infection on Sunday morning! You said you were leaving it for Dr. Weston to handle. Randy called you three times last night and you refused to come in!"

Dr. Malik looked flustered. "Well, I.. I...just, I didn't realize how serious it was," he stammered. "I would have come in then."

"Liar!" I spit out. "Randy said 'you need to come look at it now'." I gritted each word through my clenched teeth. "I was standing at the desk when he said it."

Mom and Shelby were staring at me with their mouths open. Dr. Malik was looking very uncomfortable and Dr. Weston's face was turning as red as mine.

He turned toward Dr. Malik and walked up until he was standing chest to chest with him. Dr. Malik wouldn't even look him in the eye. Dr. Weston let loose a string of colorful words that he had probably learned in the military. The general idea of the sentence was 'get out and don't come back.' Dr. Malik scurried out of the room like a dog with his tail between his legs.

Dr. Weston took a couple deep breaths and then turned around to us. I was still shaking in anger and I could feel tears welling up in the back of my eyes. I knew I wasn't acting professional but I couldn't take it anymore.

"Sorry, ma'am," he said to mom. "Ladies," he added, nodding his head in our direction. I assume he was apologizing for the language.

"Allie, thank you for speaking up," he said sincerely. "I'm glad to know what really happened. Can you fill in the details?"

I told him how mom had noticed the tan drainage on Saturday but the nurse wouldn't change the dressing. I told him that mom said dad 'just wasn't right' starting on Saturday and much more so on Sunday, but the nurses told her not to worry. I told him that Dr. Malik had pulled back the dressing and looked at the incision on Sunday morning, but said he would leave it for Dr. Weston to handle. I told him about the incision coming apart when dad was moving back to the bed. I didn't need to tell him what happened last night, he had already heard it in my tirade.

He listened to everything I said, nodding as I talked. When I had finished, he turned to mom.

"Betty, I'm sorry it happened like this," he said. "You did the right thing by speaking up. I wish they had listened to you."

He sat on the edge of the bed by dad's feet. "Bob, you're going to make it through," he said. "You're a young, healthy guy and this is just a bump in the road."

Dad nodded. "The next twelve hours are crucial," Dr. Weston continued. "That medication is already bringing your blood pressure up. We need your kidneys to kick in again and the antibiotic to get a toehold in on the infection. Then you'll be back around the corner."

I glanced at the monitor and saw that dad's most recent blood pressure reading was 98/56. That was a slight improvement. I knew they could increase the dose if they needed to.

"I'm going to go see a couple other patients," Dr. Weston said. "I'll be back around in a couple hours to check on you."

He stood up and walked out of the room. Dad was smiling at me softly.

"Well, someone let the tiger loose," he said.

"Sorry I yelled at your doctor, dad," I started to apologize. He just shook his head.

"You stood up for your old dad when he couldn't do it himself," he said, proudly. "I'm real happy to have you in my corner."

"Yeah, Lis, you were awesome," Shelby chipped in. "A little scary, but awesome!"

Mom giggled. "When you said 'Liar' I thought you were going to say 'pants on fire'," she said, laughing. "You always used to say that to your brother."

Well, I was glad no one was upset with me for blowing up. It probably hadn't been necessary, because Dr. Weston was already back and he would have taken care of dad. But maybe the next time a nurse told Dr. Malik he needed to come in, he would actually do it. My family was certainly entertained by it.

Dad was looking a little more pink, now that his blood pressure was coming up. That gave me hope that he would turn around quickly.

Lana walked back in and grinned at me. "That was quite the tongue lashing you gave Dr. Malik," she said. I started to apologize for my behavior but she cut me off. "He needs it," she said. "He is so lazy and he always blames the nurses for his screwups. We were loving every minute of it!"

Apparently, the staff had heard the whole thing. I guess I wasn't exactly being quiet. And Dr. Weston had been at full volume when he lit into Dr. Malik. They wouldn't soon forget the Sanford family in the ICU.

"I can't wait to tell Wade about this," Shelby said, laughing. I cringed at that thought.

"Seriously," Lana said, seeing my face. "All the nurses thought it was awesome. You don't need to be embarrassed." I appreciated her saying that. I still felt a little bad that I had lost control like that.

It was getting close to shift change, so we had to leave while they did shift report. We all hugged dad and headed down to the cafeteria. It was bustling now and smelled delicious. Bacon and coffee and pancakes all swirled together. I was suddenly starving. We went through the line and I loaded up a plate. I got bacon and eggs, oatmeal, an orange and some toast. I grabbed a carton of milk, too. We headed for the table by the window again. Shelby was having a huge blueberry muffin and a banana. At least it was some fruit. Mom had some oatmeal and the juice I bought her earlier. We all had a steaming cup of coffee. It tasted better this time than it had earlier. Must have been my outlook on the situation.

We were finishing our breakfast when I looked up and saw Randy walking through the tables. I waved at him and he smiled when he saw us. He walked over and sat down with us.

"How's Bob doing?" he asked. He looked genuinely concerned, even though he wasn't the nurse responsible anymore. That meant a lot to me.

"He's on Levophed and antibiotics," I told him. "His blood pressure is a little better and he looks a little better. Still not much for urine output."

"I'm glad he's finally getting treated," Randy said. "I'm sorry I couldn't get him some help sooner. I honestly think the only reason Dr. Malik said to transfer him was because he wanted me to quit calling him." He shook his head at that.

"Well, Dr. Malik won't be screwing up again," Shelby crowed. "Lis tore him to pieces!"

Randy looked at me, shocked. "You?" he asked. "You're so calm."

"Well, usually I am," I said. "But Dr. Malik was trying to tell Dr. Weston that the infection had come up quickly and he didn't even know about it until last night. I just lost it. I don't know what came over me."

"So Dr Weston told Malik that he was never covering his patients again," Shelby continued. "And he slunk out of the room like a rat. And all the nurses loved it!" She was really having too much fun with this.

Randy just laughed. "I'm so glad someone finally stood up to him. He always tries to blame the nurses when stuff goes wrong." That was the same thing Lana had said. I guess I was glad I stood up for the nurses, then. And since I wasn't an employee, I wouldn't get in trouble for it.

We said goodbye to Randy and he headed home to sleep. We went back to the ICU to see who was on for days. We already knew it wasn't Wade, since Shelby had been texting him last night and he said he had today off. He was going to come up and visit later.

We got buzzed back into the ICU and headed to dad's room. The desk was bustling with activity as usual. We walked in the room to see Marcia looking at the IV pump.

"Marcia! Hi!" I said with genuine enthusiasm. I was so relieved to see a good nurse. Now I felt like I could relax for the day.

"Well, hello again," she replied, smiling. "Sorry we keep meeting like this." She was adjusting the dose on dad's medication. His blood pressure was now 109/64 and his heart rate was 115. He still didn't have much urine in his catheter bag, but that took a few hours to catch up.

Mom sat in the chair by the bed. I grabbed the recliner quick before Shelby could. She tried sitting on me but I just tickled her and won that battle easily. She stuck her tongue out at me and then sat on the floor in the corner.

My phone beeped loudly that I had a text message. I forgot I had the sound turned way up so I would hear it if it rang. I turned it back to vibrate and looked at the message. I tried to fight a smile when I saw it was Jake. 'How is your dad doing?' he asked. I appreciated the concern, but that was a long answer to text. 'Ok. Long story' I replied.

My phone buzzed a minute later. 'Can you call?' he asked. My heart flip flopped at the thought of calling Jake. But he was being a good friend and I needed some support. I told mom and Shelby I was going out to the waiting room to make a phone call. Mom just nodded. Shelby jumped up and took my spot in the recliner. I stuck my tongue out at her.

I walked down the hall to the waiting room, feeling nervous and a little out of breath. This was ridiculous, I told myself. It's just Jake. I'm calling to tell him about my dad. It's practically a professional conversation.

He answered right away. "Hi Allie," he said. "How are you?"

That caught me off guard. I was ready to tell him all about my dad. How was I? Well, I've been better, that's for sure.

"Um, okay, I guess," I replied. That didn't sound convincing.

"You're not really selling that," Jake said, laughing. I wasn't very good at lying.

"I'm tired," I sighed. "And I'm stressed. I screamed at a doctor this morning."

There was a long pause. "You....what?" he asked incredulously. "You never yell. What did he do?"

I gave him the whole saga about the infected incision and dad getting septic and ending up back in ICU. I tried to downplay the episode with Dr. Malik. I told him that dad was starting to look a little better but wasn't out of the woods yet.

"Wow, no wonder you're stressed," he said when I was finished. He didn't have to ask how I was holding up. I had let everyone know very clearly that morning that I was not holding up well at all.

"I think you were right to say something," Jake said. "If someone doesn't speak up, the guy is just going to keep on being a crappy doctor. You stood up for all his patients, not just your dad."

Jake was making me sound like some kind of hero. Defender of the weak and infected. I liked the positive spin he gave that. I wasn't embarrassed that I stood up to the doctor. I just wished I could have done it without losing my cool.

I was starting to notice, though, that I was the only one who was upset about my tirade. Everyone else seemed to be entertained or even impressed by it. Maybe I was overreacting. As usual.

We chatted for a while about nothing at all. He was going to go hiking with his dog and some buddies later today. I was going to sit around a hospital room again. I couldn't wait for this to be over so I could go for a long mountain bike ride. I needed some one-on-one time with nature.

I finally got off the phone with Jake so I could go back in and check on dad. Actually, I needed to check on mom. Dad had nurses taking care of him. Jake told me to call anytime I needed to talk and I promised him I would.

I headed back in to dad's room. Shelby was half-asleep in the recliner and mom was half-asleep in the chair next to dad's bed. Dad was actually asleep and about the same as when I left. I perched on the counter by the sink and tried to think of something to do all day. It was only 9 o'clock and I had a lot of free time ahead of me.

I really wanted to boot Shelby out of the recliner and take a nap in it. My adrenaline was gone and my coffee wasn't holding me either. Shelby seemed to feel the same way, though, so I didn't think I was going to convince her to give up the recliner. Maybe if I waited until she had to go to the bathroom. I could steal it from her then.

A little after 10, Wade showed up. Shelby jumped up and ran to hug him. I took the opportunity to steal the chair from her. She stuck her tongue out at me.

"How's everyone doing?" Wade asked, looking around the room. I knew he was subconsciously checking out dad's vital signs and IV fluids, even though he wasn't the nurse on duty. It was just a habit.

Shelby filled him in on the details of the night. She really enjoyed telling him about me yelling at Dr. Malik. Wade just laughed and laughed. He also said that Dr. Malik deserved it and he was proud of me for standing up to him.

Marcia came in to check on dad and seemed surprised to see Wade there. Then she realized he was holding hands with Shelby and the light dawned. She just smiled at him and he grinned sheepishly.

"I need to wash Bob's leg and change his dressings," she said to us. That was our exit cue. I didn't want to see the wound again anyway. We told Marcia we were going to go for lunch and we would be back later.

I was glad to get out of the hospital for a little while. I was starting to feel closed in. We ambled through the parking lot, trying to decide where we should go. The sun was warm on my skin and I really wanted to go somewhere we could still sit outside.

"Well, let's go back to that sandwich place, then," Shelby said. "Then you can get a chocolate chip cookie." She grinned at me.

I stuck my tongue out at her.

Chapter 16

No Need to Worry

We enjoyed our lunch in the warm, sunny weather. I resisted the chocolate chip cookie. We wandered around the strip mall that the restaurant was in, looking in windows. Mom had to be getting cabin fever by now. I'm sure she never left the hospital during the days we were gone. She seemed to appreciate being outside and enjoying some mindless activity.

We finally headed back to the hospital. Dad was still resting in bed. His blood pressure was still good and his heart rate was down to 100. His catheter bag had some urine in it and it was now yellow. I was heartened by all of that. Dr. Ghanda was right- we caught it in time and he was turning around quickly. I was still irate over his comment about shock being fatal though. I guess, at 5 a.m., no one has their A-game on.

Wade had a climbing gym he wanted to show Shelby, now that we knew dad was doing okay. Mom was looking pretty wiped out. I don't think she slept much last night either, and she was getting run down. I suggested she go back to the hotel and take a nap.

"Oh, I don't want to leave Bob alone," she said, for about the hundredth time in a week.

"I'll stay here with him," I promised her. She agreed then. I knew she was glad for the chance to catch up some sleep. I wouldn't have minded a nap myself. I pulled the recliner over so I could see the bed, in case dad needed something. Marcia had given him his call light, but I wasn't sure he would use it.

I kicked the recliner back and told myself I was just going to relax for a bit. I woke up an hour later with a stiff neck. I think I had even drooled. I was really tired. I didn't feel completely rested up but I did feel a little better.

Dad was awake and watching me. He seemed to be feeling better too.

"You don't have to stay here all the time," he told me kindly. "I'll be fine."

"I know," I said. "But mom doesn't want you to be alone. She needed to get some rest and this was the only way I could convince her."

He nodded. "When you girls were gone, she wouldn't leave the room hardly," he said. "I'm glad you're back. Now she'll get a break.

"I'm not sure why she's so antsy," he continued. "I think maybe she thinks I'm going to die."

I didn't know how to answer that. She had told me that she was worried she might lose him at one point. But I figured we were past that fear. Maybe not.

"I thought I might kick the bucket myself for a little bit there," dad confided. I looked at him with concern. I didn't want to hear that kind of talk.

"Dad, you're not going to die," I said emphatically.

"Well, when the chopper landed here, those nurses in ER jumped on me like a chicken on a june bug," he said.

"The way they were zipping around, I figured I must be in pretty tough shape. Then I got wheeled into this strange room and went to sleep. When I first woke up, I felt really weird and I didn't know where I was. Thought I might be in heaven for a second. It was really bright. But it was cold and then I realized my back hurt. I didn't think that would happen in heaven."

I chuckled. My dad was so practical.

"How about you, Allie?" dad asked. "Did you ever think I might not make it?"

I almost blurted 'No!' out of habit. But I paused for a moment and thought back over the past week. I hadn't ever consciously thought it, because I wouldn't let myself. But there was more than once that I wasn't 100% sure he would pull through. I had just pushed those thoughts to the back of my mind and focused on helping my dad and mom.

"I tried not to think about," I finally confessed quietly. "I knew mom needed me to be strong."

"You are a tough one, that's for sure," dad said. "You got the most grit out of the three kids."

We just sat there in silence for a few minutes. The monitors were chirping and IV pumps were beeping. I heard a phone ringing in the distance. Maybe silence wasn't the right word.

"Y'know," dad finally spoke, "you are my greatest accomplishment. No matter how many things I screwed up in my life, I could always look at you and know that I got one thing right."

I was stunned. I couldn't think of anything my dad had ever screwed up. He had two other kids that had turned out okay. I didn't understand what was so special about me.

Dad must have read my thoughts. "Oh, the other two are good kids," he said. "But Andrew was floundering in school and drinking too much before he met Nicole. She's the reason he turned out like he did. And I love that little Shelby to death, but she's floating through life, taking the easiest path she can find.

"But not you. You put your head down and worked through nursing school all on your own. And you do that job better'n most. You really care about people and you're always thinking of someone else instead of yourself."

"Well....thanks," I finally said. I wasn't sure what the proper response was to that.

"When God gave you to me thirty-one years ago, he knew I would need you for this," dad continued. "I don't need a guardian angel as long as I have my Allie-cat watching out for me."

I almost cried. I had never heard my dad talk like this. I didn't know if it was the pain meds or the near death experience. Maybe he figured he better say it now, just in case he didn't get a chance again.

"I'm glad I could be here," I said. "I've been so focused on mom I didn't really stop to think about you. I figured the nurses had you taken care of. I guess I was wrong."

"Most of them did," dad reminded me. "It was just a couple bad ones, and you fought for me, even if it didn't work. Taking care of your mom for me was the biggest help of all. She'd be a wreck by now if you weren't here."

I couldn't argue with that. Mom was not of stern constitution. She relied on my dad a lot and when he wasn't there, she was lost.

As if thinking about her had conjured her up, mom walked in right then. She looked a little more rested.

"Hi honey," she said, to both of us. The generic term of endearment covered everyone in the room.

Dad smiled up at her as she walked over to give him a kiss. "How was your nap?" dad asked her.

"Good," she sighed. "It felt so fantastic to close my eyes. I couldn't stay asleep for very long, but I feel so much better."

I could agree with that. I felt better after my little catnap, even if it was in an uncomfortable hospital recliner.

I got up to make a trip to the bathroom. I wandered around in the hall for a while, stretching my legs. It felt good to move. I could feel all the tension in my body starting to release. I ended up with muscle cramps any time I was stressed. And stressed was the key word to describe the last week.

I finally headed back to dad's room. I didn't know what else to do with myself. I wondered how Shelby was doing at the climbing gym. I had thought about trying that. It looked like fun and with a harness and a helmet, even I should be fairly safe.

I was walking back toward the ICU when Dr. Weston came out of a side hall and started walking down the hall with me. It turns out he was headed to check on dad. We got to the door of the ICU and he swiped his badge to open the doors. We walked in to dad's room, where everything looked pretty much the way it had when I left. Dad was sitting up at the bed and mom was in the chair by his bed, holding his hand.

"Bob, you look much better," Dr. Weston said. "I just looked at your labs. I'm very happy with them."

Dad nodded and mom smiled at that news. "Let's take a look at that leg," Dr. Weston continued. Marcia had already done the dressing change, so Dr. Weston just pulled it back a tiny bit to see the part at the top that had been so red.

Dr. Weston nodded in satisfaction. "It won't really look much better for a couple days," he explained. "But it doesn't look worse and that means the antibiotics are kicking in."

He explained that the incision would take a couple weeks to heal, between the infection and part of it opening back up. Dad scowled slightly at that news.

"You don't need to sit in a hospital for that," Dr. Weston hastened to explain. "You can go home and have a home health nurse come take care of it." Dad looked a lot happier with that plan.

"If you keep improving like this, I'll move you back out of the ICU tomorrow," Dr. Weston said. "Let's hope for leaving the hospital on Thursday."

Mom nodded in agreement. It would only be three days longer than we had originally planned. I had heard horror stories of patients being in the hospital for weeks and months. We would be out in nine days, if all went well.

I was scheduled to work on Wednesday. I was nervous to leave again, though. I was torn. Dad was really stable and I didn't need to stay. But I had thought that when I left the first time. I was having an argument with myself inside my head and I wasn't getting anywhere.

"You should go back," dad said, out of the blue.

"What?" I asked. "Go back where?"

"To work," he replied. "You don't need to stay here until I leave."

For a moment I wondered if I had been arguing with myself out loud. How did he know what I was thinking? Was I really that transparent? No wonder I was horrible at poker.

"He's right, Allison," mom chimed in. "It's going to be fine this time."

I knew they were right. Dr. Weston was going to be like a pit bull, making sure dad got great care. I had no reason to worry. Not that that had ever stopped me before. When worrying became an Olympic event, I was a shoe-in for the gold medal.

"When do you work next?" mom asked.

"Wednesday," I replied. "I could stay tonight and go back tomorrow." If dad was well enough to leave the ICU I would have a little more peace of mind.

"I have the weekend off," I told mom. "I can come over and help you get settled in."

"We'll cross that bridge when we get to it," mom said calmly. "Don't worry about that right now."

Well, it seemed everyone wanted me to not worry. I was picking up that theme. I wasn't sure I knew how to do that, was the problem.

Wade and Shelby came back in the late afternoon. They looked so cute together. I felt a pang of jealousy. I wanted a handsome and wonderful boyfriend. Not Wade, obviously. I was happy for Shelby but I didn't see why we both couldn't have a boyfriend. We could go on double dates.

I sighed. Wishing wasn't going to do me any good. 'If wishes were horses, then beggars would ride' my grandpa used to say. My crude great-uncle had a more colorful expression about wishing in one hand.

It was close to supper time and mom wanted to go back to the Thai restaurant. I was interested in trying it out as well. We all said goodbye to dad and headed out to the parking lot. Wade drove a pickup, so we didn't all fit in it. He was too tall to fit into my car, so we took two vehicles and I just followed him. We parked on a side street and walked into a tiny restaurant squeezed in between a jeweler and an art gallery.

The place smelled wonderful. There were just a few booths and a couple tables crammed into the tiny room. It was nearly full but there was an open booth near the back and we squeezed in there.

A waitress came zipping by and dropped off menus and glasses of water. I looked over the menu, trying to remember which things I had tried before. I liked curry, which was a good thing. It was in most of the dishes. I also liked the spicy peanut sauce. Most of all, I loved all the vegetables they put in their food.

We decided to each order something different so we could all try each others. Wade just fit right in to the picture, which was good. Being a male nurse, he probably spent a lot of time surrounded by women.

When the food arrived, we dug in. I hadn't done anything today to work up an appetite, but the food was so delicious, it didn't matter. We ate until we were about to burst.

I finally had to stop. If I ate one more bite, I was going to rupture something. I sat back in the booth and sighed.

"I just love this place," mom said. "I wish we had one like it in Madison."

"You can cook it pretty easy," Wade said. "Most stores carry the spices."

"I'm not sure Bob would like it," she said.

"It has lots of veggies in it," I pointed out. "It fits right in to his new heart healthy diet."

"That's true," she agreed. "Maybe I'll give it a try."

I had been trying not to talk about dad during dinner. We all need a mental break from the events of the day. I wanted to act like everything was normal for an hour. But reality snuck back in, as always.

"When are you going home, Lis?" Shelby asked.

"Tomorrow," I replied. "I work on Wednesday."

Shelby nodded thoughtfully but didn't say anything. "When are you going back?" I asked her.

"Well," she started out, "I work Wednesday at 11. I might stay one more night."

I was pretty sure that her decision to stay one more night involved more than just concern for my dad. That was ok. She would be around if mom needed her, and she might as well spend some more time with Wade while she was here. Living 100 miles apart would make it tough to see each other.

Wade and Shelby decided they were going for ice cream after supper. I was stuffed full but ice cream still sounded delicious. However, I didn't think they wanted company on that ice cream excursion. Mom and I headed back to the hospital to check on dad.

Dad was looking better every time I came back. Lana was back on duty for the night shift and she was in his room all the time to check on him. I knew she wouldn't let anything slip by her.

"Well, it looks like you're in good hands, dad" I said. He grinned.

"She's a busy little bee," he said. "She never stops."

Mom and I decided to head to the hotel. We both had a short night of sleep last night and needed an early bedtime tonight. I drove back to the hotel, thinking about the stark contrast between the situation last night and now. I was relieved that things had changed so much. Last night was horrible, and I had no desire to repeat it.

I still felt a flutter of nervousness when I went to put my phone on the charger. What if it rang again in the middle of the night? I was turning up the volume when I noticed I had a text message.

It was from Jake, wondering how my dad was doing and asking if I was doing ok. I sent a quick reply that dad was much better and mom and I were headed to bed for the night. He sent a message back right away telling me to sleep tight and pray my hotel didn't have bed bugs. I laughed at that. It was kind of nice to have someone to say good night to.

I suddenly remembered that Shelby didn't have a room key. Which meant she would be waking me up when she got in from her ice cream date with Wade, since she couldn't get in the door. I groaned. I didn't want to get woke up at midnight. I wanted a solid night's sleep.

Just then, I heard a knock on the door. I got up and looked out the peephole and Shelby was standing there.

"Hi," I said, swinging the door open. "I was just thinking about you."

"That's scary," she said. "I forgot a key." She walked in and set her purse down. I guess she was in for the night.

"How was the ice cream?" I asked. It seemed odd that she came back to the hotel so early.

"Good," she said. "I had butter brickle." I think she was being deliberately vague. She knew I wasn't asking about the ice cream.

I just stood there and stared at her, like only a sister can do. She finally caved.

"Wade works in the morning, so he wanted to get to bed early," she said. "What, did you think I had screwed it up already?!"

That was exactly what I had been thinking. In my defense, her track record with men was not that great. She only kept the losers. She dumped the decent guys in about a week.

"Lis, you worry too much," she told me, shaking her head.

"He is going to be dad's nurse," she continued. "He said he makes sure to get a full night's sleep before a shift so he's not tired. He doesn't want to make mistakes."

That was a great idea. I felt the same way. Sometimes people gave me a hard time that I wouldn't stay out late the night before a shift. I didn't need to be treating ER patients with not enough sleep. I needed to be at the top of my game. Score a point for Wade.

We all crawled on the beds and Shelby filled us in on some details about Wade. It almost felt like a high school sleepover. We finally decided we better get some sleep.

The next morning, dad was looking back to his usual self. The IV medication for his blood pressure had been turned off and his vital signs were great. He would transfer to the stepdown unit later that day. Dr. Weston had already informed the nurses there that he would not tolerate any slip ups.

I was still a little concerned about leaving. I knew I had no reason to be. Shelby would be here to back up mom. Dr. Weston was going to watch over my dad like a hawk. I wasn't needed here.

Maybe that was the problem. I was used to being the one who handled the problems and I was having trouble letting go of that. I needed to trust God and I needed to be less of a control freak. I wasn't the only one capable of taking care of my dad. I didn't have to be a one-woman show.

I was hanging out in dad's room, trying to decide when to leave. Nothing was really going on, I was just having trouble tearing myself away. Dad finally spoke up.

"Allie-cat, you better get headed home," he said gently.

"Well, I will here in a bit," I countered. I wasn't quite ready to go. I wasn't sure I was ever going to be ready to go.

"Everything is going to be fine," dad said with certainty. "You don't need to worry." He sounded so sure when he said it. I couldn't really argue.

I hugged everyone good-bye and stopped at the desk to talk to Wade.

"Thanks for taking care of dad," I said. "I'm going to head out now."

"He's going to be fine, Allie," Wade assured me. "I promise to check on him. Don't you worry."

This was getting to be quite the broken record. I walked out the front door of the hospital for what I hoped was the last time. I still felt a nervous flutter in my stomach, but I reminded myself I was trusting God and I kept walking.

I got in the car and headed toward the highway. I turned on the radio and hit the preset for a country radio station. I forgot for a moment that I wasn't in Brighton and the stations were different here.

Instead of country, I got Bob Marley singing "Don't Worry, Be Happy." I laughed out loud as I pulled on to the highway.

Everything was going to be fine.

About the Author

S tormy Fanning has been a registered nurse for over fifteen years. Her experiences as both a nurse and a patient led her to write this story about a woman who experiences both sides of the hospital situation. Stormy lives in Sheridan, Wyoming.